Published by Inkub
www.inkubatorbc

ISBN (eBook): 978-1-83756-471-2
ISBN (Paperback): 978-1-83756-472-9
ISBN (Hardback): 978-1-83756-473-6

To my husband, Scott. Thank you for your hard work and dedication into renovating our new home. We may not have a big garden, but I'm pretty sure there's nothing dodgy buried anywhere ...

PROLOGUE

March 2017

Harriet Greene was sitting by her lounge window, her face turned towards the warmth of the evening sun, which was setting over her garden. There was a time when she'd spend many hours pottering about in her garden, growing beautiful plants, feeding the birds and admiring the wildlife who visited and called it their home. Now she was getting on in years and her eyesight was failing her, she made do with sitting by the open window and listening to the sounds of the garden instead. Every now and then she'd hear a car in the distance, driving up the lane, but most of the time a chorus of birdlife could be heard.

Harriet was nearing the end of her life. She knew it. Everyone knew it. Or at least her independent life. The idea of giving up her home, where she'd lived almost her entire adult life, was one she struggled with daily. But during the past six months, a lot had changed for her both physically and mentally. What choice did she have? Her fingers were riddled with arthritis, and thanks to her bad eyesight, she'd had a nasty fall down the stairs less than a month ago, resulting in a cracked rib, which had landed her in hospital for three days.

Despite her stubbornness to cling on for as long as possible, she knew she didn't have long left in this house. A care home was her only suitable option now that she was struggling with the simplest day-to-day activities. Yew Tree House had seen better days, the same as her. Both were falling apart at the seams and had more than a little wear and tear around the edges. Perhaps it was time to say goodbye to the old house after all.

She'd been told by her new solicitor that she had to make her final will and testament within the next few weeks; then she'd be moved to a nearby care home in Newcastle. The house was to remain empty until she died. But who was to inherit the house when Harriet eventually passed away? She didn't want to leave it to anyone outside of the family. She thought of Henry, the kind man who often did building jobs for her and would pop by for a cup of tea and a chat from time to time, but he wasn't family. He was, however, the only person who seemed to care about the old woman living alone in a large, run-down house. But no, Henry might have been a pleasant man, but he didn't deserve the house.

There was only one family member left that Harriet knew of who'd be eligible to inherit the house, her estranged sister's daughter. But Harriet had never met her niece. And her sister had died several years ago, so she couldn't very well ask her. She might have never met the girl, but she was still family. Plus, if she left the house to her, it would be a beyond-the-grave slap in the face to her deceased sister, Frances, whom she'd fallen out with many years ago.

It was settled.

Harriet would rewrite her will. She'd leave Yew Tree House to her niece, Natasha Moore. It would be a nice little surprise for the girl, but it wouldn't happen yet. Harriet wanted to leave the house empty while she was still alive. Maybe Henry could keep an eye on the old place for her, but she didn't want to part with it yet.

Not yet.

When she finally passed away, then and only then would Natasha Moore receive a letter to say she'd inherited a house in the country.

Harriet smiled as she thought of what her reaction would be; her own niece, whom she'd never met, would get the chance to completely change her life if she had the drive and courage to do so.

Yew Tree House was no ordinary house.

It would provide Natasha Moore with a life-changing opportunity ... whenever Harriet eventually set aside her stubbornness and died.

Harriet flinched when a shout pierced the growing darkness. How long had she been sitting here listening to the evening sounds of the garden? Raised voices disturbed the peace and birdsong. Harriet listened, her hearing a hell of a lot better than her sight.

'Don't you dare leave me!'

Goodness. Someone was angry.

A man.

'Stop!'

A woman's voice. Terrified, pleading.

Harriet turned her head towards the shouting.

A man and a woman were arguing somewhere nearby, but she didn't recognise either of their voices. Then, almost instantly, their voices stopped.

A long silence followed, but then birdsong returned to bless the beautiful evening, and Harriet returned to enjoying one of her last nights in Yew Tree House.

PART I

1

May 2024

I'm a woman who rarely changes her daily routine because I'm not one who enjoys surprises or change. Some people may crave it, need it in their lives to add a spark of excitement, but not me. I prefer to know what's happening and what's coming next. Yes, it's dull and monotonous at times, even I'll admit that, but without my solid routine, I feel out of control, like I can't catch my breath. And that scares me. Without my routine, I turn into an irrational and anxiety-ridden lunatic who can't seem to segregate her actions into what needs doing now, and what can wait.

I've always been like this. As a child, my mum used to call me 'Natty Nat'. The name even stuck throughout school and followed me into my teenage years, when my anxiety over losing control of my routine grew so bad that I had to see a therapist and take medication to calm my spiralling mind. However, neither of those things worked for me at the time despite using them for several years. Therefore, the easiest thing for me to do was to just keep to my normal routine day in and day out.

But, again, that went out the window when I became pregnant at seventeen. Now, seventeen years later, I've learned to adapt slightly, thanks to having a child so young, but in another way, my anxiety around my son and whether he's safe gets so bad that it makes me physically sick.

I do see a cognitive behavioural therapist from time to time, and my doctor has me on a daily dose of 200 milligrams of sertraline. However, I find the therapy a bit redundant now because I've just learned to adjust to my anxiety rather than try to live with it. My therapist says I need to avoid using my safety behaviours such as my routine, but I struggle to see the problem when I know it works to keep me calm. The medication keeps me on a level playing field. Who knows what I'd be like without it. I never do my therapy homework. I don't see the point. I don't have a problem. I'm just an anxious person. Always have been. Always will be.

The only part of the day I can control and manage in the way I like are the mornings. The rest of the day does seem to change, often without warning, but at least the mornings are cemented in stone. Therefore, every morning starts in the same way. Without fail. Having a calm and organised morning is the only part of my life that makes sense right now. It's the only part I can truly rely on. I depend on my morning routine like a nicotine addict. Without it, I risk falling apart and losing my direction in the world.

Perhaps it's too late for that.

At times I think I've already lost my direction, and I'm merely going round and round in circles, wondering which turning I should take, but then if I do take a direction, the road's blocked, and I must turn around and come back, always back to the safety of my routine.

Sometimes I resent it, wishing I had a better sense of direction. On one hand, my routine provides me a safety net, but on the other hand, it feels as if I've been repeating the same day over and over, like *Groundhog Day*.

I don't know. I'm confused and lacking any sort of get-up-and-go lately. I often find my brain is a bit slow and foggy. Perhaps my routine is part of the problem. I know it traps me and keeps me from doing anything normal, but being a single mum is hard enough, let alone when you add crippling anxiety on top. My doctor (when I saw him) used to tell me that pushing boundaries and stepping outside of my comfort zone once in a while is one way of proving that my anxiety doesn't control me. It can be a good thing. I disagree, especially when even a simple thing such as someone knocking on my door in the morning and disrupting my routine is enough to send my heart rate sky-high.

Okay, so maybe I do need some excitement in my life, a surprise occasionally. But how surprising can my life be when I've been living in the same run-down building in the middle of Birmingham for the past decade, where the same peeling paint adorns the hallways, and the landlord still hasn't changed the blown lightbulb in the stairway since it blew three years ago?

My morning starts with my phone alarm blaring to life, jolting me out of my deep slumber. I sometimes dream of tropical sandy beaches, strong pink, fruity cocktails and perhaps a handsome, dark-haired stranger who sweeps me off my feet and twirls me around. Dreaming is my one and only escape from the harsh reality of my life. My dreams are the only place where my anxiety doesn't control me, and my mind is free to do whatever the hell it likes, never worrying or stressing about what will happen next. I like going to sleep because when I'm asleep, I don't have to think about how I'm going to pay the next gas bill, or how I'm going to afford to pay for the MOT on the car that's coming up sooner than I'd like. In my dreams, everything is always perfect – even my naturally auburn, wavy hair, which always looks like a L'Oréal advert in my sleep.

Except for last night's dream.

It was a very different experience, one I'm not used to.

The alarm sounds at seven o'clock on the dot, and my body automatically jerks upright in bed. I clutch my chest with one hand while the other reaches over and turns off the noise. Keeping my hand on my heart, I feel it pounding through my chest. I count each beat, hoping it doesn't explode.

Everything around me slowly comes into focus. The window with the wonky grey curtains. The single wardrobe in the corner with a door missing. The chair next to it, piled high with clothes that need sorting out and putting away, something I don't do until it's necessary. Some might say that if I put my clothes away as soon as they were dry, it would cause less anxiety, but I'm not one of those people. It might seem chaotic, but it's my chaos, and I'm in control of it.

I blow a strand of hair out of my face.

It's okay. The dream wasn't real. My son isn't dead. He's alive. He's sleeping in the next room, probably half hanging off the edge of the bed that's too short for his lanky frame, and festering in his own bedsheets, which he refuses to let me wash every week. It's an eternal, uphill battle to get that boy to wash anything. I refuse to touch his dirty sheets because God only knows what happens under them. He's seventeen years old. I'm not naïve, nor am I a prude, but to change his bedding, I'd need to be dressed in a hazmat suit and use a pair of tongs. Usually, he takes his sheets off and dumps them on the floor for me to pick up, but I've been asking for nearly three weeks now, and he still hasn't done it. It may be time for an intervention. Or I may have to just burn them.

I reach across to the bedside table and pop out my daily dose of sertraline, medication I have to take every day for my anxiety. I swallow it down with a sip of water from the murky glass on the side.

A sigh escapes my throat as I swing my legs over the side of the bed, feeling the rough, bare floorboards under my feet. I can't afford new carpets. When I moved in ten years ago, I had to rip the old carpets up because they stank of cat piss, but they've never been replaced by the landlord. It means the room is cold, and sometimes I accidentally step on a wonky piece of board. The only room in the flat that has carpet is Max's room.

The dream where my son is dead in the ground continues to haunt me, rolling around in my head as I pad out to the hall and into the tiny bathroom that's barely big enough to turn around in. I groan when I see the state of the room. A wet towel is heaped on the floor. Droplets of urine sprinkle the toilet seat, and dark hair clogs the sink.

I close my eyes and count to ten, telling myself that it's wrong to murder your child over such trivial things, even though I've told him a hundred times to clean up after himself. He's not five years old anymore. He should be able to do these things, but he never listens to me.

Perhaps I'm not hard enough on him. Is this my fault as a parent, or does every teenage boy act like this? The thing is, I'm only thirty-five myself, so sometimes I don't even feel like his mother, like I'm not mature enough to have a seventeen-year-old son. I had him so young, still a child myself. I was the same age as he is now when I found out I was pregnant. It was, quite possibly, the most stressful and chaotic time of my life. I didn't know what to do. I toyed with the idea of having an abortion, but I just couldn't go through with it. I knew I had to tell my parents and my boyfriend. That was when everything went to shit, and my anxiety spiralled because having a child throws all routine out the window.

My parents disowned me, and my boyfriend dumped me. I sometimes question whether I made the right choice, especially as I pick up the damp towel and wipe the urine off the toilet seat for the eleven billionth time, but then I think about how wonderful and handsome Max is, and I find myself smiling.

Of course I made the right decision.

There's not a day goes by that I don't almost explode with love when I look at him. That is, after I've finished glaring at him, wanting to wring his neck for leaving his empty plate in his room until it grows fur, or for answering me with a grunt or a single word.

Today is a weekday, which means the morning routine is get up, shower, check Max is still alive, give him a kick and tell him to get up, make breakfast, eat breakfast, shout up to Max to get up, get dressed, go into Max's room and tell him if he doesn't get up, then he's in big trouble, then check my watch every thirty seconds while Max gets up, shoves food into his mouth and leaves the flat without a word.

That's the usual routine. Weekends are a slightly different affair, minus dragging Max out of his pit because he usually sleeps till noon.

After getting up and having a shower, I go and check that Max is still alive and to give him a kick. First, I knock lightly on the door because miracles sometimes happen, and he could already be awake and getting dressed. But, alas, there are no miracles today because I'm met with silence. I grasp the doorknob, turn it and push the door open, grimacing as a stale waft of what I can only describe as teenage-boy smell smacks me in the face. I hold my breath and step into his room.

The curtains are drawn across the grimy window, but it's letting in enough light from the spring morning to enable me to tiptoe my way around the various inanimate objects strewn across his floor, not to mention the piles of dirty laundry and random soiled plates and cups. I hate coming in his room. It makes me feel as if I'm keeping my son in some sort of pigsty or dungeon, but it's not as if I force him to live and sleep in this mess. He chooses to keep it this way. I know the council flat we live in is crap and run-down, but at least it's clean; every room apart from this one, anyway. I do my best with what I've got. In this room, there is no routine.

My eyes settle on the lumpy mattress, but something feels off.

'Max?' I call out. 'Time to get up.'

There's no response, not even a disgruntled moan or snore like normal. Already, the ball of anxiety inside me stirs and begins to grow.

I know before I even reach down and pull the covers back.

Max's bed is empty.

My heart almost erupts out of my chest. It starts hammering again, like it did when I woke up this morning. I stumble backwards, tripping over a discarded trainer, and tumble to the floor, knocking over a mug of cold tea, which soaks into the threadbare, already stained carpet.

I stay where I am, gulping in the stale air, as I attempt to steady my racing heart.

Where the hell is he? Am I missing something? Did he tell me last night that he was staying at a friend's house? Did I forget?

Often, when I'm anxious or panicky, my mind races with dozens of questions, and I can never get my thoughts in order. They appear all jumbled up, and nothing makes any sense.

Maybe he sent me a text late last night and told me. But no ... That's not right because Max was here last night. He was definitely here when I went to bed. I knocked on his door and said goodnight, and he replied with 'Night!' which is more than I normally get from him.

So where the fuck is he?

I can't seem to tear my eyes away from the empty bed. My mind races with horrible images of him dead in a ditch or kidnapped by a serial killer or trapped in a well. All stupid things that can't possibly be true, yet they flood my mind so vividly that my stomach churns with nausea.

What do I do?

I have to do something, but my body refuses to move off this damn, disgusting floor. My whole routine has gone flying out the window. Nothing is in the right order. There's no way I can get ready and go to work, not until I know that my baby is safe. If I don't turn up for my shift, what's the worst that can happen? A few people won't be able to complain to me about the service they've received, or yell at me for their insurance running out, or blame me for something that isn't my fault.

Finding Max's bed empty has altered my routine, and I can't breathe. My safety net is gone, and unplanned chaos has taken its place. All I think about are the worst-case scenarios. I can't just sit here.

Do something, Natasha!

I take a deep breath and push myself to standing, turn around to go and fetch my phone to call him – and bump straight into Max, who looks as surprised as I do.

'Max!' I can't help it. The relief I feel is like a flood. I spring forwards, grab my grown-up baby and pull him against my body, breathing in his musty scent, which isn't as soothing and pleasant as it used to be when he was a young child.

'Why are you in my room, and why are you being weird?' he asks me. I can feel him trying to pull away from me, but I hold on to him for as long as I can before eventually letting him go. He steps around me with a frown on his face.

I take a deep breath and gulp it down. 'I ... I came in to wake you up, but you weren't here. Did you sleep here?'

'Of course I slept here. I was in the bathroom.'

'Max, I've come from the bathroom. I just had a shower. It's a tiny room. I think I would have noticed if you were in there.'

He has the decency to blush and avoid eye contact. That's when I look down at his feet and see he's wearing trainers, which are caked in fresh mud. He's clearly been out somewhere and just come back. 'Where have you been?' I ask him.

Max huffs at me and slumps down on his bed, flicking his trainers off. They go flying across the room, settling on a pile of other random junk, splattering the items and nearby carpet with mud. 'Oh, get off my case, okay? I had to meet a friend before school.'

'Max, it's just after seven o'clock in the morning. You're not normally even functional at this time, let alone up and dressed and out the door. Why won't you tell me where you were?'

'Because it doesn't matter.'

'Well, it matters to me.'

Max doesn't reply. It appears we're at a stalemate. I decide to try a different tactic. 'Next time you have to go somewhere at seven o'clock in the morning, can you at least text me?'

'Whatever.'

That's as close to a yes as I'm likely to get.

'And will you please strip your bedding and put it in the washing machine? It smells so bad in here that if I didn't know any better, I'd say there's a dead animal rotting under your bed.'

'Fine.'

'Fine.'

I turn and walk out of the room, pausing to look at him before closing the door. Why do I feel as if I'm losing my baby boy more and more every day? When did he turn from a chatty, clingy toddler who'd talk my ear off for hours on end to a monosyllabic, stroppy teenager who'd rather be alone in his room than say two words to his own mother?

The ball of anxiety reduces in size as I head to the

kitchen to continue my routine. It's okay. It was just a small blip. Max is safe, and nothing bad happened. My routine is still intact.

FIFTEEN MINUTES LATER, Max appears in the kitchen, carrying his bedsheets, which he's rolled into a tight ball, and drops them in front of the washing machine. I almost open my mouth to argue with him to put them *in* the machine since it's literally only a few inches away but decide against it. Some battles aren't worth starting. He plonks himself down on a chair at the wobbly breakfast table and helps himself to a slice of white toast with peanut butter.

His eyes are glued to his phone as he scrolls through whatever it is he scrolls through for hours each day. I do wonder about teenagers these days and why they feel the need to spend so long staring at a screen, watching random videos and chatting to relative strangers. When I was his age, I was about to have a baby and was working and saving every penny to buy all the baby paraphernalia I'd need, often buying things second-hand on eBay or at car boot sales to save money. Granted, back then, there weren't such things as smartphones with internet, but still …

I sit quietly watching him, sipping my tea. Why do I feel speechless around my own son? There are so many questions I want to ask him, things I need to know about where he was this morning, but he barely says a word to me even on a normal day. It's like I'm not even here. I may as well be invisible. To him, I'm just this person who buys him food and washes his clothes.

'I need a new phone.'

His abrupt statement causes me to raise my eyebrows.

'I'm sorry, but you know I can't afford to buy you a new phone at the moment. What's wrong with that one?' I glance at the black iPhone in his hand. It's covered in scratches, and I know the screen is cracked, but I assume it still works; otherwise he wouldn't constantly be glued to it.

'It's, like, five years old.'

'But it works, right?'

'I guess, but it's ancient and slow, and the screen's cracked.'

I let out a sigh as I stand up and rinse my favourite mug in the sink. It has a picture of a smiling cup of tea on it that says, 'Got Tea?' It was the last thing my mum gave to me, so it's older than Max. Despite losing contact with her and despite how she treated me, I've kept it as a reminder that I did once have a mother of my own.

'Unless it breaks and it's incapable of sending messages or calling my phone, then you're stuck with it, I'm afraid,' I say.

Silence.

My back is still turned as he pushes his chair backwards, scraping it across the tiled floor. A door slams, and thundering footsteps echo down the hall.

I hate the fact I have no money and can't afford to buy Max nice things. It's not that I want to shower him with material items and turn him into a spoiled brat, but I'd like to be able to buy him things when he asks or surprise him with the latest video game or gadget. I see some of his school friends with the newest iPhone or expensive game consoles and notice the look in his eyes. Not jealousy, but ... sadness. Perhaps a hint of embarrassment that his mum can't afford to buy him things. And I hate it.

I look out the window across our housing estate. We've

lived in Birmingham ever since Max was born. We moved around a few different council flats for several years when he was a baby, until we were given this one. We've lived in this shitty hellhole in the bad part of the city ever since. There's a drug addict who lives below us, and next door lives a couple who constantly fight and smash each other to pieces, screaming at all hours of the night. I've had to call the police on numerous occasions because it sounds as if they're trying to kill each other, but nothing is ever done about it. The next night, they go back to their usual ways. Once, they bashed my door down and then screamed at me, accusing me of eavesdropping on their lives. I haven't called the police on them since. If they end up murdering each other, then that's their problem, not mine.

The drug addict who lives below us is actually a nice guy. He's never been rude to me or caused any trouble, but I don't like the idea of him dealing drugs in the same building where my son lives. How he hasn't been raided and charged yet, I have no idea. I'm not sure what he deals either, but there are people coming and going at all hours, in and out of the building, looking a bit shifty. I stay out of it, but I don't like it. I hate living here, but it's all I can afford. The social rent is cheaper than anywhere else I've seen, so I put up with the horrible neighbours, funky smells and bloodstains on the pavements.

It's bad enough I have to work two jobs to pay the bills. Sometimes I need to make a choice whether to pay for electric or buy food. We've been threatened with legal action several times due to late payments. I always manage to make it work somehow, but year by year things get more expensive, the rent goes up, bills increase, and the vice around my chest gets tighter and tighter.

The worst thing is that Max is changing too. Not only is he growing into a man before my eyes, but I know he resents me, maybe even hates me because I can't give him the life he deserves. He wants more from me. He's disappointed I'm his mum and we can't afford to go on holiday and have nice things. Hell, he's still got a Pokémon duvet cover from when he was seven because I never bought him another one. I'm failing him. Every day, I fail him a little bit more. Now he's lying to me and hiding things, creeping out at night to do who knows what.

I've seen him hanging out a few times with a load of other teenagers from the neighbourhood, and they are bad news. I'm not ashamed when I say they are awful human beings. Several times, I've had the school ring me and say Max hasn't turned up. Six weeks ago, Max and two other boys were arrested for joyriding and drinking. Luckily, the police let him off with a warning, but ever since then I've had a gnawing sensation in my gut, telling me that's not the end of it. It's only a matter of time before Max does something worse. I hate myself for thinking that, but it's the truth. I keep telling him I don't want him hanging out with those boys, but I may as well be talking to myself.

My son needs help. I need to do something to ensure his safety, but I don't have a clue what. I've tried talking to him, but he clams up and storms off, muttering under his breath. If I don't do something soon, I fear my baby boy will slip away forever.

I can't let that happen.

But how do I help him? How do I save him if I can barely save myself from my own anxiety? If something bad happens to him, or he does something to someone else, I'll never forgive myself. It will be my fault too because I should be more involved with his friends and what he's doing, but it's been easier to bury my head in the sand and ignore all the warning signs than stand up and take responsibility for his and my actions.

I hate myself. I hate what the anxiety around losing my routine, and the fear of the unknown, has done to me. It's turned me into a selfish mother who would rather do the same thing every single day than risk upsetting my life and confronting the issues around my son's behaviour.

I can't lose Max.

I'd rather lose my routine. And that's the truth. I'll deal with the anxiety if I have to, but I must make sure he's okay.

I'll do anything to keep him safe.

Anything.

2

I somehow manage to drag myself through the rest of my morning routine and get to work only five minutes late, which is enough to give me heart palpitations. I always imagine the worst: that I walk through the door late and get fired on the spot or get shouted at in front of the whole office, but when I arrive, out of breath and sweating, no one even bats an eyelid, which proves to me that my over-dramatic imagination needs to calm the fuck down and get a grip. My boss waves at me and smiles.

Luckily, the rest of the day goes smoothly, bar a missed phone call from the school and three phone calls from the same unknown number. It's been happening a lot lately, especially over the past few months, but I never answer them for two reasons: one is that answering the phone to someone I don't know causes me to have a small panic attack, and two is because the person on the other end is most likely going to demand money from me. I call the school back during my lunch break, crossing my fingers in the hope that no one answers.

'Oh, hi, you called me earlier? It's Natasha Moore.'

'Ah, yes, Max's mum. I'm afraid he hasn't turned up again today. That's the fifth time in the past two weeks. I think you need to come in and have a chat with the head teacher.'

My heart sinks, and I get an adrenaline spike. 'I had no idea. I'm so sorry.'

I can practically hear the judgement ooze from the woman on the phone. 'Please email with your preferred days and times this week to have a chat. Max will need to be there too.'

'Okay, I will. Thank you.'

I hang up and almost burst into tears. Where the hell has Max been going if he's not been going to school? Then I have a sinking feeling, like the floor is disappearing beneath my feet. What if he hasn't been studying towards his A levels? Shit. He is in year twelve now and is due to get his predicted grades at the end of the summer term, but I have no idea what level he's at or what his attendance has been like.

I am the worst mother in the world.

And the worst thing is, I don't even have time to go to a meeting at his school because I'm always working, and how am I supposed to drag him along too?

By the time I've finished my customer service shift at three and dragged myself to my next job, ready to start working in the pub at four, a headache is forming behind my eyes, thudding like a bass drum. I have time before my evening shift starts, so I take up my usual position in the alleyway behind the pub and sit on a small crate. I only work three hours at the pub, but add that onto the six I work at my customer service role; I work nine hours a day during the week. Plus eight hours at the pub on a Saturday. That's fifty-three hours a week, just above minimum wage. Yet I still can't seem to make ends meet. It gets sucked up in overdraft fees, loan repayments and everything else. The amount of debt I'm in causes me non-stop tension headaches and mild panic attacks whenever my email alert pings or the phone rings, in case it's someone who wants to take me to court or take my crappy home away from me.

I check my phone in case Max has messaged me, but there's nothing. As usual. I don't know why I bother checking for a text from him. I type out a quick WhatsApp message, telling him we need to talk later when I get home, that there's leftover pie in the fridge for his dinner, and I'll be back as usual at half past seven. I add a couple of kisses, but then decide against them and press delete. I don't want him to feel as if I'm stifling him with my affection. He won't appreciate my kisses anyway. Plus, I'm not feeling particularly affectionate towards him right now after what I've just found out. I don't want him to throw away his education, but that's exactly what he's done, isn't it? And I've barely noticed because I've been so anxious and constantly on high alert regarding the money situation.

Max immediately responds by liking the message. That's it. All I get from my son now is a thumbs up notification from him. He doesn't even feel the inclination to respond with words. At least I know he's alive, I suppose.

'Hey, Nat.'

I look up at the sound of my name and see Phil, the owner of the pub, walking towards me. He's about sixty years old, has a long, grey beard, and despite telling him several times over the years I've worked for him, he still refuses to call me Natasha. It's always Nat. It makes me sound like a bug. I've never liked it, and every time he says it, my stomach clenches, remembering the nickname I used to have, 'Natty Nat'.

'Hey, Phil. How's it going?'

'Can't complain. Want a fag?'

'If you've got one going spare.'

'Always have one for you, Nat.' He winks as he hands me a cigarette and lighter. I fight the urge to cringe as our fingers touch. He disappears through the back door of the pub, leaving me to smoke in peace. I'm not proud of the fact I smoke. The truth is I don't smoke often. I can't afford to. Usually, I just bum smokes off Phil, who's always happy to oblige. I know it's not trendy to smoke anymore. Most people these days vape, but I've never got used to them and prefer the feel of a real cigarette between my fingers and lips.

I'm not addicted to nicotine like most people are. I can take or leave a cigarette, and sometimes I go weeks, even months without one, but today is one of those days that I can't refuse, especially after the shock of this morning, finding Max's bed empty, my routine being momentarily steam-rolled, and now the fact he's been missing school and has probably failed his exams.

The scene from this morning repeats over and over in my mind. I can't imagine what I would have done had Max not walked in that second. The panic was suffocating, over-whelming and painful. I let out a long puff of smoke and then inhale another, licking my dry lips afterwards. I've never smoked in front of Max and never will, but I know he's started doing it. His clothes often smell of smoke, and I found a lighter in his bag once.

I sigh, realising it's yet another thing I'm failing at. I didn't even confront him about it because how could I? I'd be a hypocrite if I did. I stub out the fag and flick the butt into the bin next to me before brushing myself off and heading inside.

'Natasha, love, can you give me a hand real quick?'

I turn and see Phil's wife walking towards me. Carol is the same age as Phil, but easily looks twenty years younger. I don't know how she does it. I must ask her what her secret is to stop the ageing process because the other day I found my first grey hair, and I am not happy about it. Nor am I happy with the fact more and more wrinkles appear around my eyes every time I look in the grimy bathroom mirror. Not even thirty-five yet and I'm already feeling and looking like an old woman. I don't have the time or money to have my hair dyed, not even with a box dye job at home. Then again, I do love my auburn hair and pale skin. Everyone always says I look like Nicola Roberts or Emma Stone, but growing older is yet another thing I have no control over, and my anxiety jolts me every time I think about it.

'Sure thing,' I reply.

I follow Carol into the back storage room and help her unpack a couple of new crates of beer.

'Got some new beers in from a local brewery that's just opened,' she tells me, holding out a bottle to show me the label, which is quite striking with its black and gold colouring.

I take it and have a good look, turning it over to look at the back label too.

'Looks nice,' I say. To be perfectly honest, I've no idea about beers and what's considered good or not. I've never liked drinking it, especially since at age sixteen I decided to play beer pong with friends and ended up passing out in my friend's garden, covered in my own puke, and had to be picked up by my dad, who had not been at all happy, especially when he saw the length of my skirt. I haven't touched beer since, and every time I smell it, I'm reminded of that night, which happened to be the night my boyfriend got me pregnant. Wine is much more my thing, even though I haven't had a drink in a long time, mainly because I can't afford to buy a bottle, even a cheap one. I'd rather spend the five or so quid on proper food for me and Max.

'I'm going to put it behind the bar so the customers can see it. Make sure you offer it as a suggestion if they're after a pale ale.'

'Will do.'

We work in silence for a few minutes, then I ask her to pass me the next box, but Carol doesn't answer. 'Carol? Carol!'

Her head snaps up. 'Oh, goodness, sorry, I was miles away.'

'Everything okay?' I ask.

'Yes, fine, I was just thinking about the story I saw on the news this morning.'

'Oh, what was it about?'

'Awful business. There was another stabbing in your neighbourhood last night,' she says.

I pause as a hard lump forms in my throat. 'There was?'

'Terrible, it was. A teenager stabbed another kid in the side and left them to bleed out on the pavement. Can you believe that?' Unfortunately, I can because it happens far more times than I want to admit.

'Did he survive?' I ask, lining up the beers on the storage shelf in perfectly straight lines.

'Yes, but the kid's in critical condition.'

I nod and look down at the floor. The thought pops into

my head before I can stop it, and I imagine Max standing over a body with a knife in his hand. A horrible chill floods my body. Why did my mind automatically put Max as the stabber? Is that what I think of my own son? That he's capable of stabbing another kid. The guilt makes my stomach flip over, and shame washes over me.

'You okay, love? You've gone awfully pale. I mean paler than usual.'

'I'm fine. Sorry. It's just so sad ... about the stabbing. I can't help but think, what if it was Max?'

Carol reaches out and gives my shoulder a light squeeze. 'I know. It doesn't bear thinking about, does it? But Max is a good kid. I'm sure he doesn't hang around with people like that.'

'Right,' I say, swallowing the bile rising in my throat.

By the end of my shift, I don't feel any better. I feel worse, thanks to my friend anxiety twisting and dissecting every tiny detail and blowing it out of proportion. It's gone eight by the time I drag my sorry butt up the stairs to the flat because Carol asked me to stay behind a bit later and help clean the kitchen floor, walls and ceiling after a huge tub of sauce exploded when it was dropped. I also had to stop at the corner shop. I'm carrying a pint of green-topped milk and my handbag.

I slide the key into the lock, but it gets stuck when I attempt to turn it. I wrestle with it to get the damn door open. My handbag slips from my grip, and the items inside spill across the floor. Sighing, I bend down, scoop everything up and then head to the kitchen and place the milk in the fridge, making a mental note to buy more bread tomorrow when I see there is none left. I listen for any sounds coming from Max's room, but it's suspiciously quiet. He sometimes stays in his room all evening. I'm not quite sure what he does in there because he doesn't have a games console or computer.

I can't hear anything, but it's not unusual for him to still be out at this time of the evening. The pie I told him about is still in the fridge, uneaten. I check his room. It's empty. Again.

I check my phone, but there's no message from him. His *last seen* time was over five hours ago.

The dreaded anxiety is there in the background, ready to explode at any moment, twirling and swirling in constant circles. It's exhausting living with it. I wish more than anything that I could control it, tell it to fuck off and leave me alone, but it seems to like hanging around me, constantly keeping me on edge.

Leaving the pie in the fridge for Max, I make myself some pasta, spoon in a glob of pesto and eat it on the scruffy sofa while watching the television. We don't have Sky TV or Netflix or any fancy channels, so I flick through the terrestrial channels until I find something half-decent that isn't a soap opera, and settle in for the evening.

At some point, I fall asleep and then wake up with a start, checking my phone for the time.

It's gone eleven.

I get up and go to Max's room. He's still not back, and the pie is still there.

That sinking feeling in my stomach appears again as I type out a message, asking him to call me back straight away. Why isn't he here? Where could he possibly be at eleven o'clock on a school night? Should I go out and look for him?

If something bad happened, then the police would have called me, right? But what if he's lying dead in a ditch somewhere?

For the second time today, I almost hyperventilate as my anxiety spins out of control, throwing up a multitude of questions and different scenarios. I can't get a grip on any of them. I have no idea what to do or how to handle this. What the hell is going on with Max?

I turn the light on in his room and glance around. Perhaps it's time to take matters into my own hands, but can I really search my teenage son's room without his permission? What would I even be looking for? What do I think I'll find? If he walked in on me right now, I'd be so mortified I'm not sure I'd be able to look him in the eyes. Even being in here without him knowing is making my palms clammy.

His bed is unmade because I haven't had the chance to re-make it yet. The small desk in the corner, which should be used for homework, is overflowing with clothes, rubbish and a few trinkets. I walk up to the desk and bite my lip as I slowly slide the top drawer open, holding my breath, saying a silent prayer that I don't find anything dodgy. Papers, more rubbish and about a hundred pens.

I let out my breath and close the drawer.

The guilt and pressure are overwhelming. My heart is pounding so hard in my chest that I can barely breathe as I wonder what my next move should be. My eyes scan the desk again. I pick up the clothes, recognising them as the ones I washed last week. He hasn't even put them away. They've just been dumped on his desk with his dirty washing.

I give up.

There's no helping this boy.

Hang on, I do the same thing ... I suppose I shouldn't judge him.

The sound of keys rustling in the front door makes me jump. I turn the light off and then launch myself out of his room and into the bathroom, slamming the door just a little too hard. I lean against the door and take several deep breaths, attempting to calm my racing heart. That was a close call.

His footsteps sound outside the door.

'Mum?' His voice sounds weird. Small. Weak.

Something's wrong. A mother can always tell.

'Max?' I open the door and peer out at my son. A loud gasp erupts before I can clamp a hand over my mouth to stop it. Every mother's worst nightmare is that her baby gets hurt, and my nightmare has come to life before my eyes. My anxiety slaps me hard in the face, and I have to fight hard to stop from crying and collapsing to a heap on the floor.

Max stands in front of me. His T-shirt is ripped, and there are smears of what I can only assume is blood across his chest. Dark blood is caked around his nostrils and mouth; a black bruise is blossoming around his left eye, which is so swollen he can't even open it. His cheeks are stained with blood and tears, and he's clutching his left side, stooping over as if he can't stand up straight.

'Max! Baby! What's happened?' I rush forwards, but I don't know what to do first. In my panic I accidentally bump into him, and he winces. He's in pain, he's filthy and bleeding, but I need to know who did this to him. I'm going to kill them with my bare hands.

'M-Mum,' he whispers, tears swimming in his eyes.

He very rarely calls me mum, and I haven't seen him cry since he was twelve. He needs me to be his mother right now. He doesn't need an interrogation. Max collapses against me. Tears finally erupt from his eyes as he buries his bruised face in my shoulder and weeps like a child. We slowly sink to the floor, our arms wrapped around each other, both crying and shaking. I stroke his soft hair, hoping he's not feeding from my own anxiety.

'It's okay. Everything will be okay.' I say the words over and over, but I don't believe them. The thing I've been afraid of the most has happened. Max has been hurt, and I wasn't there to protect him. I'm trying to soothe him like I did when he was a baby, but he's seventeen years old now. I have no idea who my son is now. My gentle tones and lullabies won't work anymore.

We stay on the floor for several minutes while his sobs fade, and he eventually pulls away from me. I grab hold of his T-shirt, too afraid to let go. It's the first time he's hugged me in … I don't remember when my son last gave me a hug. I want to hold him close forever and never let go. I want to breathe in his scent, feel his heart beat against mine, like when he was a baby and slept on my chest, but I know that's just a fairy tale now, in a time and place far removed from today. I slowly let go of his top and allow him his space. He looks at me and sniffs loudly.

'Let's get you cleaned up,' I say.

He nods and walks into the bathroom, taking a seat on the closed toilet lid. Due to the bathroom being so small, there's not a lot of room to manoeuvre, and his long, lanky legs take up a lot of the space. He keeps his head bowed, unable to look me in the eyes. I don't have much in the way of first aid items, bar a few plasters, which won't be of much use, so I make a start by wiping the blood off his face with a warm flannel so I can see what the damage is and whether I need to take him into A&E for stitches. He flinches a few times, but otherwise doesn't make a sound. I don't think his nose is broken, but it's certainly bled a lot. It's clotted now. There is a cut above his eye, but I don't think it warrants stitches.

I help him take his T-shirt off, stifling a gasp as I see the bruises on the left-hand side across his ribcage. He is black and blue. I can't help but be relieved there isn't anything worse, like a stab or bullet wound.

'I think you may have a broken rib,' I say, bending down to get a better look. I gently touch his skin with my fingers, and he immediately jerks away in pain. 'I'm sorry. Let me get you some painkillers.' I rifle through the bathroom cabinet above the sink and find an old blister pack of paracetamol. Once he's got them down and had a drink of water, I begin to clean the blood off his chest and arms, being careful to keep my movements slow and gentle, rinsing the flannel whenever it gets too dirty. It doesn't take long for the warm water in the sink to turn pink.

When I'm finished, I fetch a clean T-shirt and help him into it, then assist him into his room. I haven't yet put clean bedding on his bed, so he sits on his chair and watches me while I do it. All the time my heart is racing, as if I've just sprinted around a running track, like I did at school. I used to be a decent track runner, but that soon went to hell when I fell pregnant. A lot of other things went to hell then too. My anxiety keeps threatening to overwhelm me, but I squash it down. My son doesn't need my inner demons causing trouble right now. He needs me to be calm and level-headed, something that's very difficult for me to do, given the situation.

'Mum,' he says quietly, 'I think I'm in trouble.'

I take a deep breath, fighting back tears. He's opening up to me. I don't want to say or do the wrong thing, so I just listen; the only thing I can do right now.

'I don't know what to do. I tried to handle it on my own, but ... I did something bad.'

The air in this stuffy room disappears. No. No, not Max. Please ...

I finish making the bed and turn to face him. 'What did you do?' My heart rate doubles yet again.

'I ... I've been skipping school to sell drugs.'

My mouth opens, but no words come out, so I close it again. That was not what I was expecting him to say. Drugs? My mind went to the worst place: that he'd killed someone. I hate myself for thinking it, but after the stabbing last night, it's all I've been able to think about all evening.

'What kind of drugs?' I ask. I realise I should question him regarding his exams, but it's not the most critical issue right now.

'Does it matter?'

'Well, if it was weed, then I would still be worried, but not as worried as I'd be if you were dealing class A drugs, for example.'

He doesn't respond and avoids eye contact.

'Shit,' I mutter.

Max sighs as he stands up and crawls into bed. I pull his duvet over his legs and chest and fluff his pillow while he makes himself comfortable; then I sit on the edge of his bed.

'Tell me everything,' I say. 'I need to know how bad this is so I can figure out how to handle it.'

Max nods slowly. 'I've been hanging out with these guys for a while, smoking weed and stuff, drinking. All harmless stuff, really.'

'Are these the same boys who got you arrested the other week for drinking and joyriding?'

'Yes, some of them.'

'I thought I told you to stay away from them?'

'I don't have any other friends around here.'

'I'd hardly call them your friends.'

He shoots me a look.

'Sorry. Go ahead. Continue.'

'Anyway, one of them said he needed help to sell some drugs. I thought he meant weed, but then it turned out to be cocaine.'

I inhale sharply. 'Please tell me you haven't used any?'

'No, I've just smoked weed, I swear.'

I let out a breath.

'Anyway, tonight I was supposed to take this coke to a drop-off point, meet this guy, collect some money and return the money to the dealer.'

'Okay ...'

'I got jumped when I arrived at the drop-off. Three men with masks on grabbed me, took the coke and ran off. I didn't get the money. When I returned, the dealer wasn't happy. He had two other blokes beat me up and said I needed to pay him back the money by the end of the month, or he'd kill me.'

I squeeze my fists at my sides, fighting the urge to jump to my feet and demand he tell me who these guys are so I can go and kill them myself, but the sensible side of me manages to take control. I know I'd probably get myself killed in the process if I did anything rash. Then again, I'm not sure my anxiety could take standing up to a drug dealer.

'Okay,' I finally say. 'How much money are we talking about here?'

'Five grand.'

'Five grand,' I repeat. Even if I saved every penny I earned until the end of the month, it wouldn't cover a fraction of that. I only earn just over two grand after taxes, and I certainly don't have anything close to that in savings. In fact, I don't have any savings.

We sit in silence again. I don't know what to say. How can I make this better for him? Should I lie and say everything will be okay? Should I tell him I have the money and not to worry about anything? Should I tell him the truth, that we're completely broke, and there's no way in hell I'll be able to raise the money for him to pay the dealer back.

I opt for the truth.

'I don't have that kind of money,' I say.

'I know, Mum. I wasn't asking you for it. I know you don't have the money.'

'I'll think of something.'

Max looks at me and rolls his eyes. I'm losing him. He's slowly turning into the teenager I recognise. Whoever that boy was who hugged me earlier and wept in my arms is gone now. I miss him already.

'Forget it, okay? I'll handle it. I can, I dunno, ask the guy for some extra work or something. Pay him back that way.'

'Absolutely not. God knows what he'll have you doing. It's bad enough you agreed to deal drugs in the first place, Max. I thought I taught you better than that.' Shit. That's the wrong thing to say.

Max tuts. 'Yeah, right, just like all the other important things you've *taught* me.'

Tears threaten to spring from my eyes. I admit I struggled when it came time to teach him to shave, but I did my best. I even offered to teach him to drive, but he refused. Plus, I couldn't afford to buy him proper lessons.

'I'm doing my best, Max,' I say.

He doesn't answer me.

'Max ... I need you to listen to me, okay? Does this person know where you live?'

'Yes.'

'This is bad.' As if answering the door wasn't anxiety-inducing enough. Now, I have to worry about a drug dealer bashing down my door and murdering my son. 'What's going on with school?' I ask, deciding it's now or never to confront the issue.

'I've skipped a few days here and there.'

'Yes, but what about studying for your A levels? You'll be getting your predicted grades soon, right?'

'Why do you care?'

'I'm your mother. Of course I care.'

Max shrugs. 'I doubt my grades will be very good. I don't care anyway. They're only stupid A levels.'

'But ... But ...' I stand up, ready to explode in rage, but I feel like a hypocrite. It's my fault this has happened. I should have paid more attention to what was going on.

Max sighs. 'Look, I'm really tired and in pain. Can you let me sleep for a while?'

I nod slowly. 'Yes, of course. We'll talk more in the morning though, okay? About everything. We'll sort this out together, I promise.'

Max grunts again in response as he pulls the duvet over his head.

And he's gone.

I walk out of his room, close the door, then sink to the ground and lean my back against the door; otherwise I fear I may topple over. I pull my knees up to my chest and wrap my arms around them, resting my chin in the nook between my knees. I feel completely useless. How could I have not seen this coming? Why have I been so blind to my son's whereabouts and extracurricular activities? But I had seen it, hadn't I? I knew, deep down, something bad was going to happen sooner or later, but I didn't do anything about it. Why didn't I? Why did I hide away and ignore what was going on? Because I'm a coward, that's why. It was easier to ignore everything. I should have spoken to Max, made sure he was on the right track. Instead, I buried my head in the sand and pretended like everything was normal. I trusted him to be making the right decisions. I was afraid of facing up to my own failure as a mother.

Because I have failed him.

Now, his life has been threatened by a drug dealer.

How am I supposed to come up with five thousand pounds in less than two weeks? I have nothing I can sell. My car is probably worth about two hundred quid. I can't take out any more credit cards until the others are paid off because my credit score is practically zero. The bank won't give me another loan because I've already failed on repayments. I'm way into my overdraft with no hope of paying it back any time soon. My pay cheque barely sees the light of day before it's gone again.

I have nothing to my name.

Nothing.

I weep quietly outside my son's bedroom door, where I stay all night, like his guardian and protector. At some point I fall asleep with my forehead resting on my knees, and the morning light wakes me up. My butt is numb and sore as I drag myself to my feet and wipe a slither of drool from my mouth. My neck is stiff too, so I reach up and massage the back of it with my fingers, stretching it from side to side to try to release the tension. But no amount of self-massage and stretching will get rid of the build-up of tension and anxiety I'm carrying. I've learned to live with it over the years.

I open the door a crack and peer in. Max is fast asleep, cuddled under his duvet, snoring lightly. I close the door again. I can't believe he's been skipping school. He used to be a smart kid, but for the past four years, his grades have continued to slip. He clearly has no plans to go to university after he finishes school. What does he want to do with his life? I've never asked him. Should I have tried harder? Max has no prospects now. He may want to get a job, start a career, but without qualifications, what sort of career is he expecting to start?

I feel so stupid. How could I have allowed this to happen? I'm his mother. I should have tried harder to keep his grades up. I should have encouraged him get a job, rather than allow him to hang out with his so-called friends, who have now turned him into a drug-dealing criminal and threatened to kill him. Should I go to the police and tell them what happened? Or would that just make things worse? The last thing I want is to make the police aware that my son is dealing drugs.

Maybe I can find a way to handle this myself without incriminating Max or having to pay back the money. I won't allow Max to work off his debt with this person, but I could do it instead. It's not perfect by any means and will probably mean I'll have to do some dodgy dealings myself, but if it gets Max off the hook and keeps him safe, then there's nothing I wouldn't do for my son.

My customer service shift starts in two hours. I need to

do a hundred and one things before then. My routine is non-existent now, and usually I'd have had a shower by now, but I can't seem to get my thoughts in order. Nothing makes sense in my head anymore. I don't know what to focus on first. All I know is that I have to protect Max. My maternal instinct is on overdrive.

I hold my breath as I push open his bedroom door again. His phone is lying on the floor beside his bed. I gently pick it up and then scurry out of the room, feeling like a petty criminal.

I input the code he used last: my birthday. But it's the wrong one.

Damn it.

He's changed it without telling me. I agreed for him to have a phone as long as he told me the code in case I needed access to it in an emergency. I've never looked through his phone without his permission. Never. But this is an emergency, and the fact he hasn't told me he changed his password is disconcerting. There are clearly things on his phone he doesn't want me to see.

I try his birthday.

Wrong.

I sigh heavily and look up at the ceiling, hoping for another idea as to what the code might be; then I stare back down at the phone at the picture on his home screen. It's not a picture of him or me, but of a fairground attraction, a Hook a Duck.

I remember the day we went to the fair like it was yesterday. Max was twelve, and despite only bringing ten pounds in change because that's all I could afford, we had an absolute blast. We spent all the money on that damn Hook a Duck game because Max was determined to win one.

And he did.

I smile at the memory. As far as I know, the rubber duck is still in his room somewhere under all the paraphernalia, unless he's thrown it out. It was the first of July. I remember it well because it was the last time Max and I laughed and had fun together before he started drifting away from me as he entered his teenage years.

I input 0107, and the phone unlocks.

Perhaps that date means a lot to him too. A glimmer of hope sparks in my heart at the thought of my son not hating me completely.

I open his text messages.

There's one from a private number, which says:

> You got my money yet, bitch?

I grind my teeth as I type out a reply:

> No, but let's talk.

It takes two minutes for a reply to arrive:

> Come to the warehouse on Monk Street in one hour. You better have my money.

This is a bad idea.

But I'm all out of good ones, so it's the only choice I have left.

My own phone blares to life in my hands, and I flinch so badly that I drop it. It's the same unknown number again. They just won't give up. Whoever it is leaves a voicemail, but I ignore it. They can bloody well wait. I have enough to deal with right now.

3

My body trembles uncontrollably, like I'm shivering in a blizzard, as I pull up in the warehouse car park. I don't know where to look or what I should be doing now. I'm still in the same clothes I wore yesterday, not even taking a shower before I returned Max's phone to his room after jotting down the dealer's number in my own phone and heading out the door. I'm so far out of my comfort zone that I debated taking an extra dose of my anxiety medication before I left, but I did that once before, and it took me days to level out again. Taking an extra dose is almost as bad as forgetting to take it. I've done that before too, and I had the worst headaches and brain fog.

What the hell am I doing? Only sheer desperation has forced me to do something this stupid and reckless. I know I'm potentially walking into a dangerous situation, but my racing brain cannot think of anything else to do that makes sense. This isn't me, but a switch has been flicked inside, and I'm ready to defend my child at all costs, even if it means putting myself in harm's way.

Still in my car, I stare at the warehouse. My pulse quickens. I take a deep inhale, but that makes it worse, so I stare down at my trainers. They are caked in dirt and are wearing thin in the heel. I wish I had the money to buy new ones, but I bought Max new shoes instead several months ago because his had fallen apart, and there was only so much gaffer tape I could use to keep the soles together. I lean my forehead on the steering wheel and silently scream.

Just get out of the damn car, Natasha!

Before I can chicken out, I throw open the door and march up to the double doors of the warehouse and knock hard three times. The sound seems to echo around the entire area, making it twice as loud, almost like I'm trying to bang down the door. This doesn't look like a used warehouse. There are no cars around and no signs of life. Lots of old cars and discarded rubbish piled everywhere.

I'm about to turn and sprint back to my car, back to safety, but then the doors slide open.

It's too late.

'Who the fuck are you? Where's Max?' There's a mean-looking man standing in front of me with a chiselled jaw and short, dark hair. He's wearing a black tracksuit.

My bladder releases a small about of wee. 'I ... um ... I'm his mother.'

The man bursts into laughter. Then two more tough-looking blokes appear at my side, having come from behind me without me noticing. I shriek in alarm and attempt to step to the side, but the nearest one steps in front of me, blocking my way. I feel about an inch tall, sandwiched between three very large, very angry-looking men.

'Maxy boy sent his mummy to do his dirty work, huh? That's fucking hilarious,' says the first man.

The two men next to me inch closer towards me, forcing me to step inside the warehouse. As soon as I do, the doors slam shut.

I open my mouth to take a breath, but the air seems to have disappeared. 'Look,' I say in a voice reminiscent of a mouse, 'I don't have the money right this minute, but maybe we can come to some sort of arrangement.' The two men next to me tower over me by at least a foot and a half. They are huge and muscular, like bodyguards.

The man in front of me sniffs loudly, then spits out a globule of phlegm at my feet. I flinch, but don't move my feet as I swallow back a gag. 'What sort of arrangement are you thinking, huh?' He reaches for his crotch and rearranges himself.

I fight the urge to gag again. 'I ... I'm not sure, but perhaps I can work for you until I pay off his debt. I don't care how long it takes.'

The man looks me up and down. 'Listen, you seem like a decent chick, but I'm not doing a deal with Maxy boy's mummy. Either you pay me the five grand your no-good son owes me, or I send my boys round, and then shit will get ugly. You know what I mean? He's lucky he survived the first beating. He won't survive the second.'

My body betrays me and starts shaking again, but not with fear. I see myself exploding towards this man and wrapping my hands around his neck, squeezing the life from him. I see myself lunging forwards and shoving him hard in the chest, then kicking him over and over while he's rolling around on the floor in agony. But it's all in my mind. There's no way I can do any of those things. He's twice the size of me and probably three times stronger. Plus, his two bodyguards are merely inches away. He knows it too because a crude grin spreads across his face as he takes a step towards me, so close that I can smell his beer breath.

'You have two weeks to come up with the money. You're lucky I'm being so lenient. Two weeks. For every day you go over, I add a hundred quid. Got it? I'll be watching you. I know where you and Maxy boy live.'

Tears leak from my eyes. 'P-Please ...'

The man doesn't respond. He looks at each of the men next to me and then nods. They turn like obedient dogs and go and stand further away. The man in front of me leans in close to me again.

'With one word I could set my boys on you. What kind of idiotic woman willingly walks into a situation like this? Are you stupid?'

'I ... I just want to keep my son safe,' I say as tears stream down my face.

'Then maybe you should teach him to stay away from people like me, yeah? Two weeks. If I don't see my money, then Maxy boy gets thrown off a roof, and you get fed to my boys, and trust me, you don't want that, do you?'

I shake my head and take a step backwards, but both his hands lash out and grasp my jacket. I scream as my legs buckle, but he holds me up easily, pulling my face in close. 'Get out of my sight,' he murmurs. Then he drops me, and I collapse in a heap on the concrete floor.

I crawl to my feet and somehow manage to reach the exit. One of the thugs is holding the door open for me, and the second I'm through it, he slams it shut. The noise it makes is so loud that it vibrates my brain.

I slump back to the ground, unable to summon the strength to get to my car.

There's no way I can find that sort of money.

My parents are both dead, and even if they were alive, they wouldn't help me out. I didn't hear from them after they told me to get out and not come back unless I got rid of the baby, not until their solicitor called me and told me they'd both died in a car accident. They left me no money in their wills or even acknowledged the fact I existed. That was eight years ago.

I'm an only child and have no other family members to call. My parents had small families and were both only children themselves. Plus, my grandparents died young. As far as I know, I have no living relatives.

I don't have friends I can rely on. At least, not ones I can ask for that big a loan. I doubt my boss would give me the money or pay me up front for the next five months.

I manage to drag myself to my car, locking the doors once I'm behind the wheel. I drive on autopilot back home. I don't even remember the journey.

BY THE TIME I make it through the front door of the building, sweat is dripping off me. The weather looks like it's going to be decent all week with the temperature climbing each day. May is usually my favourite month of the year, but I can't stop to admire the gorgeous flowers in bloom or the smell of freshly cut grass. None of it registers in my mind because all I can think of is the situation I now find myself in.

Before heading up the stairs to my flat, I check the mail slot, grimacing at the menacing-looking envelopes that no doubt contain more demands for money I don't have. There's even an envelope that looks like it's from a solicitor and says urgent on the front. Why can't these people just leave me alone? My phone already has another missed call this morning from the same unknown number.

'You okay, love?'

'Huh?' I blink out of my trance and see one of the more senior residents of the building looking at me. She lives on the ground floor.

'You looked like you were miles away there,' she says with a slight smile.

I blink several times.

Oh my God. That's it.

'Thank you!' I say and then rush up the stairs to my flat. She has just given me an idea.

I can potentially move away, far away where they can't find me or Max.

It's not a perfect plan, but it's the only one I've got that doesn't involve bank robbery.

My shift starts in less than an hour; I don't have long. Max is still snoring, so I allow him to sleep. He'll probably be in a lot of discomfort when he wakes up. I leave him a note on the kitchen worktop, reminding him there's a small bit of leftover pie to eat, and include a packet of painkillers, adding that he can have one dose every four hours if necessary. I have a very quick shower, despite it not being at the usual time, and change into my work clothes, then spend the rest of the time looking through the application form to move council housing, but it's more complicated than I thought. I need a legitimate reason to want to move out of town. I'm not sure putting that my son owes a drug dealer a lot of money is a valid or legal reason.

So, paying full price on a rental property is my only other option. There's no guarantee it will even work. Besides, if I found a place to rent in my price range (which is next to nothing), I wouldn't be able to move out in less than two weeks. What other choice do I have?

I search nearby towns for cheap places to rent and send off a few emails to estate agents while I walk to work. Phil offers me a cigarette as soon as I walk in the door, but I decline.

'Suit yourself,' he says.

'Phil, is it possible to be paid up front for the next five months?' I may as well ask.

Phil laughs out loud and walks away.

I guess that's a no.

AS THE DAY DRAGS ON, I constantly check my phone for a response from one of the estate agents. One does respond with a few properties that are available in the area, but all are almost double what I pay now, and they aren't far enough out of the city for me to feel safe. I need to move miles and miles away. Maybe to a remote area of Scotland. I've always wanted to go there, but everything costs too much. I don't have the money for a deposit.

My shift comes to an end at three and, with it, my plans to move and run away.

It's just not possible.

Everything is fucking hopeless.

I stop by the shop on the way home and buy more bread, pasta and Max's favourite chocolate bar. I can't give him much, but hopefully the small gesture will cheer him up. When I arrive home, the place is quiet. I check the fridge, and the pie is gone, so at least I know he's eaten today.

I knock on his bedroom door. 'Max, you in there?'

'Yeah.'

'Can I come in?'

'Yeah.'

I push the door open, grimacing at the stale, pungent odour that hits me in the face. 'Could you maybe open a window and let in some natural light and air?'

Max is lying on his bed, scrolling on his phone. I'm glad I deleted the text messages I sent earlier before I replaced his phone back on the floor. I doubt it would have gone down well had he found out his mother tried to make a deal with his dealer. Not to mention the fact I was able to crack his new passcode.

He makes no sound to say he's heard me, nor does he move a muscle, so I lean across his bed and pull the curtains open, illuminating the huge array of mess and chaos in the room. In the daylight, it looks even worse than before. I open the window and then take a step back, catching sight of the small, yellow duck he won at the fair resting on a shelf above his bed.

I smile to myself before turning to face him. 'How are you feeling?'

'Fine.'

'Do you need more painkillers?'

'Already took some.'

'Are you hungry?'

'No.'

I know that's a lie. My son is always hungry. He's like a scavenging hyena. He'll eat anything he comes across. I don't have a lot in the fridge or cupboards though. A pang of guilt hits me. Max has always been skinny, but maybe if I'd been able to feed him more, he'd be bigger, more muscular perhaps, more able to defend himself.

'I guess you don't want this, then.' I hold up his favourite chocolate bar.

He flicks his eyes up, and a small smile appears across his lips. 'Thanks.'

I chuck it on the bed, and he tears into it.

Smiling, I turn and exit the room. I walk into the kitchen and see the pile of unopened bills on the kitchen table. They just don't stop coming. Tears spill down my cheeks.

My phone vibrates in my pocket.

Something inside me snaps.

I need a release. Having been threatened by three scary-looking men earlier and having no way of paying them back or running away, it's enough to push me over the edge. In fact, I'm so far over the edge now, there's no way of me ever getting back up and on solid ground.

I grab my phone, see the same unknown number, the one that won't stop calling me, and jab my finger at the screen. 'Will you stop fucking calling me!' As soon as the words are out of my mouth, I feel momentarily better.

'I'm sorry, ma'am, but—' comes the quiet male voice.

'But what? What could possibly be important enough for you to call me half a dozen times a day and fill up my voice-mail?' I've lost it. I've totally lost it. This isn't me. I don't scream and shout at people down the phone. I'm sure this poor guy is just doing his job, but a part of me doesn't care anymore. I'm done.

'Um, ma'am ... have you actually listened to any of my voicemails?'

'No, and I don't plan to. Now, will you please leave me the fuck alone?' I'm about to hang up, but his next words stop me in my tracks.

'It's about the last will and testament of Ms Harriet Greene.'

4

The name means nothing to me, so I don't say anything back to whoever it is who's on the phone. I don't want to be on the phone anymore. I need to hang up. The only reason I freeze is because I have no idea why this man is calling me about someone called Harriet Greene.

'Are you still there, ma'am?'

'I ... I don't know who you're talking about. You must have the wrong number.'

'I don't believe so. You should have received a letter from Harriet Greene two months ago, and I've also written to you.'

'I ... No, I haven't. Sorry, but ... I have to go. Don't call me again.' And I hang up.

As soon as I'm off the phone, my jaw unclenches and my shoulders relax, but something keeps niggling away at the back of my mind.

Harriet Greene.

My mother's maiden name was Greene.

None of this makes any sense, but something tells me not

to ignore it straight away. It's like a beacon blinking in the darkness. My eyes land on the pile of unopened mail on the side of the kitchen counter, the pile I've been ignoring and adding to for months. It's so big that it has collapsed several times, and all I've done is scoop it up and plonk it back on the side, so it'll all be out of date order.

The guy on the phone said I should have received a letter two months ago. I might have thrown it straight out. Then again, I might not have and just added it to the pile to be opened later. I know I need to address the pile of bills and post, but it's just too much to deal with, so it's sat there and grown. It causes too much anxiety, so I find it's sometimes best to ignore it.

I walk over to the pile of post, pick it up and start flicking through it, not opening any, but glancing at the front of each envelope to see if anything jumps out at me. There are the usual bills with scary red lettering on the front and then the thick envelopes, which are the credit card statements.

I've almost reached the end of the pile, about to put the whole strange situation out of my mind, but then a plain white envelope catches my eye, along with another that looks official and scary. There's nothing about the plain one that stands out. Just my name, address and a simple stamp. The postmark says it was from almost two months ago.

My breath catches in my throat.

Is this it? Is this the letter from Harriet Greene?

Who the hell is she, and why is she writing to me? If it's regarding her last will and testament, then that means she's dead.

I sit down at the kitchen table, grasping the letter, and stare at it for a long time before my curiosity overrides my anxiety, and I tear into the envelope.

I scan the handwriting on the page, unable to decipher a lot of the words straight away due to her scribbling penmanship. It's signed Harriet Greene at the bottom. Yep, this is it.

Dear Natasha,

This letter may come as a surprise to you, but I hope that it will be a nice surprise. However, I must be honest with you from the start; if you've received this letter, it means I'm dead. Don't fret, dear, I had a wonderful life.

Upon my death, this letter was to be immediately posted to your last known address, so I hope it finds you. I'm an old woman now, and I have no children of my own. My niece, Prudence, left me several years ago to marry a man I didn't approve of. She was, up until the day she left, my primary carer and the sole beneficiary of my will. However, since she decided to run away, I decided to cut her out of my will. Some might say it's harsh, but she made it very clear she didn't want anything from me.

And so, I give everything to you. Your mother was my older sister, so you're my niece. I may never have met you, but you're still family.

I don't have a lot, but I do have a house and some money in an account. However, that money has slowly been dwindled away on care home fees, burial arrangements and the running cost of Yew Tree House, but whatever's left now I'm gone is all yours.

My family solicitor, Adrian Stanton, will have access to the will and all the details. I expect he'll attempt to contact you a few weeks after you receive this letter, to arrange ownership of the house, which is yours as soon as I'm dead. It's yours to do with as you wish.

I am sorry we never got the chance to meet.

With fondest love,

Harriet Greene

I stare at the words on the page, but don't have time to reread them because Max pads into the kitchen.

'What's that?' he asks. 'Another overdue bill?' He smirks at me. Normally, I'd snap at him and tell him off for being rude, or attempt to hide it and deny there was anything wrong, but I can't do anything to hide the shock on my face.

'Um,' I say. 'It's a letter from Harriet Greene.'

'Who?'

'She was my mother's sister.'

Max stares at me for several seconds. 'Huh. Weird.' Then he opens the cupboard. 'Where are the biscuits?'

'We ran out.'

'Bummer.' He slams the cupboard door shut. Clearly, having demolished the chocolate bar, he's craving more sugar. Finding none, he stomps back to his room, leaving me still sitting at the kitchen table, grasping the letter. Did he hear what I said? Does he even care? I could really use his help with deciphering this strange letter, or at least to make sense of it. Then again, Max probably isn't the best person to speak to about this.

Adrian Stanton.

I'm assuming he was the man I shouted at on the phone earlier, and who's been calling me several times a day for the past couple of months.

He's clearly the best person to speak to about this. I'm still convinced they've tracked down the wrong Natasha Moore. Yes, my mother's maiden name was Greene, but as far as I know, my mother never had a sister, let alone two.

I flick the kettle on and take a seat back at the kitchen table with my phone, navigating to the last number logged. My heart is hammering hard, and I've got the familiar anxious feeling in my chest I always get when talking to a person on the phone. Maybe it's because it's just not the done thing anymore. Even for my customer service job, most of the communication is done via instant chat message. I do speak to people for my pub job, but I can't remember the last time I spoke to a person over the phone outside of work. Even the companies who are after late payments don't call me very often. They prefer to send threatening letters and emails. I've become allergic to speaking on the phone and will do anything to avoid it.

Doing just that, I type the name of the solicitor into Google, and up pops a business website called Stanton & White Family Solicitors. I browse through to the profiles and see a picture of Adrian Stanton, who has salt-and-pepper hair, a strong jawline and kind eyes. There's a short biography about him and one for Johnathan White, who is around the same age. I guess he's legitimate. It doesn't help me feel any better though because now I have hope blooming in my chest, and I've learned not to depend on hope. It's only a glimmer, a mere spark, but it's enough to send my pulse racing.

This house could be the answer to all my problems.

Moving to a remote location without paying a penny is a dream come true for most people, but to me it would mean freedom and safety for my son. Owning a house would mean I'd have access to money, and I could pay the drug dealer back, ensure Max is free from his debt, and start a new life away from Birmingham.

I press dial and listen to the ringing, holding my breath.

'Stanton & White Family Solicitors. Adrian speaking. How can I help?'

'Uh, hi ... um ... My name is Natasha Moore. I ... we spoke earlier.'

'Ah, yes, of course, Mrs Moore. It's nice to hear from you. I had a feeling you might call me back.'

'Actually, it's Miss Moore.'

'My apologies, Miss Moore.'

'Are you sure you've got the right Natasha Moore?'

'What's your birthday?'

I pause.

'I can assure you that this isn't a scam, Miss Moore. Is your birthday the 20th of September 1990?'

'Yes.'

'Was your mother called Frances Greene, and married your father, William Moore?'

'Yes.'

'Then I believe you are the correct Natasha Moore.'

I rub my eyes. 'B-But I've never heard of anyone in my family called Harriet Greene. In the letter she sent me, she says she's my mother's sister, but my mother never told me she had a sister. And if this woman Prudence is her niece, it means my mother had a second sister too. My mother died a few years ago, and before that, I hadn't spoken to her since I was seventeen. I was never very close with her anyway, but I can assure you she never told me about having a sibling, let alone two.'

'I see,' says Adrian. 'Well, she had two sisters, Frances and Joan, which makes Harriet your aunt. Harriet Greene died in a care home on the 30th of March this year. I was appointed as her solicitor in 2017. She lived in Yew Tree House since she was a girl, and according to her will, when she died, she wanted to leave it to her niece Prudence Greene, Joan's daughter, who looked after her into her old age. But unfortunately, Prudence left her seven years ago. She left Harriet a note saying she was running away to marry someone, but there was no record of her anywhere after that. Harriet requested to have her will be changed, and she wrote you a letter, which was to be sent to you when she died.'

'Ohhhkayyyy ...' A million questions explode in my brain. I stumble over a few words, unable to make up my mind on the start of my sentence.

'I realise this must have come as a bit of a shock to you, especially since you didn't know about Harriet to begin with. I am sorry I've been calling you so often, but I really want to ensure Harriet's wishes are carried out. Do you have any questions?'

'Only about a million.'

Adrian laughs. 'Understandable.'

'How did Harriet even know about me? I've never met her.'

'That, I'm afraid, I don't know. I assume your mother must have told her about you at some point. However, I must tell you that it states in the will that if you can't be found or you don't wish to have the house, then it will be sold, and the proceeds given to the care home who looked after her in her final years. Are you interested in inheriting the house?'

I cough a few times, choking back my immediate reaction of 'Yes!' But perhaps I should think about this for a moment. Can I afford to run a large house? Moving away is so far out of my set routine that I can't even think about what to do first, but owning a house is the only way I'm going to be able to pay back the drug dealer and escape this toxic environment.

Fuck it.

'Yes, I'll take it. When can I move in?'

'There're several logistical hoops to jump through and documents to sign, but there's no reason why you can't move in straight away if you wish. It's legally yours, but the official paperwork will take a bit longer to complete.'

'Where are you based?'

'Near Newcastle-upon-Tyne. The solicitor's and house are in a small village called Haymere Bridge just outside of Newcastle.'

I swallow back the lump in my throat. I've rarely driven more than a few miles in any given direction for years. The idea of travelling so far to somewhere I don't know, to a house I've never seen ... It all sounds too much, too risky, too complicated, but it can't be riskier and more complicated than the situation I'm in now. My baby's life is in danger.

This house is the answer to all my problems, a place to hide and start afresh.

'Miss Moore?'

'Yes, sorry. I can be there tomorrow to sign the paperwork, and I'll move in straight away.'

'Perfect. If you have any other questions, bring them with you, and I'll do my best to answer them when we meet.'

'Thanks, Adrian. See you tomorrow afternoon. I'm not sure how long it will take me to get there.'

'We're open till seven in the evening on Tuesdays. Bye, Miss Moore.'

I hang up and place my phone on the table. I stare at it for a long time, unsure what my next move should be.

Holy crap, I'm moving to a house in the country.

Max and I are free. Is this a dream? Can I really make this work? I need to get Max out of here as soon as possible. What's the best way to do this? Should I just up and leave this flat without telling anyone, without telling the council or landlord? The last thing I want is anyone knowing where we are going, or that we're moving at all. If anyone comes here looking for Max, I don't want the landlord telling them we've moved. I need to be sneaky about this. Plus, at some point I'll need to get Max re-enrolled in a new school, which could cause a multitude of issues, but that will have to wait. I'd rather him be safe and alive first.

I run my fingers through my hair and sigh deeply. There's not much to pack. I don't own a lot. Nor does Max. But how do I tell Max? We'd need to leave tomorrow morning as early as possible to give us plenty of time to drive there, including stops.

How do I tell him that I'm uprooting his life and moving us halfway up the country?

It's for his own good. I'm doing it for him. Everything I do is for Max. But I know my son. He won't take this move well. He won't want to leave his friends. He's like me in many ways. He clearly likes his routine here, but there's no way we can stay here.

I will pay the drug dealer back with the money I can take from the house, but it won't happen in less than two weeks, which means Max is in danger. We need to run and hide while I get the money together.

But I can't tell Max the plan. Not yet. Not until I get him out the door and in the car.

5

I wait outside Max's bedroom door, taking deep breaths and summoning the courage to lie to his face. I don't really have a plan. My brain can't seem to sort anything out in a logical order. I just want to get out of this flat, out of this city, get to the new house, and then go from there.

I knock lightly. 'Max, can I come in? I need to have a chat.' I know there's still the whole school situation to sort out, but if we're moving away, then the whole thing is moot. Once we're free, perhaps he'll want to focus more on his schooling and try to bump up his grades to attend university next year.

My palms are sweating as I push the door open when Max allows me entry. I'm glad to see that the curtains and window are still open, so it smells slightly better in here. Max is lying on his bed, scrolling through his phone again. He doesn't acknowledge my presence in the room.

'Um ... I've just read that letter from Harriet Greene. It

turns out she's my mum's sister, and she's invited us to visit her, so I thought we'd travel up tomorrow morning.'

Max doesn't respond at first, so I clear my throat loudly.

'I heard you,' he says.

'Okay, good. I thought we'd stay for a night or two. Three at the most.'

'No.'

'Excuse me?'

'No, I'm not going. She's your relative, so you can go and see her. I'm staying here.'

'That's not happening. You're coming with me.'

'Why?'

'Because ...' I'm stuck for an answer. He's old enough to stay home by himself, but I wouldn't trust him to stay behind alone. I feel like a hypocrite standing in front of him. The truth is I'm terrified, but I can't tell him that. I can't show my son weakness because I've always wanted to prove to him that I'm a strong, independent woman, as cliché as that sounds. He knows I've raised him by myself. I've had a few boyfriends over the years, but none have stuck around long enough to be considered a permanent male figure in his life. I've done everything myself, worked two jobs for most of his life, and even though I've had to resort to using food banks from time to time to ensure he was fed and clothed, I've never backed down from a fight, never run away from my problems. Yet here I am. Doing exactly that. And lying to his face about it.

'Max, you're coming with me whether you like it or not,' I say. The wobble in my voice almost gives me away. 'I think it will be good for you to get some space from this city.'

Max lowers his phone and stares at me. 'I don't want to go and visit some old woman. What about my friends?'

I bite back a snort of laughter. 'You mean your friends who forced you to sell drugs and now want to kill you if you don't pay them back?'

Max's nostrils flare. 'No one forced me. I wanted to do it.'

'You wanted to ... Max, I haven't raised you by myself for seventeen years for you to throw your life away dealing drugs on the street.'

'That's funny. You've hardly raised me at all, have you? Especially not in the past few years. I hardly see you. You're always working. We never do things together. The last thing we did together was go to a funfair when I was twelve. You never take me anywhere or let me go on school trips or take me shopping for things I need.'

'Because I have no money!' I shout. I shake my head, lowering my voice. 'Max, I'd love to hang out together more and go places and do things together and buy you all the things in the world, but things cost money. And if I didn't work two jobs, then we wouldn't have any money at all. We'd be out begging on the streets.'

'Then why won't you let me get a job? I could have helped.'

I sigh. 'I know, but I wanted you to focus on school and get some decent grades so you could perhaps go to university. You'd be eligible for a grant because of my low income and because you come from a single-parent household. I still want that for you, Max, to go to university and have a better start in life than I did, but you've thrown it all away.'

'You mean because I ruined your life by being born?'

'No! I didn't say that. You didn't ruin my life. You changed it for the better.'

Max mutters something.

'What was that?'

'Nothing. Doesn't matter.'

Another sigh escapes before I can stop it. My son infuriates me at times. I want to grab his shoulders and shake some sense into him. Why doesn't he see that I've been slowly killing myself to keep him alive, to give him everything I possibly can in life, but it's still not enough for him.

'Max ... I'm sorry you'll be leaving your friends, but ... it's only for a few days until things blow over. That man and his gang know where we live.'

'I don't care. I'm not going.'

I almost burst into tears. There used to be a time when Max would do as I asked without question, but he's become so headstrong. I know I'm asking a lot for a teenage boy to visit an elderly relative he's never met with his mother, but he has no idea of the repercussions of what he's got himself into. It's like he doesn't see the danger he's put us both in.

'You are, and that's final,' I say. 'We're leaving tomorrow morning at nine.'

Max opens his mouth to say something, probably to argue with me that I'm being unfair or unreasonable, but then he rolls his eyes and closes his mouth again. 'Whatever.'

'Now, I need you to get a good night's sleep and then get up early and pack all the things you'd like to take—'

'Why did this woman write to you again?'

'Um ... she just found out about me and wanted to meet. She's the only family I have left.' Every lie I tell makes my stomach twist further into a knot.

'How far away does she live?'

'About two hundred miles.'

Another grumble, but he doesn't say anything else. He's already focused on his phone, typing away. 'Please don't tell any of your friends that you're going away,' I add.

'Why not?'

'Because ... I don't want any information getting back to that drug dealer friend of yours, and please turn off your location settings.'

'Whatever.'

I back out of his room and take a deep breath once I'm safely on the other side of his door. That went about as well as I expected. I have no idea how he'll react when I finally reveal the truth: that we're moving away and not coming back.

I'm not even going to tell my work about my decision to move. In fact, that's my next thing to do. I call both my jobs and hand in my notice, saying I've got a new job. I get off the phone as quickly as possible, making a note to buy a new SIM card as soon as possible and change my number. Now, I just need to destroy Max's SIM card or phone. I don't trust him not to share his whereabouts with his friends despite me warning him not to.

I don't know what's going to happen over the next few days. It's the most unplanned I've ever been, and it's scaring me. I feel physically sick, but moving away from this toxic environment means I won't have to worry about Max every time he steps out the front door. Maybe I'll finally be able to breathe easier at night, knowing he's away from this place and the horrible people who don't care about him and his well-being. He may hate me for it, but I'm saving him from himself. One day, he'll thank me. One day, he'll see that this was the best decision we've ever made.

I just hope I'm right.

I DON'T SLEEP A WINK. My brain refuses to switch off, and I find myself going over and over random scenarios that may or may not happen. We could die in a horrible car crash on the motorway. We could end up getting completely lost down a country road and get ambushed by a serial killer who then peels our skin off and hangs it on his wall. We could break down in the middle of nowhere and starve to death trying to find the way back to civilisation.

By the time it's time to get up, I'm already exhausted. I take a shower, realising it's the last time I'll have one here. My routine is about to be non-existent, and it causes tears to fill my eyes, mixing with the running water.

I don't own a proper suitcase, so I end up stuffing most of my clothes into black bin bags. I don't intend to take a lot of material items, but I do have a few things I can't bear to leave behind, my favourite mug, for example. I can't make it look like I'm properly moving, otherwise Max will get suspicious, so I hide my bags in the boot and hope he doesn't question why I've brought the kettle and toaster. I have no idea what state the house is in, so I'm preparing for the worst, although the worst would be that there's no electricity, but Harriet's letter makes it sound as if the house is furnished and liveable, but I can't be sure about anything. Max packs a few clothes, but since he thinks we're returning to the flat, he's left behind a lot of items I'd rather he take, so while he's having a shower, I pop into his room and grab a few of the sentimental items, including the yellow duck I saw earlier.

. . .

By the time nine o'clock rolls around, we're all ready to go. The anxiety in my chest and stomach has been gradually building for hours. I try all my coping mechanisms and safety behaviours, including pinching the skin on my arms and the bridge of my nose and counting my fingers, but nothing quells the rising panic of the long drive ahead on unknown and busy roads. I haven't had to drive for more than half an hour at a time since living here, so the prospect of a two-hundred-odd-mile journey fills me with dread, especially driving on the motorways, something I haven't done for several years. I've always worried over the years that my anxiety and worries will rub off on Max, but he seems perfectly at ease about the whole thing, although he has no idea about the full extent of our journey. When we arrive at our destination, later this afternoon, I'll have to tell him the truth and just hope he doesn't blow up at me.

Max gets into the front seat, immediately reclines it and closes his eyes, his arms folded. I look up at the grey, depressing building I've lived in for the past decade, the place I've raised my son on my own, done my best to look after him and provide for him. I can't say I'll miss the place, nor the neighbourhood or loud parties into the long hours of the nights. But I will miss the memories it holds. Like when, at eight years old, Max decided he wanted to start an ant farm, and he thought that catching ants would be easy, so he put out a load of food on the floor and waited for hours for ants to come along, but they didn't arrive. A mouse did, and then I spent two days trying to catch the damn thing. Looking back now, it was a time I cherish, and it always puts a smile on my face.

I shut the car door and turn the ignition on, sitting for a

few moments, listening to the turnover of the engine. My car is on its last wheels. I doubt it will pass its next MOT. I hope to God it makes it through the next couple of hundred miles without exploding or spluttering to a stop. One of the unlikely scenarios in my head could actually happen, and we could break down in the middle of nowhere and starve to death. My mind whirls with worries. What if we break down on the motorway? That's even worse. We'd be stranded. I don't have breakdown cover. What if a tyre blows? I have no idea how to change one.

'Are we going or what?' asks Max without opening his eyes or moving an inch.

'Um, yeah, in a minute.'

I scan the car park, taking note of the number of cars. Only two. Most people have already left for work. It's good to leave now before everyone starts coming back home later this afternoon. There's one blue car and one red one with a missing bumper.

Putting the car in gear, I pull away and leave our shitty life behind. I start following the signs out of the city and following the satnav on my phone. It's crazy how much faith I'm putting in a piece of technology. I've already checked five times that I've put in the right address. What if the satnav breaks and we end up travelling in the wrong direction?

I have the radio turned down low. My fingers are grasping the steering wheel so hard that they're turning white.

A flash of red catches my eye in the right-hand side mirror.

That's weird.

It's a red Vauxhall. Is it the same car I saw earlier parked in the car park at my building? The clock on the dashboard tells me I've been driving for ten minutes, and I've made several turns since then, yet the car has been behind me for a while. At least, I think it has.

Something isn't right.

I think I'm being followed.

I decide to do a couple of test turns, so I indicate left down the next road, then right.

The red car follows.

Shit.

'Max,' I say. No reply. 'Max,' I say more forcefully.

'What?'

'I think we're being followed.'

'Huh?'

'Will you sit up and listen to me?'

Max groans as he adjusts his seat into an upright position.

'I think the red car a few cars back has been following us since we left our building.'

Max checks the side mirror. 'Are you sure?'

'Pretty sure. Do you recognise the car?'

'No. You're being paranoid.'

Am I though? It could very well be the same car. Plus, the drug dealer made it very clear that he knows where we live and that he'd be watching us. What if they were watching us while we packed the car?

I turn the next corner, taking it a little faster than is deemed necessary. The wheels shriek. I put my foot down as I accelerate out of the corner, and I wrestle with the wheel to keep it on track. Max grabs the edges of his seat and presses on an imaginary brake pedal.

'Jesus, Mum.'

I ignore him. Every few seconds, I glance in the rear-view mirror. I can't seem to see the red car anymore, but now there's a black car right up behind me; too close.

The roads are getting busier, and there's a set of traffic lights coming up. I'm certain I can make it. I put my foot down, the engine revving.

The car hurtles towards the green light. It turns red, but I don't stop, but the black car behind me does. I hold my breath as we race through the red light. A car horn blares, and my first reaction is to slam on my brakes and yank the steering wheel to the left, trying to stay clear of the traffic. Another long beep.

'Mum, what the hell are you doing!' shouts Max.

I skid to a stop as cars drive past, their owners shouting expletives at me. I keep my gaze straight ahead while my chest heaves up and down. I can't believe I just did that. I could have killed us. Tears swell in my eyes as it dawns on me how close we were to having an accident, and I haven't even made it out of the city yet.

'I'm sorry,' I say, putting the car in gear.

As I pull out into traffic, the realisation hits me that I haven't taken my anti-anxiety medication today. If I took it now, it would only be a few hours late. Is that enough to cause an adverse reaction? I have skipped it before. I blame my lack of routine. It's one of the first things I do upon waking up each morning. Come to think of it, did I even pack it? Have I, in my haste to get away, forgotten the one thing that could help control my spiralling thoughts?

'Mum?'

My son's voice jolts me back to the present. 'Sorry. Yes.'

I turn my attention back to the road, flicking my eyes to

the rear-view mirror every few seconds just in case I see another tail.

Max's phone buzzes.

'Turn your phone off right now.'

'No, you can't make me.'

Then I do something both dangerous and stupid. I flick the locks on the passenger door, roll down my side window, snatch Max's phone out of his hands, and hurl it out onto the road, where it falls underneath a car. All in the space of less than a second.

'Mum! What the fuck!'

'It's to keep us safe, Max. I'll get you a new one when I can, I promise.'

Max grabs the door handle and yanks on it. We're now heading towards the busier roads and the motorway, but my focus is on Max when I know it should be on the road.

'Max, calm down; it's only a phone.'

'I'll never forgive you for this!' He gives up trying to get the door open, crosses his arms and glares out the window, pouting like he used to do when he was a toddler.

'I'm sorry. I'll make it up to you, I promise.'

Max is practically vibrating with anger. I don't attempt to engage him in conversation.

Once we get on the motorway, I find myself more tense than ever, my eyes glued to the road. Each time someone overtakes me, I flinch and imagine us dying in a fiery explosion.

Max resumes his position and closes his eyes. My heart is beating wildly, and that spike of anxiety is still there, keeping me alert. However, as the minutes pass, the better I feel, and with every mile that goes by, the weight on my chest decreases.

I've made the right decision. I know I have.

No one is following us.

No one can know where we're going.

We're on our way to a better life, a house of our own and the prospect of a fresh start.

I wonder what Haymere Bridge is like.

It's got to be better than Birmingham city centre.

6

We stop after two hours at a service station for a McDonald's as an early lunch/late breakfast. I'm glad to be off the motorway for a while because my anxiety has been through the roof since I got onto it. I kept to the speed limit, maybe a few miles under, but even so the constant changing of lanes and idiot drivers were enough to fill me with mind-numbing fear. Twice, I had car horns blare at me for no reason I could decipher, so as I indicate into the services, my pulse returns to a somewhat normal state. My paranoia still hasn't completely gone away though. Several times I thought a car was following us, but Max was oblivious to the battle going on inside my head. He kept his eyes closed the entire time, refusing to talk to me after what I did to his beloved phone.

We eat in silence in the restaurant. I pick at my chips, unable to stomach anything more than a few bites, whereas Max inhales his double cheeseburger and chips as if he's never been fed before. He barely stops to chew.

I use the toilets and buy myself a strong coffee from the

Costa. While I'm waiting in line, I notice a man keeps glancing over at me, and it immediately makes my stomach flip. I continue to face forwards, ignoring him, and as I scurry back to the car with my coffee, I check my surroundings. The man has followed me out to the car park. Why is he following me?

Sliding into the car, I take a deep breath and tell myself to stop being so silly. Max doesn't say a word as he scoffs my leftover chips in the passenger seat, and I pull back onto the motorway, praying that the traffic clears and no further incidents make me want to wet myself.

I slurp my extra-shot coffee, but to be honest, I don't even need the hit of caffeine. The adrenaline is enough to keep me awake and focused on the drive. Max falls asleep once he's finished his meal and begins to snore.

I glance over at my beautiful boy and smile. I've loved watching him sleep ever since he was a baby. The way his eyes lightly flutter while he's dreaming, his shallow breaths as his chest moves up and down, even his gentle snores. I used to lie awake when he was sick and study the freckles on his face and count the eyelashes framing his closed eyes.

Now, he's a far cry from the baby and toddler I remember. He has chin stubble, for a start. He's still my beautiful boy though. I know he's been giving me a hard time lately, but it's my own fault. I've not been there for him. I've allowed my insecurities to blind me from what he's been doing behind my back, but now I'm saving him. He might hate me, but I'd rather he hate me than get himself killed.

By the time I arrive in Haymere Bridge where the solicitor's building is located, it's just gone half past two in the afternoon. I park up outside the building and switch off the engine.

Too many emotions and thoughts race through my head, all jumbling together. Despite the weight on my chest being less than before, it's still there, a steady pressure that's restricting my breathing and movement. I'm not sure if it will ever go away completely. I suppose, as a parent, it never really does. There's always an underlying pressure on your body that has nothing to do with you personally. Kids do that to you. They rip out a piece of you and keep it as their own without realising it. Max literally has a piece of my heart with him everywhere he goes. The heart in my chest couldn't beat without him.

When I got pregnant, I knew it would be hard, especially without my parents' support. They told me I was making a mistake, that I would always regret keeping him. But it's not true. They were right about one thing though: it never gets easier; the challenges just change.

Right, I can't just sit here. I need to tell Max the real reason we're here.

I nudge him awake. 'Max, we're here.'

'Huh?' he grumbles and yanks his arm away from me.

'I, um ... I have a confession to make. We're not really here to visit my aunt. My aunt's dead.'

At this, Max opens his sleepy eyes. 'What the hell are you talking about? Where are we?' He looks around at the nearby buildings.

'We're in a place called Haymere Bridge, near Newcastle. I'm sorry I had to lie to you, but I didn't think you'd agree to come if I didn't. I've inherited a house from my aunt, and we're moving here to live. I just need to stop by the solicitor's to sort out some paperwork.'

Max frowns as if he doesn't understand English. 'You're fucking with me, right?'

'No, Max, I'm not. We're really going to live here.'

'Let me get this straight. You lie to me about visiting a relative of yours, who turns out to be dead. You almost kill us on the drive over here. You throw my phone out the window, and now you're telling me I'm never going back to Birmingham to see my friends, and we're going to live in this shitty country village? What about the stuff I've left in my room?'

My God, he makes me sound like a monster.

'I'm sorry,' I say again. 'I grabbed a few things from your room, but most of it was junk.'

'Yeah, to *you*, maybe. You've lost it,' he says with a laugh. 'Unlock my door. Now.'

'Max …'

'Let me out!' He rattles the door like he's in a cage.

His loud voice makes me jump, and I quickly flick the central locking off. He forces the door open, gets out and storms up the road. I scramble out of the car and call out after him, but he doesn't stop.

Shit.

I stop shouting, aware there are people staring at me as I do so. Not the first impression I want to make. There's nowhere for Max to go. He has no phone and no money. He just needs to cool off. I'm sure he'll come back once he's had time to process what I've just loaded on him.

For now, I may as well sort out the house paperwork while he's blowing off some steam.

I head inside.

Adrian turns out to be a bubbly, attractive older guy who makes me a cup of coffee while he sorts out the legal paperwork and explains more about the house. I nod along as he clarifies all the technical jargon and details, most of it going straight over my head. He does do his best when my eyes start glazing over.

Adrian pushes a load of paperwork across the desk towards me after twenty minutes of going through the details. 'Right, all that's left now is for you to sign where I've put a tab. Any questions?'

'Um ... I guess not. This is all a bit overwhelming, to be honest.' I take the pen, scanning the pages.

'I'll be happy to help with anything you need. You name it.'

I smile as I sign my name on the first line. 'Thanks.' I'm touched by his eagerness, but I'm a little unsure about revealing too much detail about my life. He keeps smiling at me and seems very attentive to my needs. It's more attention than I care to receive.

'Once you've got to the house, just let me know if you have any questions, okay?'

'Sure.'

At that point, the bell on the front door pings. I continue to sign my name and date where it says. Adrian asks, 'Can I help you, young man?' I turn and see Max walking towards me.

'No,' Max says curtly.

'Sorry, this is my son, Max.'

'Oh, my apologies.' He nods hello at Max, who doesn't return the compliment. I'm just glad he decided to return to me rather than me having to go and search for him.

Once I sign the last piece of paperwork, I push the pile back across the desk towards Adrian, take a deep breath and lean back in my chair. 'So ... what happens now?'

'I'll grab your keys,' replies Adrian cheerfully.

While Adrian goes into a back room, Max slides onto a chair next to me. 'This place is in the middle of nowhere.'

'Yes,' I say. 'That's kind of the point.'

'Are you going to pay the dealer back, or are we going to hide out here for the rest of our lives?'

'I'm going to pay him back once I can leverage money from the house, but it will take several weeks or more. Once I have the money, I'll contact them and sort it out; then we'll be free to live here.'

'We're seriously not going back to the city?'

'No. We have nothing keeping us there.'

Max grunts, gets up and walks out of the building. I watch him, wondering if he's going to storm off again, but he doesn't. He just leans against the car with his arms folded, staring at the ground.

Adrian returns with a folder full of paperwork and a set of house keys.

'Thanks,' I say again as I rise to my feet and take the items. I hold out my hand, and Adrian shakes it.

'Great to meet you, Miss Moore.'

'And you, Adrian. Please, call me Natasha.'

We exchange smiles. 'Remember ... you need anything, you give me a call, yeah? Happy to help. Now you've signed the paperwork and provided your account details, Harriet's money should be in your account within five working days. There's just under ten thousand pounds left.'

I nod, attempting to hide my surprise.

Oh my God. I can pay off the dealer straight away with that money! I just hope he doesn't come looking for us in the meantime while I wait for the money to arrive.

I say goodbye to Adrian and head back to the car.

I drive slowly through the main village, taking note of where everything is: the post office, food shop, bank, doctor's surgery and dentist. It seems nice, pleasant, but the house is not situated in the centre of the village, rather on the outskirts, which is picturesque and peaceful. As I drive over a cute stone bridge, I glimpse the dilapidated sign for Yew Tree House immediately after it. I slam on the brakes. Max jerks forward and tuts.

'Bloody hell! Are you trying to give me whiplash?'

'I missed the turning. Sorry.'

The lane leading up to the house is uneven, full of potholes and overgrown on both sides. By the looks of it, no one has been up this lane in years. Harriet left the house and moved into a care home seven years ago. Why didn't she sell the place back then? Or give it to that woman, Prudence, while she was still around?

My mind drifts to Prudence. It's strange to know I had family members whom I knew nothing about. Now, both she and Harriet are gone. Plus, there's Prudence's parents. Joan and whoever her father was. Where are they? Are they dead too? Moving into this house is going to be like stepping into a different world, their world. Who were Harriet and Prudence? Why did I never hear about them from Mum when I was younger?

The driveway is covered in gravel and a fair amount of debris. I pull to a stop, switch off the ignition and look up through the windscreen at our new home.

Fuck. My. Life.

What have I got myself into?

'What a shithole,' says Max.

I couldn't agree with him more. The house looks like it's been taken over by the forest, covered in thick ivy, black vines and tangled weeds. One of the ground-floor windows is smashed, and a tree is growing through it. The house really has been taken over by nature. Random pieces of furniture have been haphazardly piled out the front, some of it broken, but all of it covered in weeds and rot. Dozens of beer bottles, cans, rubbish and what look suspiciously like condom wrappers litter the area. Eww.

If this is what the front of the house looks like, I don't even want to guess what the inside looks like. What the hell have I done?

The grounds of the house are overgrown and unkempt, but spacious. There's a wood off to the side just begging to be explored, and there looks to be a small pond, which is mostly just green algae, but has some gorgeous white lilies growing from it.

Max opens the car door and gets out. I copy him, and we stand side by side, staring up at the house, neither of us knowing what to say or do first.

'Harriet's letter didn't say anything about the house being in such a bad state,' I say at last. Even Adrian didn't mention it. Maybe he didn't know. It's not like it's his job to keep an eye on the place. He merely sorted and held the paperwork. If Harriet moved into a care home seven years ago, that means it's been unoccupied all that time. Clearly, no one has been here other than kids with no regard for personal property.

'You seriously expect us to live here?' asks Max. 'It doesn't even look like there's electricity.'

My heart sinks. Looking at the state of the house, it's obvious it needs a lot of work to make it liveable. Plus, there's the broken window on the ground floor. Anyone could get in whenever they want.

'Well ... I guess we can think of this as an exciting adventure,' I say with no enthusiasm whatsoever in my voice.

Then it hits me. How the hell am I supposed to pay for all the repairs? The five grand or so I'll have left over won't go very far. Perhaps I can take out a loan from the bank using the house capital.

Max mutters something and walks towards the front door.

I follow him, then slide the key into the lock, holding my breath, wondering what the hell I'm going to find on the other side. I can already smell the damp and something else, something ... rotten. Mouldy food, perhaps.

'What's that smell?' asks Max as he steps around me and enters the first room on the right.

I sniff the air and follow the smell into the kitchen, where I find a half-decomposed rat on the floor. I clamp a hand over my mouth, fighting a gag as I back out of the room and join Max in the lounge. This is the room with the broken window and how, I assume, the local kids have gained access to the house over the many years it's stood empty. The tree outside the window is growing in and around the wooden bookcase, and a thick pile of rotten leaves lies on the floor, after years of growing and then falling, creating a thick carpet of foliage.

Luckily, we're moving in during the spring and not the dead of winter. The first thing I need to do is see if we have running water and electricity.

'Um ... let's check some of the light switches,' I say, walking up to the first one. I mentally cross my fingers and flick it up.

Nothing.

'Well, that's just great,' says Max, heading out of the room and into the hallway. I hear him stomp up the stairs, sending echoes through the empty house.

I head into the kitchen and start opening cupboard doors. Old cans of food, pots and pans and various kitchen appliances have all been left here. There's an old toaster and a kettle on the side, both covered in thick dust and still plugged in. I'm glad I brought my own because no amount of scrubbing will make them suitable to use. It almost looks as if this house has been frozen in time. Harriet didn't even bother to pack anything away before she moved into the care home.

I find a roll of bin bags in a drawer, so I dispose of the dead rat in the overflowing bin around the corner. Then I try another light switch.

Nothing.

Figures.

I'm hoping the fuse box has just been tripped. I don't know a lot about electrics, but several times I had the electricity turn off in the old flat because of dodgy wiring, and it turned out the main fuse had been tripped.

I begin my search for the fuse box.

FIFTEEN MINUTES LATER, I discover the fuse box under the stairs, covered in cobwebs and dust. I flick a few of the switches. A loud bang from upstairs makes me jump and shriek. Did something just explode? Some of the switches stay up, but others stay down. What does that mean?

I close my eyes and take a deep breath.

Who the hell's been paying for the electric and utilities for the past seven years? Then I remember Harriet's letter and the fact she mentioned a bank account with money in it that had been used to pay for her care and to keep the house running and the bills paid.

Now the fuse box has been reset (I think), I flick the nearest light switch and almost whoop with glee as the bulb above my head flickers to life.

I walk around the house, testing light switches. Some work and some don't. It's like a light lottery.

I take note of the dust-covered furniture, all of which reeks of must. There are several dozen old pictures on the walls, a couple of which have fallen off and are lying broken on the floor. I bend down and pick one up. It's a picture of an elderly woman and a younger woman with her arm draped over her bony shoulders. I'm guessing this is Harriet and Prudence. I can see the resemblance to each other in their eyes and the way they're standing. I even recognise my mother's features in Harriet's nose and the shape of her thin mouth. Neither of them has auburn hair like mine. Mum always said my hair was a surprise when I was born. As far as I know, no one in my family has auburn hair.

'Mum!' My son's loud voice jolts my wandering mind.

'Yeah?'

'The toilet's blocked!'

'Of course it is,' I mutter.

It's times like this I could really use a glass or two of wine.

Max and I congregate in the kitchen.

'Max,' I say timidly, 'I'm sorry this place is in such a state, but if we both work hard, I believe we can make this a comfortable place to live. Adrian told me that Harriet has left me some money, which will arrive in my account within five working days, so I'm going to use it to pay back that dealer and then some of it to start the renovations.'

Max runs his finger across the worktop, picking up a thick layer of dust. He grimaces.

'And ... I think it would be a good idea if we both get jobs as soon as possible. The leftover money won't last for long with the amount of work it's going to take to fix this place up.'

'You're not thinking of doing it up yourself, are you?'

I shrug and look around. 'It might be a good project for us.'

'Right ... because you're so good at DIY. I've never even seen you hang a picture on a wall or use a screwdriver. What makes you think you can renovate a whole house?'

'Thanks for your vote of confidence.'

'Just being realistic.'

'I'll have you know that I fixed the leaking toilet one time, and I put your cot together using my own two hands.'

'And how long ago was that?'

'Okay, fine, point taken.'

This is going to work. I'm sure of it. I'll make it work. No matter what it takes. I'll look for a job straight away, take out a home equity loan as soon as possible, and do as much of the renovation work myself. I don't consider myself a whizz at DIY, but I love those home improvement and garden makeover shows on television. Plus, I'm almost certain you can learn to do anything via the internet. YouTube has hundreds of thousands of videos explaining how to tile a wall or install a toilet. I once looked up how to fix a leaking toilet and managed to sort it myself when the landlord said it would be at least three days before he could get someone round to fix it. This can be the chance to learn new skills, not just for myself, but Max too.

We can learn together and do up the house side by side.

He said himself he wishes we'd do more things together. Well, here's his opportunity. I expect he won't be happy about it, not at first, but when he sees how satisfying it is to renovate a home and learn life-long skills, he'll forget all about his friends and what he's left behind.

I LEAVE Max to settle in and plug in the old fridge/freezer in the corner of the kitchen. It still works, but it stinks, so I'll need to clean it as soon as possible. There are only two outlets that work in the kitchen, so the other can be shared between the toaster and kettle for now. I then drive into town to fetch some supplies, including a bottle of bleach and some Dettol to clean with. I brought the little food we had at the flat with us, but I need milk and a few other fresh ingredients to put in the fridge. As I'm paying, I see a sign for a part-time job. I enquire and manage to get Max an interview for tomorrow morning at nine o'clock. I'll have a tough time getting my son up for that time, but I'll make it work.

As far as school goes, I'll need to apply for an in-year transfer for Max, but I'm worried about the fact he's missed so much learning over the past few weeks or months or however long he's been hanging out with those friends of his back in Birmingham. There is a local school here, so my best bet is to have a chat with the headteacher and see what she suggests we do. However, I've got so many balls in the air at the moment that I can't focus on everything. I think a job will be good for him to clear his mind. Maybe taking a break from school is a good idea, and he can perhaps catch up over the summer.

Next, I walk into the Fox and Hound, the local pub across the road, and ask about a job for myself. Since I already know how to work in a bar, it seems the most obvious place to start. Darren, the manager, hires me on the spot! Apparently, he's desperate and wants to hire a more experienced (aka older) bartender because he was fed up with being let down by young kids in their twenties who kept taking advantage of the staff discount.

I start tomorrow at two.

Talk about jumping in at the deep end.

I feel like a different woman than two days ago. I'm still full of anxiety, unease and general stress, but I'm working my way through it. I'm making things happen. I'm making decisions I never knew I'd have the confidence to make. Because I don't have any choice. If I don't, then things will just get on top of me again. I can't let that happen.

I don't recognise myself. Nothing this crazy has ever happened to me, other than finding out I was pregnant at seventeen, sending my plans of attending university to study medicine out the window. Looking back, I can't see myself working in medicine now. I often wonder where I'd be in life had those two blue lines not appeared on the stick, but I certainly wouldn't be here, in this picturesque town, having inherited a country house.

7

When I return to the house, I stand in the kitchen and just take it all in: the filthy worktops, the grimy windows, the two working plug sockets, the still lingering smell of the dead rat, the disgusting fridge/freezer. I brought as much as I could from Birmingham, but I'm still missing general items, such as dishcloths and washing-up liquid. During my scatterbrained approach to packing, I didn't think ahead to what I'd need when I arrived because I had no idea the place would be in such a bad state. I get to work cleaning the fridge with the products I bought so that I can put away the milk and vegetables. I'm not too sure what Max is doing upstairs, but every now and then I hear a bang or footsteps. Perhaps it's best if I leave him alone for a bit to sort his room out.

Instead of drunken shouts from the neighbours and car horns blaring, the late afternoon air is filled with creaks, groans and random clicks as well as wildlife noises, such as owls and other birds. Other than that, as the day draws to a close and darkness creeps in, it's completely silent, something I'm not used to at all. I think there might be more rats nesting in the walls or under the floorboards because I also hear the pitter-patter of tiny feet and claws. Perhaps there's even a pigeon or two in the roof.

Before I start on making dinner, I head upstairs to attempt to unblock the toilet. Luckily, the blockage isn't too far down the pipe, and after sticking an old, rusty kitchen utensil down the bowl, I'm able to release the blockage.

Right, time to wash my hands and then start on dinner.

I manage to find a saucepan that's not completely disgusting. I decide to make pesto pasta because it's a staple meal for us and something I can make quickly and without too many pots and pans. But there's a problem. The hob doesn't work, and the water running from the tap starts off a murky brown. I run it for a while, and it eventually runs clear, but who knows how safe it is to drink.

But the broken hob is a problem. It's electric, so perhaps it's merely the plug socket it's attached to that's not working. I pull the plug out of the wall socket and attempt to put it in the one that's shared between the kettle and the toaster, but the bloody cable isn't long enough.

'For fuck's sake!'

I squeeze the bridge of my nose with one hand and tap my fingers together with the other, attempting to quell the rising panic and frustration. I can't even boil water on a hob! I take a breath, then another, calming myself down.

Okay, think. I can boil water in the kettle. It's not perfect, but it'll have to do. I fill the kettle with water, wait and then pour boiling water on the pasta in the saucepan and put the lid on. I'll probably have to repeat the process several times as the water cools, but at least it's better than serving buttered toast for dinner because that's the only other food I can make right now.

A long twenty minutes later, I finally have pasta that's somewhat edible and mix a glob of pesto in it. Max is already at the table. He looks lost without his phone attached to his hand.

'Here you go,' I say, putting a bowl of steaming pasta in front of him.

He sighs, picks up a spoon and takes a bite. 'It's a bit ... crunchy,' he says.

'It's al dente,' I say.

'Whatever. It's still hard.'

I take a bite and attempt to hide a groan. I decide a change of subject is in order. 'Oh, I almost forgot, you've got a job interview at nine tomorrow morning at the Co-op, and I start work at two at the local pub, the Fox and Hound.' I take a sip of water. It tastes okay, so I'm hopefully not going to die from dysentery. I almost treated myself to a bottle of white wine at the shop, but decided proper food for Max and me was more of a necessity.

Max pauses with his fork in his mouth. 'The Co-op. Really?'

'You're seventeen years old, it's your first job, and you have no qualifications. You can't afford to be picky.'

'What about school?'

'What about it?'

Max stares at me blankly. 'Like ... am I going to a new school?'

'What do you want to do?'

Max shrugs. 'Dunno,' he says.

'I thought we'd settle in for a few weeks, and then I'll contact the local school, and we'll go and have a chat with them. Perhaps you can catch up on schoolwork over the summer, or maybe they'll get you to redo year twelve in September.'

Max chews loudly with his mouth open, then takes a slurp of water, grimacing. 'Whatever.'

'As far as your interview goes, please try to be professional tomorrow. It would help if you answered questions with more than a one-word answer. And I'd like you to wear a clean T-shirt.'

'When am I getting a new phone?'

'Once the money comes in, but there are a few rules. You can't go on social media or turn on your location settings.'

Max scoffs. 'We're not hiding from MI5. I doubt Luke knows how to track a phone.'

'Is that his name? Luke?'

Max nods.

'Fine. Well, I'd still like you to stay off social media until I say it's okay.'

Max doesn't reply to that statement. 'How am I supposed to keep in contact with you without a phone?'

'What, like you used to keep in contact with me before when you had your old phone?' I'm alluding to the fact he used to merely like my messages rather than replying to them.

He finishes his pasta and stands up. 'Where's my bedding?'

'I ... I didn't bring it.' Shit. Another thing I forgot to bring.

'I'm not sleeping in mouldy old bedding.'

'I'm sorry. I ... there's a blanket in the back of the car. You can use that.'

I feel like the worst mother in the world as I watch my son walk to the car and fetch a blanket to sleep under. I haven't even looked upstairs yet, but I already know I won't be sleeping up there. I'll be camping out in the lounge, by the broken window, in case any intruders come and visit in the dead of night.

Once I finish washing up in the warm water I used to cook the pasta in, I sit in the lounge on the sofa by myself and listen to the noises of the house. I haven't brought a second blanket, but I do find one in the large cupboard in the corner of the lounge. It smells like mothballs, but it seems clean enough. I face the open window, shivering slightly.

Even if someone does break in, what am I expecting to do? Perhaps just my presence will be enough to deter them. They'll see the car in the driveway and realise someone lives here now. It takes a long time for my heart to stop hammering at a hundred miles an hour. Sleep doesn't come easy, but eventually my eyes grow so heavy, I can't keep them open a moment longer, and I succumb to exhaustion, and I dream about our new life here and what surprises tomorrow will bring.

I WAKE up to the sounds of birds and the early morning light beaming through the broken window directly onto my face. I guess no one broke in and murdered me in my sleep. My heart jolts as I think of Max.

I throw off the blanket and race upstairs, taking the steps two at a time, praying that the drug dealer didn't find us and creep through the house to kill Max while I was asleep. I don't know which bedroom he's claimed as his own, so I start opening every door I see, eventually finding him in the second-largest bedroom, curled up on the bed with the blanket over him. It's only then that I let out a long breath.

It takes three attempts to get my lazy son out of bed. He doesn't shower (although I don't blame him because there's no hot water, and the water pressure is little more than a dribble), and he doesn't brush his hair, so I quickly try to flatten the errant strands. Why do I feel as if it's his first day of school all over again? I feed him a breakfast of toast and then usher him out the door and into the car, where I then drive him into town.

The manager of the shop gives me a reassuring smile as I wave goodbye to my son. He'll be fine. I hope. I'm not sure how long he'll be, but the manager said he'd give me a call when Max is finished. I don't start work till two today, so with nothing else to do, I drive back to the house and start making a list of the jobs I need to do first. I need to get myself back into some sort of routine, even if it means doing random jobs to keep myself busy during the times I'm not at work. If I'm still and quiet, then my brain works overtime, and it feels like all my thoughts are racing around a track, so I need to get a grip on them before they overrun me completely. This is the first day when I haven't taken my morning medication, so I'm unsure how my body and mind is going to react. I checked and double-checked the bag I packed, but I definitely left them behind.

I can't do anything until I have money in my account, but there's plenty of work I can do that doesn't require money. There's so much mess and rubbish scattered about the house, so I begin by grabbing a bin bag and picking it up. Then I walk around the house and decide which pieces of furniture to keep and which to sell for some extra cash. The house is large and full of bits of furniture I don't really need.

I also want to try to cut down the branches of the tree growing through the smashed window into the lounge, and I'm pleased when I find a rusty saw in the shed round the side of the house. It's not exactly the perfect tool for the job, but it'll have to do. I can't have a tree growing in my lounge, but with the rusty saw, I can't remove the larger branches. I don't find anything lying around that I can use to board up the window either, so for the time being, the lounge is still open to the elements.

I'm pleased with my progress after three hours, but my back isn't. It's only then I realise I haven't heard from the manager at the Co-op. Surely a job interview doesn't last three hours? I've been so busy and distracted I haven't even given Max a single thought.

I grab my phone from my pocket and am about to call the Co-op when Max arrives through the front door. His appearance makes me jump out of my skin.

'What are you doing here?' I ask. 'I thought I was coming back to pick you up when you were finished.'

'Yeah, and John called your phone several times, but you didn't pick up.'

I look down at my phone. 'I don't have any missed calls. Damn it, maybe there's no signal here.' I didn't even consider that. 'I'm so sorry. How did it go?'

'Fine.'

I wait, hoping for him to elaborate, but he doesn't. 'Did you get the job?'

'Yeah.'

'That's great! Congratulations!' I put my phone away. 'When do you start?'

'I start tomorrow at nine. I need to bring in my ID and provide a bank account.'

'Do you want to open up your own or use mine?'

He shrugs. 'I don't mind.'

'Let's get you your own account. It's time you learned how to handle your own money. I'm going to start my new job in an hour. Can I leave you to finish clearing out the dining room? There are lots of random boxes that can be moved outside.'

'Can't. Megan's picking me up in an hour. I'm just going to have a quick shower. The water's still cold, I take it?'

'Yes, it is. Sorry, but ... who's Megan?'

'A girl who works at the shop.'

'Okay ...' My mind reels with thoughts about what kind of girl Megan is. I hope she's nothing like the girls he used to spend time with. 'Um ... And where is Megan taking you?'

'Dunno. We're just gonna hang out.'

Max turns and heads upstairs. A door slams a few seconds later, and the water starts running from the shower. I rub the small of my back. My mind immediately thinks of the *friends* he used to hang out with back in Birmingham. He had a girlfriend about a year ago, but that quickly fizzled out when she overdosed by accident, and her parents moved away once she'd recovered. I hope he makes better friends here than he did there. I know I need to trust him, but how can I when he made such bad decisions in the past? I want to wrap him up in cotton wool and protect him, but he needs to learn to stand on his own two feet. Hopefully, this job will be good for him and teach him the value of hard work.

I wanted this move to bring us closer. Now, I already feel as if he's drifting away again. I've always known the day would come when he'd prefer to hang out with girls than his mum, but I just wasn't prepared for how much it would hurt.

I realise now that, without Max, I have no one. Perhaps I

should take a leaf out of his book and make some new friends, but the thought fills me with nothing but dread. I'd rather cement myself into a new routine here in this house. It'll be my project to focus my mind.

MY FIRST SHIFT at the bar goes well. It's quiet to start with while I find my feet and practise pouring drinks, but by the time five o'clock rolls around, the place fills up quickly with the locals, and I don't even have time to be nervous and worry about what Max might be doing with Megan. My anxiety about starting a new job is high, but I find that keeping busy helps dampen the rising worry.

The bar manager, Darren, takes me under his wing, and I shadow him for the rest of the night until eight when my shift ends. He doesn't look much older than me, and I find myself enjoying his company and laughing at his lame jokes. My feet are killing me, and my back keeps spasming, a mixture of the manual labour this morning and relentlessly being on my feet all day.

'Great work today, Natasha. I can tell you've worked behind a bar before. You're a natural,' Darren tells me.

'Thanks,' I respond somewhat awkwardly. I've never been great at receiving compliments.

'How are you settling into your new house?'

I told him about inheriting the house at the start of my shift when I had to complete the paperwork. When it asked for my previous address, I just left it blank, hoping he wouldn't ask for further details. I already decided I didn't want to tell people where Max and I came from.

'Um ... yeah. Fine, I guess. It needs a lot of work.'

'Ha! Yeah, Yew Tree House is a bit of a dump ... Sorry.'

I wave off his comment. 'No, you're right. It is,' I say with a laugh; otherwise I might cry.

'Where'd you move from?'

The question I've been dreading. Why does he even care?

'Um ... Manchester.' The lie slips off my tongue quickly. I still have a tingle of fear running up my spine whenever I think of that man, Luke, who's after Max. For all I know, he has people out looking for us. Despite moving a few hundred miles away, I am still finding myself looking over my shoulder, looking out for anyone who might be following or watching us. I must be careful what I say to people, how much I reveal. I've repeatedly told Max not to tell anyone about our previous life in Birmingham. I just hope he remembers. Although, our accents may give us away, so I make a mental note to try to tone mine down. Max's isn't too noticeable, but mine has been honed over the years, although I very rarely use the Brummie dialect.

'Really? Your accent isn't very Mancunian.'

Damn it.

'Oh, well, we've sort of lived all over,' I say with a nervous laugh, attempting a weird Manchester accent.

Darren raises an eyebrow, then thankfully changes the subject. 'You getting a builder in to do the work on the house?' asks Darren while drying a pint glass with a tea towel.

'Oh, well, yes, eventually I'll get a builder in, I suppose, but money's a bit tight at the moment, so I'm going to do most of it myself.' I didn't even think of hiring a builder, but it makes sense. I'm not qualified to do a lot of the work. I suppose I can do cosmetic stuff, but to fix the electrics and hot water, I'll need a professional.

'Good for you.' He switches to pouring a beer and handing it to a man who's sitting at the bar close by who nods his thanks without uttering a word. 'The grounds are nice though, right?'

'A bit overgrown but, yes, they look lovely. I'm going to start cutting all the overgrown bushes and trees down to clear a bit of space. I think maybe I'll start planting a vegetable garden.' I'm not sure why I say this because I didn't think about starting a vegetable garden at all, but it's not a bad idea. It might give me a project to keep me busy over the spring and upcoming summer. I keep spilling ideas out of my head as soon as they enter without really thinking about it. But my therapist did always tell me that keeping my hands and mind busy on tasks such as gardening and being outside is one of the best things I can do for my mental health. And that's exactly what I need right now.

'Sounds like you've got quite the renovation project on your hands.'

'Indeed,' I say.

WHEN I ARRIVE HOME after work, it's to an empty house. I don't know why I was expecting Max to be home before me, but it irritates me that he's not here. He doesn't have a phone yet, so I haven't been expecting a call, but he knew what time I was home. I still haven't got the damn hob fixed, so I stopped by the shop on the way home and grabbed some ready meals for the both of us that can be eaten cold.

After dinner, instead of going to bed, I stay up and wait for Max to arrive, silently seething and growing more and more frustrated and anxious with every passing minute that he doesn't appear. I keep myself busy by finishing tidying the dining room, the job I asked him to do earlier. Max may not appreciate my hard work, but I do. There's a sense of pride growing inside as I finish wiping down the side table and straighten up the ornaments. A lot of them are old-fashioned, some a little strange, but each one is beautiful in its own way. Harriet must have loved her possessions very much. I can't bring myself to throw them away. They must hold so many memories. They are, after all, family heirlooms I never knew I had. Each one tells its own story, yet I don't know a single one.

The crunch of tyres against gravel makes my head jerk up. I rush to the window and peer out at the darkness. A black car is parked on my driveway, and Max is in the passenger seat, with a girl in the driving seat. I can see a few of her delicate young features under the inside lights of the car. She's blonde, slim and is wearing a lot of eyeliner. Very pretty.

Guilt starts to niggle in my gut as I spy on my son and his new friend, so I step away from the window and give them their privacy. A few minutes later, Max walks in and stops in his tracks when he sees me sitting at the bottom of the stairs opposite the front door with my arms folded.

'It's gone midnight,' he says.

'Yes, I'm aware of the time, Max. Are you?'

'I just told you—'

'Might I remind you that the last time you started hanging out with people at all hours of the night, you got yourself involved with a drug dealer who now wants to kill you.'

Max huffs. 'I can look after myself.'

'Can you though?'

'What, suddenly you're worried about me? I thought this was supposed to be a fresh start? That's what I'm doing. I'm making new friends.'

'Yes, I know that, Max, but you have to understand that we're still in danger. All it takes is for word to get back to—'

'Word won't get back. I don't have a phone, so how am I supposed to fuck this up? Stop worrying, okay? You just focus on this shitty house, and I'll focus on my shitty job.'

I push myself off the bottom step, my fists clenched. 'You could at least be grateful for everything I've done for you.'

'Grateful? Grateful for what? Moving me into this run-down house, taking me away from my friends, throwing away my phone and forcing me to get a fucking job? What-ever fantasy you had for us, doing up this house together and being a happy family, it's not going to happen.'

Angry tears distort my vision as Max storms past me and up the stairs to his room. 'Max! Please don't shut me out. I'm trying my best, I really am.'

'Your best isn't good enough,' comes the seething reply.

My mouth opens, but I have nothing left. My son may as well have reached into my chest, ripped out my heart and stabbed it with a knife. I sink to the floor as sobs rack my body. I pull my hair and scream into the floor, wishing it would open and swallow me whole.

The whole situation we're in comes crashing down on me. I have no idea what I'm doing, living one moment to the next with no clear goal or routine. My son hates me and is giving me grief over everything, blaming me for being here. I need to lie low for the next five days until that money comes through so I can pay off the drug dealer. There's a gaping hole in the window in the lounge, which I'm going to have to camp in front of again, like a bouncer. The bloody oven doesn't work. The water's cold and brown.

Can it possibly get any worse?

8

The next morning, I wake up with a headache that pounds behind my eyes. If I didn't know any better, I'd say I was hungover. All the symptoms are there: dry mouth, headache, nauseous feeling in stomach, everything apart from the fact I haven't touched a drop. After I peeled myself off the hallway floor last night, completely spent from sobbing my heart out, I crawled onto the sofa in the lounge and stared at the ceiling for hours, listening to the sounds of the old house and making weird animal shapes out of the mould patterns and shadows. Eventually, I must have passed out, but I have no idea what time it was. Again, the open window provided a cool breeze, but no intruders.

I grimace at the thought of a cold shower this morning. I haven't washed since I arrived here, which I know is disgusting, but thanks to my routine being non-existent, I'm really struggling to organise my thoughts. I know the hot water needs fixing and the electrics sorted, but I just can't bring myself to start the process of looking for a builder.

Maybe that solicitor can help. It's not his job, but he did say he'd be happy to help with anything I needed. Surely, he'll know of a local builder who can do the work. It will save me having to vet a load of builders. I wouldn't even know what to look out for.

I call Adrian before I head upstairs for a shower, managing to find a pocket of signal in the kitchen.

'Natasha, great to hear from you. How are you settling in?'

'Um, yeah, great, thanks. Sorry for calling so early. I was just wondering if you knew of any local builders or plumbers who can sort hot water and electrics?'

'Yeah, of course. Let me have a think, and I'll text you the names and numbers.'

'Great. Thanks, Adrian.'

'Happy to help!'

I hang up and smirk slightly at his enthusiasm.

When I eventually make it downstairs, after the cold shower where I hated every second, I find Max eating a slice of toast at the kitchen table. In the whole time he's been a teenager, he's never once made it downstairs before me, so my guard's immediately up. He looks up as I enter.

'Hey,' he says.

I'm a little taken aback that he's even spoken to me after the way we left things last night. He's said some nasty stuff to me over the years, including 'I hate you', but what he said last night, that my best wasn't good enough, hurt me the most.

'Good morning.'

'By the way, only one side of our toaster works.'

'Of course it does,' I say with a sigh. It's bad enough that we have to keep unplugging and plugging in the toaster, kettle and various other appliances whenever we want to use one. Now, we can only toast one piece of bread at a time because my old toaster, which is at least a decade old, has decided to cut its workload in half.

'What time are you working till today?' I ask. 'Did John give you your shifts?'

'Yeah. Till three.'

'We'll need to sit down and discuss our work patterns soon. Do you need a lift into the village?'

'Megan's picking me up.'

I nod, unplug the toaster and plug in the kettle, flicking it on. It's full of limescale, but at least it still works. For now.

The sound of Max chewing fills the awkward silence. 'I'm sorry ... about what I said last night.'

I turn around on the spot.

'I didn't mean it,' he adds, a faint blush creeping across his cheeks.

I smile as relief washes over me, and the shattered pieces of my heart fuse back together. I want to run and hug my baby, squeeze him tight and tell him that I forgive him, that it doesn't matter what he said because nothing he can say or do will ever make me stop loving him, no matter how bad and hurtful it is. But I know I can't do and say that because it would embarrass him and potentially push him away again, so I merely shake my head.

'Max, it's okay. You were angry and upset. So was I.'

'Yeah, but ... what I said about you not being good enough. It's not true. I know you do your best. And the reason we're in this shitty house is because of me, so ... I'm just angry, I guess, about everything.'

'Oh, Max, it's not your fault. I should have handled it better. It's just that ...' I look around the kitchen as I continue, 'this house was a gift, and yes, it's a bit shitty now, but I'd really like to make it our home, somewhere we can be safe and happy. I could really use your help with that.'

Max swallows the last bite of toast and stands up. 'Sure. If you want me to do some stuff when I get back from work, then just leave a note of what needs to be done.' A car horns sounds. 'That's Megan now.'

'Have a good day,' I say.

He doesn't hug me goodbye, but for once I don't care.

The kettle boils, and I make myself a cup of tea, leaving the bag to stew for a few extra minutes. I have another late shift today at work, and I'd really like to finish getting that damn tree out of the lounge. There's a garage out the back, which isn't locked. The padlock holding the double doors shut has been smashed apart, probably by the teenagers who ransacked the house. Perhaps they were hoping to find something exciting inside, but all I find that I can use is a pair of gloves to protect my hands.

I get to work on the tree, dragging the branches through the house and out the front door, leaving fallen leaves and twigs in my wake.

Adrian sends me a message with three local builders and their numbers, all of whom come highly recommended, but he does say they are on the expensive side, over two hundred and fifty pounds a day, which immediately makes my stomach flip. Getting this house up to scratch is going to ruin me. When I arrived here, I was over five hundred quid into my one-grand overdraft. That ten grand I'm expecting can't come fast enough. I thank Adrian with a quick message, but decide not to call any of the builders just yet. There's no point until the money comes through anyway.

· · ·

IT TAKES me two hours to finish removing the tree from the house. I trim back the branches as much as possible, then sweep up the leaves and sawdust. I'm washing my hands in the kitchen sink when I look out the window across the driveway and see a white van coming up the lane. It's filthy, and when it pulls up, I see the faded writing on the side: *Clayton Building Works.*

Frowning, I dry my hands on the nearby towel and walk to the front door, opening it to see a very tall, broad man getting out of the van.

'Can I help you?' I ask, staying by the door, holding on to it in case I need to use it as a shield. Living in the centre of Birmingham for a decade has taught me many valuable life lessons. I once had someone turn up at my door, asking for help, and when I opened it, they tried to push past me to get inside the flat. I tried to slam the door in their face, but they put their foot in the door. I've never been so scared. Max was still young and playing just behind me, but luckily, I was able to crush the man's foot between the door and the frame, and he backed off. I didn't open the door to a stranger ever again, but right now my defences are up, especially as I'm not expecting anyone.

The man looks up as he shuts the van door. He walks up to me and stops by the front steps. He has a thick bushy beard with flecks of grey and short brown hair covering most of his head. His hairline has seen better days, and he has a slight belly on him, but due to his height, it doesn't make him look overweight. He's just very large, at least six feet two, but it's difficult to tell his age, possibly mid-forties.

'Hi, I hear you're looking for a builder,' he says.

'Um ... sort of. Yes, but ... I'm sorry ... Who are you?' He does look vaguely familiar, but I can't think where I've seen him before.

'Sorry,' he says. 'Henry Clayton.'

'Right ...'

'I heard you were after a builder, so I'm here to offer my services.'

I fold my arms across my chest, my eyes flicking from the van and back to him several times. 'Oh! Um ... that's very nice of you, but I can't afford to hire a builder at the moment, but I should be getting some money through in the next few weeks. Out of interest, how did you know I was looking for a builder?' My mind casts back to Adrian's message, and none of the recommendations were called Henry Clayton.

Henry's attention seems to be elsewhere. He's looking up at the house and casting his eyes over it, as if adding up all the money it's going to cost to bring it up to standard. 'I overheard it at the pub.'

It clicks into place.

That's where I recognise him from. I saw him at the bar the other night when I was working my first shift, and Darren served him a beer while we were talking about the house. He must have been eavesdropping on our conversation. He was quite pissed, just quietly sitting at the bar, drinking beer after beer, but he hadn't made a sound nor been any sort of problem.

'I see,' I say. 'Well, like I said, I can't afford to hire you at the moment and—'

'I work for cheap, and you don't have to pay me until you get your money through. I don't need a deposit. How's a hundred and twenty quid a day sound? Plus all the material costs, which I'll get cheaper than anyone else because I know a lot of the local building merchants.'

I almost choke. That seems exceptionally cheap to hire a builder. The builders Adrian suggested were charging much more than that, not including the building materials. Why is Henry so cheap? Red flags start popping up in front of my eyes. I've heard of people being taken advantage of by cheap builders who start a job and then leave halfway through, leaving it unfinished. Or they do such a bad job that the building work is shoddy and needs ripping down and starting again. I watched a Stacey Solomon show about it not long ago. She even helped and taught people to do their own DIY, which is what I planned to do.

'It sounds good, but ...'

'I can see you're a bit nervous. I'm sorry for just barging up here like this, but ... I don't have much work on at the moment, and it seems like you could use the help.' He looks up at the house again. 'Do the electrics even work?'

'Yes, but most of the sockets in the house are dead.'

He nods, as if he's not surprised.

I gulp back my growing anxiety. 'I ... I was going to hire someone else. I was recommended a few builders in the area, but your name didn't come up. Are you from around here?'

'Yeah. I live about fifteen minutes away. I used to work on this house back when the old girl lived here. I even did a lot of the work you see inside and out in the gardens. Not that you can tell now since it's been left to rack and ruin over the past seven years since she moved into the care home.'

'Did you know Harriet well, then?'

'You could say that. She was a lonely old bird and always made me a nice cuppa when I popped by. I even visited her in the care home a few times.'

'You did?'

'She told me about you. That when she died, you'd be getting the house.'

'I see …' My first thought is why the hell was Harriet telling her builder her life story and secrets?

Henry clears his throat, clearly nervous. He sees the broken window and points at it. 'That needs boarding up or the window replacing ASAP.'

'Yeah, I tried to find some boards or something, but there was nothing around.'

'I can get it replaced today easily enough.'

I almost choke. My immediate response is no. I just want him gone. Strangers make me nervous, and this guy seems too good to be true. No deposit. A hundred and twenty quid a day. Doesn't need paying until I get the money through. But the red flags are still waving in front of my face, warning me that sometimes if things are too good to be true, there's usually a good reason.

Why?

Why? Why? Why?

'Can you provide some good references?' I ask, putting an end to the constant nagging single-word question.

'Sure. I've worked for people all around this area.'

'How long have you been a builder?'

'All my life.'

'Why are you charging so little?'

Henry sighs. 'I don't charge so little for everyone. My usual fee is two-fifty, but I guess I'm doing it because I owe it to Harriet. She was good to me back when she was alive. Not many people are around here. I heard about her death a few months ago. It's been horrible to see this house stand here and rot for the past seven years. I'm glad someone's come along to bring it back to life. I just want to help. Plus, I've got a gap in my schedule for the next few weeks. I can't just let this house be worked on by just any old builder in the area. Some of them do a proper crap job.' His body language is relaxed, open. He's even staring up at the house as if he's reliving old, happy memories.

'I tell you what,' I say. 'If you can provide me with a couple of references and they check out, then I'll take you up on your kind offer.'

Henry positively beams at me. 'Great. Well, ask Darren at the pub. I did work on his upstairs bedrooms, and … Carter Jones who lives at number twelve Holly Lane. I dug his pond, plastered his walls and put up the fences in his fields.'

I nod. 'Thank you. If you leave me your card, I'll let you know tomorrow.'

He hands me a bent and folded business card, which he pulls out of his pocket. 'You want me to replace your window today, then?'

'Um … no, that's—'

'Free of charge. A test run so you can see the standard of my work. It won't be a super fancy window, but I reckon I've got something that'll work in the back of my van.'

My mouth drops open. I can't say no to that. 'Thank you. That's very kind.'

Henry nods and walks back to his van. I watch him as he opens the back and retrieves a bucket of tools. He's wearing a pair of grey cargo shorts and a scruffy black T-shirt, which is tight around his biceps. I'm still not convinced about him, but I have to hand it to the guy, he's very persuasive and clearly passionate about his job and this house.

I think I'll feel better once I ask Darren about him.

I wonder why Adrian didn't include him on the list of builders he gave me.

Within a few minutes, Henry has already made a start on removing the broken window and the shattered pieces of glass lying around. The truth is, Henry has already loosened some of the tension and stress I've been feeling. Now, with the window fixed, I can sleep upstairs in a bed, something I haven't done for the past two nights. My back is killing me.

Despite Henry's helpfulness, his manner and sudden appearance give me a different sort of tightness across the chest, an uneasy feeling that doesn't quite sit right. I wish there were a way I could ask Harriet about him. He says he spent a lot of time here and did work on the house for her, but there's no proof of that. I just have to take his word for it.

He seems to know what he's doing though.

I still want to do some of the work myself and learn new skills, but having Henry here will certainly lessen the load, as it were. Plus, there are certain building jobs I wouldn't be able to do, such as sort the electrics out and the hot water. I know they need a professional to fix them and sign them off to ensure everything is up to code. If I tried to rewire the electrics, the house would probably catch fire, or I'd electrocute myself.

Once the money is through, the dealer is paid off and some of the bills are sorted, I hope this tight chest will loosen more and more. A fresh start isn't all it's cracked up to be. It's stressful and expensive, and I still have no idea what I'm doing.

Plus, I haven't taken my medication for several days. I'll need to sign up to the local doctor's and get another prescription, but it's yet another job that isn't a high priority. I can deal with the headaches and brain fog that I can't quite get rid of. I've even stopped emailing my CBT therapist. I just can't face doing any of that right now.

I need to get the house sorted.

Perhaps I can help Henry with some of his jobs, and he can teach me the basics. Or Max can shadow him and learn.

Henry may turn out to be a blessing in disguise after all.

9

I drive to work and park, then quickly pop across the road and tell Max that when he gets home later, Henry will probably still be working. I explain who he is and what he's offered to do for us. Max just shrugs and replies with, 'Cool.'

I take that to mean he's happy with a strange man being at the house. Max has never had to deal with that before. The few times I dated casually, I never brought my boyfriends back to my home. In fact, Max never met any of them. They didn't last long enough to warrant an introduction. It's not that I didn't want Max to have a male role model or father figure in his life, but there was no one ever good enough for him. Even his real father wasn't good enough in my eyes, so I'm glad he's never been in the picture. I barely remember what he looks like.

Darren is at the bar when I walk in, serving a customer. I decide to ask him about Henry straight away rather than sitting on it all day and allowing my mind to run free with worry. I wait until he's finished with the customer and then approach him.

'Hey, Darren, I'm thinking of hiring Henry Clayton to do some work on the house. I asked him for some references, and he gave me your name.'

Darren closes the till and then wipes down the surface of the bar. 'Henry Clayton? Yeah, I know him well. He did some work upstairs on the bedrooms. Great job he did too. He's a regular here most nights.'

'Does he drink heavily, then?'

Darren laughs. 'Nah, he's just a lonely guy with nothing better to do. However, he does usually go on a bit of a bender around the time of year his wife left him. He's still a bit bitter about her leaving him for another guy. He used to be much happier before all that happened, but he's a decent builder. His quality is the best I've seen. His attitude and bedside manner could use some work at times, but otherwise I can't fault him. You could do a lot worse.'

I join him behind the bar and begin tidying up the empty glasses. 'He was married?'

'Yeah, I forget her name. A nice chick.'

The fact he was married surprises me, but I decide not to press any further for details. It's none of my business. 'Do you know anyone called Carter Jones? He's another reference Henry mentioned.'

Darren frowns. 'No, not heard of him.'

'He lives at number twelve Holly Lane.'

'Nope. Sorry.'

'No worries. Thanks anyway. I'll take over here,' I say, nodding at the bar area.

'Thanks, Natasha. I'll be in the back if you need me.'

Darren leaves me to serve the next customer, and I spend

the rest of the day looking forward to seeing my new window when I get home. It will be nice not to have a draft in the house and a tree in the living room, and it means I can sleep upstairs in a bed. Speaking of which, I need to buy new bedding, but it'll have to wait a few more days.

I talk to loads of customers and introduce myself. All of them seem thrilled at the fact I'm renovating Yew Tree House. A couple of them even apologise for the mess because apparently their kids like hanging out there and drinking. We share a laugh, and I avoid telling them about the empty condom wrappers I found.

Harriet Greene seems to have been a well-liked woman too, but no one mentions Prudence, her niece who disappeared and left her to fend for herself, resulting in her having to move into a care home in her later years. I don't bother asking questions about Prudence because, at the end of the day, she did me a favour by running away. If she didn't, then I wouldn't have this house, and Max and I would still be back in Birmingham, being threatened by a drug dealer, so I decide that, rather than worrying about her for no reason, I'll put it out of my mind and enjoy the fact I have a house to call my own.

Prudence Greene isn't an issue.

WHEN I FINALLY GET HOME LATER THAT night, exhausted from eight hours on my feet, I smile when I see the window has been replaced. It's not a brand-new window, but it's clean and, therefore, looks completely out of place against the rugged, old walls of the house. At least no woodland animals or feral teenagers can get in and cause a mess now. It looks perfect.

There's a light on inside. I walk into the kitchen to find Max at the kitchen table and ...

'Ah, here she is!' exclaims Henry before taking a loud slurp from my favourite mug, which I brought with me. My eyes linger on the mug longer than is deemed polite, and my jaw clenches at the thought of him having his mouth on it.

Why is he still here ... and with Max ... so late at night? It can't have taken him all day to fit the new window.

'Um ... Hi. I didn't think you'd still be working,' I say, eyeing the tools and items laid across the kitchen worktops.

'I'm not, but Max and I got to talking, and he gave me a hand with fixing the hot water.'

'You fixed the hot water too?' I can't hide my shock.

'Yeah, thought I'd take a quick look at it for you. Max mentioned you haven't had a hot shower since you've been here, so I took it upon myself to fix it for you. Now, you have hot water for a shower,' he says with a smile.

'Wow ... um ... thank you.'

'Max tells me you've moved from Birmingham,' says Henry, rising to his feet and walking to the kitchen sink. He rinses the mug under the running water and then plonks it down on the draining board. I wince, expecting it to break, but it doesn't.

I glare at my son. How could he have been so stupid to tell Henry the truth about where we came from? I don't want details of our old lives spreading around the area, especially since I've been telling people we moved from Manchester.

Max shrugs and stands up. 'Well, I'm going to head to bed. See you later, Henry.'

'Bye, kid.'

Max takes a few steps towards the stairs. I give him an

extra ten seconds, expecting him to say goodnight to me, but he doesn't.

'Goodnight, Max!' I shout up the stairs.

'Night!'

I sigh as I turn to Henry, who is leaning casually against the kitchen counter. His body language and smile appear friendly and perfectly innocent, but it still niggles at me about why he's been here alone with my son for over five hours.

'You got a good kid there, Nat.'

I can't remember if I told him my name, and we certainly don't know each other well enough for him to call me Nat, which I still hate. Then I remember he told me that Harriet had told him about me.

'Thanks. Yeah, he's all right ... considering.' I say it as a joke, but Henry frowns at me and clears his throat.

'He tells me that he ran into a bit of trouble and that's why you had to move. From the looks of that black eye, it was bad. Is his dad not around to step in?'

I can't believe Max has been careless enough to tell this to Henry.

Fear grips my insides as I steady myself against the back of the nearest chair. 'Um ... no, his dad isn't around. What did Max tell you about what happened?' Surely, my son hasn't offered up the information willingly and of his own accord? Has Henry been questioning him about our background?

'Nothing much. He's not a huge talker, is he?'

I don't mention the fact that it sounds as if Max has said more words to Henry in the space of half a day than he's spoken to me in the past year.

'No, he can be very private,' I say.

Henry nods, and we fall into an uncomfortable silence. 'So ... did you check out my references? Do I get the job?' He sounds so hopeful, so excited.

'Er ... yes, I did.' I take a deep breath. There's no obvious reason why I shouldn't hire Henry straight away. He's working for cheap and doesn't require money up front. He clearly wants to be here, but his overeagerness makes my stomach clench. However, having him here fixing things would certainly lessen the load on me and put my mind at ease. Plus, a hot shower is a hard thing to turn down.

'Yes, you're hired.'

Henry beams.

'I'm extremely grateful for your kindness and for fixing the window and hot water, and your offer of working for a lower fee, but I must ensure there are some boundaries while you work here. This is my home, and ... I'm afraid I'm not comfortable with you being here with my son if you're not actually working on the house. I'm sorry, but—'

Henry holds his palms up towards me and steps towards the front door. 'Hey, I totally get it. I apologise. It's just that the kid arrived, and he seemed interested in what I was doing, so I asked him if he wanted to lend a hand, and he said yes. I didn't see the harm in giving him some work experience. It might be good for the lad.'

'I agree, and I'm more than happy to have him shadow you. In fact, I'd like to help too if you'd be willing to teach me.'

Henry nods. 'Absolutely.'

'Great.'

'I guess I'll get going, then. I'll be back tomorrow to sort out the electrics. I'll leave my tools here for now if that's okay. I'm surprised this place hasn't caught fire with the amount of bad wiring running through it. The last time I worked here, I told the old girl that the wires needed updating and replacing, but she refused to listen, and that was, like, ten years ago.'

'If the electrics need replacing, then please go ahead. Would you mind running the costs past me though before you order anything?'

'I told you that you don't have to worry about paying me until you get your money through.'

'Yes, I know, and that's very generous of you, but ... I'd still like you to tell me the costs of materials and labour at the end of each day so I can keep track of the outgoings.'

Henry nods again. 'No problem.'

'I really do appreciate you working for next to nothing,' I say, lowering my gaze away from his. Despite him making me feel a bit weird and on edge, I can't deny that he's literally saving my life right now.

He waves it away. 'Think nothing of it. As I said, I guess I owe the old girl. And now, it's you who owes me. Oh shit ... sorry, I didn't mean for that to sound weird and creepy.'

Too late.

I look up at his choice of words and attempt to wave it off. 'Don't worry, I know what you mean.'

Henry blushes. 'Bye, Nat.'

'Goodnight, Henry.'

He lingers a moment longer and then walks out the door. I wait until I hear the van door slam before letting out a long breath.

Then, ignoring my hunger pangs, I race up the stairs and bang on Max's door a little harder than normal. My heart is racing, and I see spots dancing in front of my eyes as I wait for his reply.

'Yeah?'

I grasp the door handle, but it's locked. 'Can I come in?'

The door opens a crack. Max is topless but wearing his pyjama bottoms. 'Mum, I'm about to go to sleep. What do you want?'

'What exactly did you say to Henry?' I ask.

'What? Nothing much.'

'Nothing much? Because it sounds like you told him rather a lot. He knows we moved from Birmingham and that you got into trouble, and we had to move. I thought I told you to keep quiet about all that.'

'Yeah, so? He asked where I got my black eye. I couldn't very well just lie to him, could I?'

'So ... I told you to be careful what you say to people around here. We need to keep a low profile. We don't know anything about Henry. He could be ... I don't know ... dangerous or something.'

'You hired him to work on our house. How dangerous can he be?'

'Yes, but ...' I take a deep breath, realising my son is making a valid point. 'His rates were very reasonable, and he didn't require payment up front.'

'So, basically, you hired the cheapest and easiest builder there was available.'

'No, I ... Well, yes, but ...'

'Okay, fine. Whatever, I'll just keep my mouth shut, shall I, and not talk to anyone ever again?'

'That's not what I'm saying ...'

'Whatever.'

I swear if he says that word one more time, I'm going to lose it.

I allow my shoulders to relax and step backwards. 'Just ...

please be careful what you tell people, okay?' I say somewhat half-heartedly. 'I'm glad you seem to get on well with Henry, but please just be careful. The last thing I want is word getting out about why we had to move. I don't want you getting into trouble here.'

'Fine. Whatever. Can I go to sleep now? I'm on the early shift.' Max goes to slam the door, but I wedge my foot between it and the door jamb.

'Do you need dropping off?'

'Megan's picking me up.'

I remove my foot. 'Of course she is,' I mutter as he slams the door in my face.

I head back downstairs and sort out some food for myself, which ends up being two slices of peanut butter on toast because I don't have the energy to make myself anything else. I sit at the kitchen table, staring at the wall while I munch away, going over and over a few of things that Henry said earlier.

He tells me that he ran into a bit of trouble and that's why you had to move.

I guess I owe the old girl.

Now, it's you who owes me.

He might have gone back on what he said, but he still said it.

10

The next morning, I get up early and head to the bathroom for a hot shower and to wash my hair, silently thanking Henry for fixing it yesterday, even though I didn't ask him to. It was a kind gesture, but his eagerness to fix things around the house seems odd considering he doesn't even know me well. My anxiety-ridden brain is telling me I should be wary, but my heart and body are enjoying the fact I have hot water and now no longer have to worry about getting it fixed. It's done.

I'm aware this is now day four of not taking my medication in the mornings. I feel dizzy and a little nauseous, and even though it's not that warm this morning, my armpits are sweaty. Perhaps that's the main reason why my head is all over the place, and I can't seem to keep mentally focused on anything or make up my mind about how I feel about Henry turning up out of the blue and working here.

Now, it's you who owes me.

Stepping under the running water, my body sighs with relief as the warm jets fall on my shoulders. The water pressure still isn't great, but I can deal with that. I wash my hair and body and give myself a pep talk, ready to start the day despite my foggy brain. I have a hundred and one things to do, but I can't really do any of them without money, so I may as well focus on the stuff that costs nothing to do, such as cleaning and tidying, putting things in some sort of order so I don't get heart palpitations every time I look at the amount of rubbish in this house that needs sorting.

I turn off the running water and squeeze the excess moisture from my long hair before wrapping a towel around my chest and stepping out of the tub. I wipe the condensation from the bathroom mirror and lean in close to get a better look at a spot on my face near my nose. I always break out in spots when I'm stressed, or when it's coming up to my period. I guess that's why my emotions have been all over the place over the past few days, or maybe it really is the medication withdrawal. That, and moving to a new house, getting a new job, and Henry turning up randomly.

This morning, I plan to sort through the main bedroom, where I slept last night, and strip the beds and chuck all the bedding in the wash, providing the washing machine in the kitchen works, something else I need to check. There are four bedrooms in this house. Max has taken the one furthest from mine. There's a lot of stuff in my bedroom that needs clearing out and sorting.

Henry is due to arrive soon. He didn't tell me what time he'd be arriving, but I assume it'll be in the morning so he can get a full day's work in. I expect he'll get straight to work on the electrics today. It will be nice to be able to use the other plug sockets in the house without the risk of blowing a fuse or starting a fire.

I may do a spot of gardening today too. Nothing fancy,

just clearing the weeds and chopping down the overgrown bushes that have taken over the front garden. I may find an area to start the vegetable garden I told Darren about. I wouldn't consider myself green-fingered at all, but it will be nice to grow my own vegetables and fruits. Again, it's something I can learn and will give me a project I can work on independently.

Once I'm dressed, I skip breakfast and just make a strong coffee instead. The house is silent. Max left for work earlier this morning. I'm slightly surprised I didn't have to kick his door down and drag him out of bed to get to work on time. It seems having a job, something to get up for in the mornings, is doing him the world of good. That, and having a pretty girl come and collect him. Next time I see her, I must try to say hello. Max hasn't mentioned anything about introducing me yet though, so I don't want to tread on his toes before he's ready.

My first job is to tackle the wardrobe in my bedroom. As soon as I open the double doors, I'm met with a waft of stale, musty air. It smells like, and I hate to use this phrase, an old person. If Harriet moved into the care home seven years ago, then these clothes have remained untouched ever since.

I run my hands across a few of the pieces, all of them old-fashioned, but quite pretty. It's a shame that none of her relatives can take them. They'll all be going to the local charity shop, although I doubt anyone will buy them, considering their out-of-date style.

One by one, I remove the dresses and items from the wardrobe, slipping them off their hangers and placing them inside a black bag. There are several sets of shoes too, which are very faded and worn. They'd be better off in the bin, so I make two piles. One for charity and one to throw away.

Once the wardrobe is empty of Harriet's old items, I clean the sides and remove all the dust at the bottom, then hang up my few pieces of clothing. I didn't bring a lot. Most of it is things I've owned for more than a decade. Never having any sort of fashion sense, I've stuck to what I feel comfortable in, leggings or jeans, T-shirts and hoodies. I have one dress, which is blue; something I haven't worn for a very long time.

I cart the black bags of Harriet's clothes downstairs and find Henry in the hallway with the understairs cupboard door open. He's wearing the same clothes as yesterday.

'Oh, hi, I didn't hear you knock,' I say, setting the bags by the front door, ready to put in the car.

'Sorry, I did knock, but there was no answer, and the door was open, so I let myself in. I hope you don't mind. I assumed you were busy somewhere,' he says, backing out of the cupboard and looking up at me. He's tinkering with the circuit board under the stairs.

'No problem. I was just sorting some bits upstairs. Can I make you a cup of tea or anything?'

'Already made myself one, thanks.'

I look down and see my favourite mug on the floor. I didn't wash it up earlier when I finished my coffee, which means he must have reused it on purpose rather than getting a clean mug from the cupboard. Am I thinking too much into this? Why that mug in particular? How does he know it's mine? I can feel my irritability brimming under the surface.

'Everything okay?' he asks.

I look up. 'Oh, yes, sorry. I've just been clearing the wardrobe from the main room. Got lots of clothes to take to charity and a few bits for the bin; then I think I'll do a spot of gardening while you're working inside. It's such a lovely day. Seems a shame to waste it.'

'Gardening, huh?'

'Yeah, I was thinking about starting a vegetable patch.'

Henry stands up straight, which causes his T-shirt to ride up slightly on his belly, revealing hairy skin. 'I'm a keen gardener myself. I'd be happy to help you.'

I wave him off. 'Oh, thank you, but I think you've got enough to be getting on with today. Maybe another time?'

'Sure,' says Henry, his face falling slightly. Is it just me, or does Henry seem to want to be around me as much as possible? Almost like a needy, clingy dog. In fact, he sort of reminds me of a dog, a big one, like a mastiff.

'Just a word of warning about the garden. There are lots of water pipes running through the area, so be careful how far down you dig.'

'Oh, um ... I was just going to clear the ground today. It's like a jungle out there.'

Henry smiles and nods, then returns to the circuit board.

I watch him for several seconds, but then I start to feel self-conscious, so I head back upstairs and finish bringing down the black bags with the items to throw away. I take the bags out to the bins. I must remember to find out when the council come and collect the recycling and rubbish.

I check the shed where I found the saw yesterday, but there's nothing else of use in there, so I approach the second small shed near the bin storage and try the door, but it's locked with a rusty padlock. I can't imagine the keys are around anywhere, so I head inside and ask Henry if I can borrow a hammer and then smash the padlock apart with it. It only takes two hits before the metal snaps and the doors are free. I pull them open after I've cleared the brambles, which are doing their best to seal the doors shut as if it's a secret, forbidden building.

It's like opening the doors to an unknown world, but when I finally get them open, I find myself disappointed by what I find. Old tools, buckets, a broken mower and other random pieces of junk. However, there is a spade hanging on the wall and a pair of shears. They are rusty, but still usable. I don't have the money to buy new ones, so these will have to do.

I grab them and get to work.

THREE HOURS LATER, I stop and assess what I've accomplished. I'm proud of how much ground I've managed to clear by myself. I've had a few nettle stings and scrapes, but I've created a lovely area to begin my vegetable garden. Unfortunately, there's the remains of an old patio blocking any further progress. It was buried under all the undergrowth, but it doesn't look like it will put up much of a fight to remove it. The slabs are disintegrating in places and are uneven. Whoever laid it didn't do a very good job. Perhaps I can dig the slabs up and use the ones that don't fall apart someplace else in the garden. I've always fancied a patio on which to sit in the sun and drink wine on a summer's evening.

I place both hands on the small of my back and lean backwards, arching and stretching my stiff joints. Glancing towards the house, a dark shape stands in the top left window. I pause, bringing a hand up to shield my eyes against the sun. Was that Henry upstairs watching me? A cold tingle ripples across the back of my neck. Almost as soon as I notice the dark shape, it moves away.

It's a warm day, and my dry tongue and sore throat remind me I haven't had anything to drink or eat since my coffee this morning, so I decide to call it a day and head back to the house to check on Henry's progress.

The house is silent when I step through the front door. 'Henry?' I call out.

A door slams upstairs.

So it was him in the upstairs window. But why was he watching me? I shake my head, telling myself to stop being so suspicious of him. These withdrawals are not helping at all. It was clearly a mistake to come off them without speaking to my doctor, but after everything that happened in Birmingham, I just needed to get away as fast as possible.

Footsteps sound, and he appears at the top of the stairs and looks down at me. 'Hey, how are you getting on?' he asks.

'Fine. Think I'm done for the day. My back is killing me. I was just coming in for some food and a drink.'

Henry jogs down the steps in front of me. 'Ah, I'd love to join you, but I was checking the plug sockets in the bedrooms, and while the electrics upstairs look good, I need to pop into town to buy a few bits for the new circuit board. I'll be back in an hour or two.'

'Okay,' I say, silently relieved that he's not staying to have a drink with me. It feels too ... friendly, somehow.

Henry walks out of the house, leaving the front door open. I wait until I hear his van tyres on the gravel before racing upstairs and into my bedroom, scanning the area. I'm not sure what I'm looking for, but nothing seems to be out of place. Everything is where I left it.

Then why do I have such an uneasy feeling in my gut?

I'm so paranoid that I'm annoyed at myself for being so stupid.

Just let the man work, Natasha!

AFTER A CHEESE SANDWICH, a cool drink and a brief sit-down, my back feels better, and I decide to carry on for another half an hour or so. I return outside to the old patio with a crowbar I found in the shed. I have two hours before I need to be at work, so I plan to get most of the slabs up in that time, but they can stay piled up where they are to be moved at another time. It's tough work. A lot harder than I imagined it would be, but with every movement I make, I feel the stress and pressure releasing, despite my dizziness and nausea from the lack of meds. Manual labour is proving to be very cathartic for me. I've not had time to exercise since having Max. I always told myself that working two jobs and bringing up a child by myself was enough of a workout to keep me fit, but as I break apart the slabs, I realise just how unfit I am when it comes to cardiovascular and muscular endurance.

I bend over and grab a large patio slab, hooking the tips of my fingers underneath it, but it's stuck, and I barely move it an inch. My hands are filthy, my fingernails caked in mud, so when I brush a stray strand of hair from my face, I smear dirt across my forehead. I pick up the crowbar, stick the end underneath the slab and attempt to make some sort of lever. I press down on the bar with one foot and do a little whoop as the slab gives way and lifts from the rock-hard ground. It cracks in half, but at least it's loose now.

Once I've dragged the slab and the broken pieces to the side, I return to grab the next one. There's a small blue piece of material sticking out of the ground. It looks like a plastic tarp. Maybe this area was used as a dumping ground years ago. I take hold of it and give it a tug. It doesn't move. I lean back as far as I can, hoping my body weight will dislodge it, but all it does is rip apart in my hands, and I fall backwards onto my bottom with a thud.

I sit and rethink my plan, annoyed that there's another thing I have to dig up now. Perhaps digging up the patio wasn't such a good idea.

I decide to remove all the slabs first and then dig over the ground, remove the tarp and any large stones so it's ready for me to start planting seeds. I'll admit, I have no idea how to start a vegetable garden, or how to prepare the ground properly, but I'm proud of my efforts. It's also best to have a clear area to start with.

Half an hour later, the slabs are all piled to the side. Most of them I was able to remove without breaking them, but several did disintegrate as I pulled them up, so the rubble has gone into the rubbish bins. I grab a rusty spade from the shed and begin to dig around the blue tarp. Every now and then I stop digging, grab hold and give it a pull, slowly but surely removing it from the ground. It's a long and sweaty process. My hands keep slipping, but I don't give up. My hair sticks to my face, which gets on my nerves very quickly.

I stomp on the spade and hear a sharp ripping sound, followed by a loud snap.

Oh shit, what have I just broken?

I chuck the spade to the side and kneel on the ground, grasping the tarp again and tugging. Another rip makes me lose balance and land on my bottom again.

A musty, rotten odour wafts up from the dry soil. Okay, maybe I should stop pulling and digging. I may just be making it worse. Henry was right when he said I need to be careful where I dig.

I crawl forwards to get a better look at the hole I've made in the earth. The smell is stronger the closer I get. That's when I see something that makes my stomach churn.

There's a small amount of hair and something that looks like ...

I retch as I realise it's the body of a decomposing animal.

I can't just leave it here. I have to remove it. The poor thing's been stuck underneath the patio for God only knows how long. I curse under my breath, regretting this whole stupid idea as I dig around the area, following the outline of the tarp.

I frown as I look down at the shape. Bloody hell, it must be a big animal. Maybe a large dog or a pig or something. I hold my breath as much as possible, but luckily most of it seems to be just bone and hair. It's hard work, and I end up puffing and panting as if I'm sprinting.

The more I dig, the more I'm convinced this is a pig, but I see a flash of purple material with flowers on it, and it stops me in my tracks.

I gasp, clamping a hand over my mouth as I retch again and lunge to the side.

It's not a pig.

I've just dug up a dead body.

A dead ... *human* ... body.

PART II

11

Every muscle in my body tightens and convulses as I retch, leaning on my thighs for support. I quickly pull my hair out of the way as bile flies out of my mouth, splashing across the weeds in front of me. I suck in huge gulps of air, trying to catch my breath, but my body is fighting against me, wanting to purge itself of everything I've eaten today. I need to calm down, get a grip, think about this, but my muddled brain fog is stopping me from thinking about anything other than the shape of the degrading bones in the soil.

The human mind is a strange thing. It can play tricks on you. I know that. Perhaps I'm wrong. Perhaps my confused mind saw something that wasn't really there. I didn't dig up and find a dead body. It's just a dead animal wrapped in a piece of clothing, then wrapped in a tarp and buried under a patio. People wrap their dead pets in clothing or blankets all the time. It's time to think about this rationally and logically ... if my cloudy head allows it.

Once I've finished retching, I wipe my mouth with the

back of my hand, smearing more dirt and spit across my face. Slowly, I turn around to look at the hole and the blue tarp and material. Holding my breath, I take three steps closer, unable to pull my eyes away from the area.

The material looks thin, possibly cotton or silk. It's very dirty, but definitely purple with small flowers dotted in the design. Doesn't look like a blanket.

Reaching out my hand, I grip the material between two fingers and gently pry it away from the ground, revealing more of what is hidden within its folds.

I gag again, clamping a hand over my mouth.

It's a decomposing human body.

There's no mistaking it. There's no fur or anything to suggest it's an animal. I can't see any blood, but I imagine it must have been down here a while. It's not fresh, that's for sure. It's mostly just bone with some random bits of God only knows what. There's also some long, black hair tangled in amongst the material and tarp.

Oh fuck. It really is a person, isn't it?

A woman, if the long, black hair is anything to go by.

A small whimper escapes my lips as I hold back a sob.

Potential images flash before my eyes.

Images of police swarming the area, digging the body up, journalists asking questions, my face on the news, Max being questioned, my new home being overrun with crime scene investigators, the house being taken away from me, the drug dealer finding out where we are, Max being killed ...

I can't stop them.

The overwhelming, and most ludicrous, thoughts overrun my mind, and I let out a muffled scream into my hands, staring up at the sky. What have I done to deserve this? Moving to this house was supposed to be good for us, a chance to start over. I was supposed to get the money, pay the drug dealer back and be free from any restraints and pressure.

Now, it's all ruined. All because I wanted to dig a Goddamn vegetable patch and spend time in nature.

'Nat?'

Fuck!

I spin around on the spot, fear gripping my insides so hard, I can barely breathe, and I almost retch again. My feet get tangled in some long grass, and I topple over but manage to right myself before I fall into the hole I've just uncovered.

Henry is walking towards me from the driveway with a frown on his face.

'Henry, stop!' I shout.

'What?'

'Stay where you are!' I hold up my hands as if I'm trying to stop traffic.

But he doesn't. He keeps walking closer to me, closer to the hole, closer to the body, a look of concern etched on his face. He must think I've truly lost the plot.

'Looks like you've been busy,' he says with a chuckle. 'Bloody hell, that's an impressive hole you've dug.'

Another sob escapes, and I clamp a hand over my mouth again. I'm crying, and the tears are running into my mouth. How can I make him leave? He can't be here. He can't see this.

Henry stops beside me and peers down at the hole. 'Looks like you've dug up a dead animal,' he says, his face deadpan.

I hold my breath, watching his body language, waiting for the inevitable moment that the truth clicks into place. He's staring at the tarp, at the purple material, the black hair and the dirt-stained bones. I can see the cogs turning in his head as his brain attempts to understand what he's seeing. It takes several long seconds to connect all the dots.

He's quiet as he flicks his eyes to look at me. 'Fucking hell,' he whispers.

He doesn't say anything else. We just stand there, completely still, staring down at the body in the ground. Side by side. I have no words. I'm due at work in less than twenty minutes, but my body refuses to move other than to tremble violently.

Henry finally clears his throat. 'Well, I guess that explains where Prudence disappeared to.'

'What?' The short question pops from my lips, and I shake my head. I haven't even spared a single thought as to whom the body could belong to, but now he's just said her name, it makes perfect sense.

Prudence left seven years ago with her boyfriend and hasn't been seen or heard from since. Is this really her? Was the whole thing about her leaving something that Harriet made up? Did Harriet kill her to stop her from leaving? I can't stop the jumble of thoughts and scenarios that pop into my head, none of which make any sense.

'Oh my God,' I say. 'I can't believe she's been here all this time. Are you sure it's her though? How can you be sure?'

Henry bends down and looks closer at the tarp and material. He picks up a stick and uses it to move the material aside, revealing a further mass of dark hair. I avert my eyes. I wish I'd thought to use a stick rather than touch it with my fingers.

'Obviously, I can't say for sure it's her,' says Henry, 'but she did have long, black hair, and I can't think who else it would be. It's also definitely a woman, considering the clothing.'

I bite my lip, turning back around as Henry stands up straight. That's all we have to go on. The fact she had long, black hair and she's a woman. I doubt it would hold up in court.

'Should we call the police? What should we do?' I ask. Of course, I know the right thing to do would be to call the police, but it's the last thing I need right now, so I'm hoping Henry has a better idea.

Henry blows out his cheeks. 'Well ... I suppose you should, yeah.'

I bite my lip again, another coping strategy I sometimes use to distract myself from my swirling anxiety. Sometimes, I bite my lip so hard I draw blood.

Henry turns to me. 'Nat ... why do I get the feeling you don't want to call the police?'

'I just ...'

'You don't want them here, do you? You don't want them poking their noses around your property.' Henry turns to face me.

I can't even look at him because he's right. From the moment I first laid eyes on the body, all I have thought about was the police poking around and asking questions I can't answer, highlighting all my irrational and mind-numbing fears. I don't even care that Henry seems to have worked all this out. Or maybe he's just exceptionally good at reading people and guessing. But can I really not report it? It's so ... wrong. This poor girl has been in the ground, lost for years. Surely, she deserves to be recognised and given a proper burial.

'I don't think I can,' I say. 'You're right, you're completely right about all of that, but ... not reporting this is a crime. I'm not sure I could live with it on my conscience as well as everything else.'

Henry sighs. 'Okay, I hear you. I do, but telling the cops is just going to cause more harm than good. I should know. I've had my fair share of run-ins with the law. What's more important to you right now? Doing the right thing or keeping Max safe?'

'I ... I don't know. I just need to think. Just let me think,' I say, turning and walking a few paces away where the smell is less powerful. However, the stench still fills my nostrils as I inhale deeply. Henry stays where he is, watching me. What he said about having run-ins with the law is probably something I should ask him about, but we all have pasts, so I can't hold that against him. I finally return to his side.

'Henry, if I decide to keep this quiet for a while, then do I have your word that you won't tell the police?'

'Nat, you have my word. I won't tell a soul.'

'You barely know me. You work for cheap. You do all these nice things for me, and now you're willing to cover up the fact there's a body buried in my garden? Why are you doing all this for me?'

Henry turns his whole body to face mine. He speaks slowly, deliberately. 'You're right, I don't know you, but I know you need my help. Look, I'll be straight with you. My old man was a cop, and he was a nasty piece of work. He thought just because he was a cop, he was above the law himself, that he could do whatever he wanted and get away with it. I don't trust cops. Never have. Never will. Whatever it is you've got yourself into back in Birmingham is clearly weighing heavy on you. The discovery of this body is unfortunate. Right now, you need to keep yourself and your son safe. And that means I have to keep my mouth shut, and this body needs to disappear again.'

'But ...' He still hasn't answered my question: why? Does he like me? Does he think that by doing this huge thing for me, I'll owe him something?

Adrenaline spikes in my chest at the thought. 'Did you know Prudence well?' I ask timidly.

'Not really. I spoke to her once or twice. She knew my wife and—' He stops and sighs, realising he's given too much away. It's the first time he's mentioned his wife. 'I mainly chatted to Harriet. She was really broken up when Prudence up and left her to fend for herself.'

'There was a note, right?'

'I believe so, but I never saw it.'

I stare down at the body and sigh. 'I guess we'd better put the slabs back on top.'

'That's not going to be possible,' says Henry. 'You've destroyed most of the slabs by digging them up. Besides, if you want the body to stay hidden, then it needs to be buried deeper. Whoever buried her here clearly didn't do a very good job. The body isn't nearly deep enough. If it had been buried deeper, and the slabs been laid properly, then you wouldn't have ever found it. By moving it to a new location, we can ensure it is buried deep enough where no one will ever discover it, even if they happen to dig up the new patio. Can I ask, why were you digging up this old patio in the first place?'

'I wanted to create space for a vegetable garden.'

'Right ...'

I look across the greenery around me, at the old pond that's full of algae and the strange-looking stone statue that's half-buried in brambles. Can I really do this? Can I really re-bury a body and pretend I never found it, all to protect myself and my son from being discovered and possibly losing the house? It's only a matter of days until I get the money, and then I can pay off the dealer. Maybe I can wait a few extra days, but what if the money doesn't come through on time? What if the news gets out about the body, then the dealer finds us before I can pay him back? What if this body means I lose the house? It's not going to be the fresh start I imagined, is it? I could lose everything.

I don't know for certain. I don't know anything. All I know is that Henry and I are the only two people in the world who know where Prudence is buried. Well, us and whoever it was who killed her, providing she was actually killed. But then she must have been because how else would she have been buried?

All this is going around and around in my head, so I flinch when Henry waves a hand in front of my face, bringing me back to reality.

'Hello, Nat ... You in there?'

'Sorry, I was ... thinking.'

'What's your decision? This is your property at the end of the day. I can go and buy brand-new paving slabs, a load of cement and rubble right now, and we can have it re-buried before Max gets back.'

My heart rate leaps. Max. Oh my God. He can't see this. He can't know about this. There's no way I could trust him to keep it quiet. He's already told Henry too much about our old lives, and who knows what he and Megan talk about.

'Yes, do it,' I say before I can chicken out.

Henry nods. 'You keep digging it up, and I'll be back with the new slabs, cement and rubble soon.' He turns to go.

'What's the cement and rubble for?'

'Laying a patio isn't just about laying slabs down on soil because soil moves over time. That's why you were able to dig up this body so easily. Slabs need concrete to sit on. Plus, I reckon pouring concrete directly on top of the body will mean it will never be found, and give a solid base if your plan is to never have it be found.'

'So what's the rubble for?'

Henry continues his lecture. 'Rubble gives the concrete and slabs a foundation on which to sit. That way, they won't move and crack over time.'

I suppose that's why he's the professional builder.

'I'll be as quick as I can.' He turns to walk away again.

'Wait!' I reach out and grab his arm. I don't mean to grab him so hard, but I'm close to losing it. The thought of staying here alone with the body is enough to make my stomach flip and my anxiety spike.

'Don't worry, Nat. You'll be enjoying your new patio and having a drink in the sun in no time.' Henry throws a wink at me, turns and leaves me standing with my mouth open. Does he seriously think I'm going to sit on a new patio with a dead body buried underneath and enjoy a glass of wine in the sun? Who does he think I am? His casualness about this whole thing makes me think he's a complete psychopath, but it's only a brief thought. The fact is, he's saved my life.

I hear Henry's van pull out of the driveway. I turn back to the body. I can't believe I'm doing this. I can't believe I've just let Henry, a complete stranger, talk me into moving a body and keeping it a secret. What am I doing? Wait ... did he convince me, or did I convince him? I can't even remember. Is this a side effect of the medication withdrawal? Memory loss and confusion?

Who's to say Henry won't turn around one day and

report that there's a body under my new patio? What if he tells people I forced him to help me cover it up and re-bury it?

I've never had to put so much faith and trust into someone I've only just met before. It's causing my stomach to ache. I bend over and dig my fingers into my side as a cramp overwhelms me. It would be fucking typical if this is period pain right now. I'm not on any birth control, since I haven't had sex in … a very long time. I doubt it's that though. It's more than likely stress related, or medication related, or a combination of both.

Darren is expecting me for my shift in less than ten minutes. Shit. I fish my phone out of my pocket and call him.

'Natasha, hi. You okay?'

'Um, actually, no. I'm so sorry that this is such late notice, but I can't make it in for two today. Something has come up with the house, and there's water leaking everywhere. Henry's here helping me fix it. I'll be as quick as I can.'

'Ah, no worries at all. Sorry to hear. Water damage is not what you need. Just give me a bell when you're on your way, yeah?'

'Will do. Thanks, Darren. Sorry again.'

I disconnect and put my phone away. Then take a deep breath, attempting to centre my scattered thoughts. I grab a shovel and get to work, imagining I'm digging up a tree root rather than a decomposing human being.

I wish it were dark. I feel so exposed out here in the garden. Luckily, there aren't any nearby neighbours, and the road is several hundred metres away, restricted by overgrown hedges and trees, but still … it's enough to make me check my surroundings whenever I hear a rustle in a bush.

· · ·

AN HOUR LATER, Henry returns. He inspects my work, nodding his approval. There's a very prominent mound on the ground that's shaped like a body. I've dug round it and down as much as I can. How the hell we're supposed to remove it, I don't know, but hopefully the tarp will keep it all together. If it's in bad condition and rips, then we're in big trouble.

'Good work,' Henry says. 'I've got the slabs, cement and several buckets of rubble in the van. Where do you want your new patio, then?'

The fact that Henry is acting so calm, like this is all part of a day's work for him, is still not sitting well with me. I look around the garden again.

'I don't think we should move her far,' I say.

'Agreed. How about over there?' Henry points to the only clear area in the garden, which is covered in long grass.

'Sure,' I say.

HENRY and I dig in the soil for two more hours. I call Darren again and explain that I need to stay and sort out the water damage before it seeps into the floor. He is very understanding and even offers to come and help, which I quickly decline. I feel bad for lying to him, but I don't have any other choice. He says to forget about coming in for my shift today and just come in as normal tomorrow. I thank him and return to digging.

Max is due home in the next hour, and we've only just finished digging the huge, deep hole we'll be transferring the body to. We still have to move it. It's the job I've been dreading. I'm already filthy, exhausted and starving. I can't stop until it's done though. Only adrenaline and sheer determination are keeping me going right now.

Henry keeps ploughing on. I can tell he's done manual labour his whole life. He barely stops to catch his breath, only a light sheen of sweat on his forehead, whereas I'm dripping in sweat and must stop and lean on my shovel every five minutes, gasping like a fish out of water. My muscles are screaming at me, and I want nothing more than to crawl into my bed, pull the curtains across the window and sleep for a week and pretend none of this happened.

This all feels like a nightmare come to life.

Finally, the hole is ready.

Henry inspects the tarp, and we wrap the body in another one I find in the shed as we transport it the fifteen feet to its new place of rest. Henry does most of the work. There's no way I would have been able to do this without him. A part of me is eternally grateful for his help and silence, yet another part of me is stressed about the fact he knows such a scandalous secret about me. He's right. I really do owe him now. But, then again, he's just as involved as I am, and it's his own choice. He could have easily walked away or called the police himself, but he didn't. He chose to stay and help me. I still can't remember whose idea the whole thing was.

With the body in its new home, Henry begins mixing buckets of cement. I watch in awe as he mixes just the right amount of cement and water, pours it in and then repeats the process, never stopping, never faltering. Once the body is covered in concrete, he starts filling the hole up with dirt. While he does that, I flatten out the original burial place so it looks like just a flat piece of earth with a few roots sticking out.

In a perfect world, Henry says he would have allowed the cement to go hard before putting the soil on top, but we don't have the luxury of waiting for it to go off.

I hear tyres crunching over gravel.

Fuck.

What's the time?

I check my watch. It's Max. He's home. Henry and I aren't finished yet. What if Max comes looking for me in the garden?

'Stay here,' I tell Henry as I start running towards the house, heart pumping wildly.

I arrive just in time to see Max and Megan getting out of a black car. Max is smiling, and Megan is laughing, but when they catch sight of me, they both freeze and stare. I must look a right state, covered in mud and sweat and God knows what else. This is not the first impression I wanted to make with Megan.

'Hi!' I say, attempting to sound bright and happy.

Max frowns at me. 'Mum ... why are you covered in dirt?' He screws up his nose.

'I've been digging the new vegetable garden,' I reply.

Max continues to frown. 'Okay ... um ... Mum, this is Megan. Megan, this is my mum.' Max gestures between us. I've probably severely embarrassed him. He's blushing.

Megan smiles, clearly far too polite to mention how filthy I am. 'Lovely to meet you, Mrs Moore.' She reaches out to shake my hand, but I laugh as I back away.

'I'm sorry, I don't want to get you all dirty.'

Megan pulls her hand back, turning pink. Max looks like he wants to strangle me.

'It's lovely to meet you,' I say. 'I'm sorry I'm such a state. I'll be done soon. Can you stay for dinner?'

Max steps forward. 'Actually, Mum, Megan needs to get back for a late shift.'

I nod. 'No problem. How about dinner tomorrow night instead? I promise I'll be clean and presentable then,' I say with a nervous giggle.

Megan beams. 'That would be lovely, thank you, Mrs Moore.'

'Please, call me Natasha. Do you have any dietary requirements?'

'No, I'm all good.'

'Great. Does seven o'clock sound good to you?'

'See you then,' she says. Max turns to her and whispers something in her ear, and she giggles. My son, the charmer.

Max and I watch her get into her car and drive down the lane.

'Why did you invite her for dinner?'

'I thought it was a nice thing to do.'

Max rolls his eyes. 'She's too polite to say no.'

'I'm sorry, I didn't think.'

'Whatever. Seriously though ... you're filthy, Mum.'

'I'm aware.'

Max gives me one last disgusted look, turns and goes into the house.

I let out a long sigh and return to Henry, who is now beginning to lay out the new area for the patio. The body is nowhere to be seen, and the ground is flat. He's done a good job.

'Do you want a cup of tea or anything?' I ask him because I don't know what else to say.

'Water will be grand, thanks. I can take it from here. Just the patio to lay now. I don't need help with that. I can lay one in my sleep.'

'You sure?'

'Yep.'

'Okay, I'll just go and grab you a drink.'

I walk back to the house, pausing to look over my shoulder at him while he leans down and lays the first slab, his muscles flexing with the effort. It's getting late in the day now, and I know he wants to finish the patio before it starts getting dark. I would suggest laying it tomorrow, but I need this day over and done with, along with the hideous events.

I can't quite believe what's happened over the past few hours. Everything was going so well, and now it feels as if there's another weight crushing down upon me. One I don't think I'll ever be able to ease. I suppose I'm going to have to get used to it.

12

I spend a long time standing in a scalding hot shower, attempting to scrub and wash away the last few hours, the smell of dirt and rot, and my own guilt and bad choices. Steam soon engulfs the whole bathroom, clearing my sinuses and enabling me to breathe a lot easier, but it does nothing to ease the weight on my shoulders and the tension in my neck.

Was it a bad choice though? As choices go, it wasn't the best one I've ever made, but I did it to protect Max and to ensure we can be happy here. If I'd told the police about the body, our whole lives would have been thrown into turmoil, and it's the last thing we need right now.

As I lather the fruity shampoo into my hair for a second time, in case the lingering stench still remains, this question keeps nagging me. I can't seem to let it go. My indecisiveness has always been one of my biggest downfalls, but it's not too late, is it? I could inform the police of the discovery of the body right now, but how would I explain the fact Henry and I have moved it to a new location and encased it in concrete and dirt and laid a patio over the top? Any possible evidence left behind has been contaminated by me and Henry. There's no salvaging it. We've covered up a murder. That's a crime in itself.

No, stop it, Natasha.

I've made my decision. It's time to stick with it and see it through. I didn't know Prudence. No one is looking for her. According to everyone in the village, she ran off with her boyfriend.

But ... what if the body doesn't even belong to her? No, it does. I'm sure.

I scream through the running water at my indecisive thoughts.

Make up your fucking mind!

It's a dark secret that Henry and I share. Forever. Henry and I are now bound together by this wretched decision. Without planning it, he's the only person who can keep Max and me safe. It's not just me who has to live with this choice.

An uneasiness settles over me as I switch the shower off and reach for a clean towel, fumbling through the steam.

Did Henry already know the body was there? Did Harriet kill Prudence and then ask Henry for help in disposing of the body? It's a sobering thought and not out of the realms of possibility. Granted, it would mean that Henry is a decent liar and actor, having looked positively white in the face when he realised what I'd dug up. Perhaps Harriet killed Prudence, and then someone else buried her. There's no way she would have been able to dig a grave by herself, not in her frail state, although it would explain why the body wasn't buried very deep and the slabs laid crudely on top. Henry said himself that the patio hadn't been laid professionally. It had been laid by an amateur, someone who didn't know what they were doing.

I open the door to the bathroom, ready to go into my room and put clean clothes on. I shriek loudly when I see Henry standing directly outside the door. I clutch the towel tighter against my chest, double-checking that nothing private is on show.

'What the hell? You scared me!'

Henry doesn't respond straight away like I would expect him to. Surely, he should be mortified and apologise, but instead a small smile creeps across his dirt-smeared face.

'It's done,' he says. 'Obviously I didn't get the electrics sorted today like I originally planned, so I'll be back tomorrow at nine.'

I nod, still breathing heavily after my shock. 'Okay, see you tomorrow.'

Henry turns to leave.

'And thanks ... for your help and discretion today,' I add.

Henry stops and glances over his shoulder at me. 'Any time.'

AFTER DINNER, Max continues to sort out his room while I head to one of the spare rooms, the one next door to mine. Max has done a good job with his own room so far, and I tell him so as I pop my head round the doorframe. I say I'm proud of him for getting a job and for helping me. He just shrugs his shoulders. He must be missing having a phone. I intend to buy him one when the money comes through.

The spare room, I immediately notice, is full of boxes, clothes and general junk. There may be some items in here that I can sell. I doubt I'll get a lot for them, but anything is better than nothing. I could do with a large skip out the front of the house considering how much rubbish is being removed. But skips cost money, so I'll just have to take several dozen trips to the dump and recycling centre over the coming months, as long as my car holds out.

I begin by opening the nearest cardboard box, which isn't labelled, but has enough tape sealing it closed to ensure it's almost waterproof. Inside, I find several trinkets and breakable items such as glass vases, wrapped in bubble wrap. I free one and hold it upside down to check who made it. Wedgwood. Bloody hell, I don't know much about antiques and fine vases, but even I know that Wedgwood is an expensive and well-known brand. This can go in the sell pile. It's not to my taste at all, and even it was, I'd still sell it. I need all the money I can get for the foreseeable future.

I check through the rest of the box, but there are no more Wedgwood items, but a few pretty porcelain figurines and china teacups, all of which can eventually be sold. Some of them have cracks, and others are missing hands or feet, but most are in good condition. Returning the expensive vase to the box, I shift it to the side and open the next one.

This one is filled with piles of paperwork in no sort of order. I pick up the first page and scan my eyes across it. It's an old car insurance policy under the name of Prudence Greene. My heart does a little flip-flop in my chest as I see her name almost jumping off the page. Seeing her name in black and white on the page makes her seem like she's alive.

How did this woman, who cared for Harriet into her old age, end up buried in the garden under a rugged patio?

The box of paperwork doesn't reveal much else. There's no sense in keeping it now, so I put it in a separate pile for recycling.

A part of me almost feels relief that Prudence is out of the picture. If she weren't, then she'd have inherited the house, and I'd still be in Birmingham, trying to keep my son safe from a drug dealer.

Prudence's disappearance and subsequent death has done me a huge favour, but searching through her belongings makes it all very real. She was a person, a real, live person, and her life has been reduced to these few boxes and items. She's been forgotten. No one misses her. No one is looking for her, not anymore. Never to be found. What have I done?

'Mum?'

'In here,' I call out as I wipe away a small tear.

Max pops his head around the door. 'I've found something interesting in my room.'

'Oh?'

Max comes all the way into the room, holding a small, metal box. He hands it to me, and I take it, wondering what on earth he's found.

I lift the lid and gasp.

Inside is a roll of cash tied up with an elastic band. Nothing else.

'Where did you find this?'

'Underneath the bed under a loose floorboard. It wasn't locked or anything.'

'What were you doing looking under the floorboards?'

'I pulled the carpet up because it was loose and damp. Henry said it all needs to come up eventually. The board came away at the same time.'

'Wow, I wonder how long it's been under there,' I say, picking up the roll. The notes are mostly twenties, a few tens but no fives. There must be a few hundred pounds here, maybe even a thousand or slightly more. 'Have you found anything else in there?'

'Not really. Just clothes and stuff belonging to a woman. I've chucked most of it.'

I stare down at the money. I've never held anything near this much cash before. I always think the new notes look like fake money. Most of these notes are all the new plastic variety, which means they can't have been stored under the bed for very long, but some of the twenty-pound notes are older, which means they can't be used as currency anymore. Perhaps I can take them to a bank and exchange them.

'Well, I suppose Prudence won't be needing this money anymore,' I say with a long sigh. 'It will certainly help tide us over for a while until we get our first pay cheques and the money from Harriet arrives.' I unravel the roll, count out one hundred pounds in usable notes and hand them to Max.

'What's that for?'

'It's for you, Max. To spend on a new phone. You won't be able to get the new iPhone you wanted, but get yourself something second-hand. There's enough left over for some groceries and things for the next few weeks. I'll have to take the older notes to a bank to exchange them. Henry is still happy to work for no up-front fee. I want you to buy something for yourself. God knows, I've never been able to give you any money for yourself before.'

Max looks down at the ground. 'Um, thanks,' he says.

I smile as Max backs out of the room, a little red in the face. I take a deep breath as I look at the money. This house keeps on surprising me. It's not enough to pay the dealer back, but it'll help with fixing the house and buying food.

· · ·

THE NEXT DAY, Henry arrives early and continues fixing the electrics, and Max and I go to work. I finish at five today, so afterwards I head to the shop and use some of the cash to buy food for dinner for when Megan comes over. I also buy a couple of bottles of wine as a treat. I'm happy to find that Henry has fixed the electrics in the kitchen, so now the oven works.

I decide to make a lasagne. It's one of the only meals I know how to cook from scratch, that and the usual pasta bake, pesto pasta, chili con carne and spaghetti. I hum a tune while I chop the onions and sip from a glass of wine, my bare feet cool against the floor tiles.

Henry is still working somewhere in the house, but I'm not sure where. I can't hear any banging or the sound of electronic tools. Max is upstairs taking a shower. I set the kitchen table for three people. I've never hosted a meal before, let alone officially met one of Max's girlfriends. My stomach is filled with nervous butterflies.

AT SEVEN O'CLOCK, almost exactly, a black car pulls up outside. I watch from the kitchen window as Megan gets out. She's carrying a bouquet of beautiful flowers. Max's thundering footsteps race down the stairs, and he flings open the front door. I watch them kiss and hug. He certainly works fast.

I turn around with a smile as they enter the kitchen. Megan is wearing a lovely, floaty white top and a pair of tight-fitting jeans. Her blonde hair is flowing loose over her shoulders, and she's only wearing a slight hint of make-up. She's beautiful.

'Hi, Megan. Welcome!'

'Hi, Mrs ... um, Natasha. Thanks for inviting me. Here ... these are for you.' She steps forwards and hands me the bouquet of flowers.

I take them with a smile. 'They're beautiful. Thank you so much.'

'The food smells amazing,' she says.

'I have to admit I haven't cooked from scratch for a long time.'

'Oh, you shouldn't have, not for me.'

'No! Not at all. It feels great to cook properly again. I hope you like lasagne.'

'Yes, thank you.'

'Would you like a drink? A glass of wine perhaps, or a soft drink?' I am aware they are both underage. Max is anyway, I'm not sure on Megan's exact age, but she looks like a sensible young lady. Plus, it's not as if it's the first time Max has drunk alcohol. I've heard him stagger in at all hours of the night back in Birmingham and cleaned vomit off his clothes.

Megan and Max swap glances. 'Wine's good,' says Max.

'Dinner is almost ready.' I turn and pour each of them a small glass of wine as they take their seats at the kitchen table. I found the glasses at the back of one of the kitchen cabinets, and after a wash, they came up sparkling. I can tell Max is a little nervous. I hope I don't let him down or embarrass him.

'Max tells me you inherited this house,' says Megan.

I hand them both a glass each, flicking Max a look, hoping he has kept to his word and not told her too much detail. 'Yes, it was a bit of a surprise to find out I had an aunt I never met.'

Megan takes a sip of wine. 'Mrs Greene was a nice lady,' she says.

'Did you know her well?'

'Not really. I saw the lady who looked after her more than anything, but I didn't know her well either. She was around your age, I think. She used to come into the shop every week at the same time of day, like clockwork.'

I fight the urge to bombard Megan with questions about Prudence. I want to know everything, but only to satisfy my curiosity. The healthy thing to do would be to put her out of my mind and pretend she doesn't exist, rather than fixate on someone who literally doesn't exist anymore.

We continue to talk back and forth as I dish up dinner. Then we all sit down around the table, and I feel a little buzz of happiness as I look at my son sitting next to a pretty girl and smiling. This is all I've ever wanted for him, to be happy. It feels as if I'm living a completely different life, like it's a dream.

Megan is delightful, and she seems to really like Max, but she's careful not to overstep the mark with too much physical touch. She tells me that she has a younger sister who is twelve and a younger brother who is nine. She, herself, was eighteen three weeks ago, so she's several months older than Max, which sets my mind at ease about her drinking alcohol in my house. The last thing I want is her parents coming after me for allowing their daughter to drink while underage. I don't know how strict they are about these things.

Apparently, her father bought her a car for her birthday. He's a mechanic and bought an old car and did it up for her. A pang of guilt hits me in the chest as I look at Max, who stays quiet. Maybe I should try to get him some driving lessons soon. It will give him some independence, but there's no way I can afford to buy him his own car yet, so he'll have to share mine, for however long it lasts.

'Hmm, something smells good in here!' Henry walks through the door, disrupting our conversation. He's covered in dust, sweat and grime.

Shit. I thought he'd left ages ago. Where has he been all this time? I completely forgot about him.

'Hi, Henry,' I say, rising to my feet. 'I thought you'd gone home already.'

'I was doing some wiring upstairs.'

I frown, confused, because I didn't hear any sound of him moving around upstairs.

Henry hovers awkwardly by the door. Oh God ... he wants to join us for dinner, doesn't he? Should I invite him to sit down? Or have I missed the mark completely?

'Um ... Henry, if you'd like to stay for dinner, there's enough lasagne for everyone.'

It seems I read the situation correctly because Henry beams and drags a chair out and sits down without a moment of hesitation. Then he quickly stands back up again. 'Ooh, best wash up, huh? Wouldn't want your mum having a go at me.' He winks at Max, who looks mortified about the whole situation.

Henry smiles as he passes me on his way to the kitchen sink and begins to wash his hands. 'Haven't had a home-cooked meal in a long time,' he says.

'I'm not a great cook, I'm afraid,' I say.

'Ah, Nat, don't sell yourself short. I'm sure it'll be great.' Henry dries his hands on a tea towel, then sits at the table.

During this time, I've noticed Megan is a little red in the face and is looking down at her hands, which are resting in her lap. I'm at a loss for words now that Henry has arrived. Only yesterday, he and I were burying a body in my garden, and now we're having dinner together along with my son and his new girlfriend.

'Let me grab you a plate,' I say, getting to my feet. 'Did you get everything done on the house you wanted to do today, Henry?'

'Yep. Electrics are all safe, and the circuit board is brand spanking new. Shouldn't have any problems now.'

'Great. Thank you. Well, when you come back tomorrow, we can speak then about what needs to be done next,' I say.

'Sounds good to me.'

I hand him a plate of food, and he takes it. 'Cheers, Nat.'

I sit back down and take a small bite of my own food, but I've lost my appetite. Perhaps Henry is lonely. His wife left him, so I assume he has no one to go home to. I don't even know where he lives. Why else would he accept an invitation to dinner?

'So, Max. How's the eye?' asks Henry, chewing loudly.

'Huh?' responds Max.

'The eye.' Henry points to his own. 'Still looks sore.'

'It's fine,' he says. 'It's the ribs that hurt more than anything.' Max shifts in his seat.

I shoot him a look.

'Broken ribs too, huh?' He looks up at me. 'Ouch.'

I feel my cheeks heat up. Max and I swap glances. Luckily, he's remembering the warnings I've given him about revealing too much information. That, or he just doesn't want to talk to Henry, which I don't blame him for. I don't want to talk to him either.

I stay silent while I watch Henry tuck into the dinner I've

made with a fork, stuffing it into his mouth and chewing loudly.

'You came from Birmingham, right?' Henry continues.

Oh God, he's still on that.

'Can be a rough area. There was a stabbing the other week on the news,' says Henry, now reaching forwards and grabbing the wine bottle from the centre of the table. 'Could you grab me a glass, Nat? I'll just have a small one. I'm driving.'

I'm properly speechless. Should I have offered him some too? Am I the one being rude here? I get up and grab a glass, feeling a little woozy after a glass myself. I'm really suffering with the side effects of coming off sertraline so quickly, and my stomach now feels like it's churning.

Then Megan speaks for the first time since Henry walked into the room.

'I thought you said you came from Manchester?' she asks, turning to Max.

'Oh, he probably meant that we originally came from Manchester. We only moved to Birmingham less than a year ago.' I swallow the lump in my throat. Shit. Shit. Shit. I'm so confused, I forgot whom I told what to.

Megan nods, but frowns.

Henry merely raises an eyebrow as he pours, slurps his wine and then continues eating.

I decide to take the lead and change the topic of conversation. 'So, Megan, how long have you worked at the Co-op?'

'Oh, about a year. Dad wanted me to get a job alongside my schoolwork for a while. I'm working there to save money for when I go to university next September.'

'Where are you thinking of going?'

'I'm hoping to go to Bath. I'm obsessed with the architecture there. I want to be an architect.'

'Wow, that's impressive,' I say. I try not to look at Max, who appears to be shrinking back in his seat. Without meaning to, I've brought attention to the fact that Megan has more prospects than my son. Maybe it's not clear to her or Henry, but Max clearly understands. He glares at me. The subject of his schooling is still a sore subject for both of us.

Then Megan turns to Max and asks, unaware that she's just rubbing salt into an open wound, 'Have you thought about what universities you want to attend yet, Max?'

'Um ... no. I've sort of dropped out of school for a bit.'

'Oh.'

I grind my teeth together, wishing the floor would open and swallow me whole.

'Well, the school I go to is really great. I'm sure they'd help you get back on track.'

Max grunts and shrugs. He's embarrassed, and I feel so bad for him. He scoops up the last of his food on his fork and stands up.

'Um, thanks for dinner, Mum.'

Megan stands, following his lead. She hasn't quite finished her plate yet. 'Um, thank you for dinner, Mrs ... Natasha.'

'You're welcome. I hope to see you again soon.'

Megan smiles, throws a quick look at Henry, who has been watching the whole debacle with an amused grin on his face, and then follows Max out the door. She leaves Henry and me in silence.

'Well, that was odd,' says Henry.

'Hmm,' I say, agreeing with him. I don't want to tell him

that it only started getting odd and awkward when he arrived at the table.

'Gives us a chance to spend some time together,' he continues.

'Um ... Henry ...' He looks up, and it makes my stomach churn again. Spend some time together? What does that mean?

'Yeah, Nat?'

How do I tell him that I'm not interested in him? Should I be? If I turn him down, will he take offence and tell people about the body in the garden? How did I even get myself into this mess?

'I, um ... I'm not exactly looking for any sort of relationship right now. You're a nice guy, and I appreciate everything you've done for me, but ...'

Henry shakes his head. 'Oh, no, I didn't mean ... Well, I did, but ... you don't have to worry about that right now. I'm happy just to be invited to dinner. Feels like I'm part of the family.'

'Right, but—'

Henry stands. 'I'd best be off anyway. Thanks for dinner. It was top-notch.' He leaves before I have a chance to get a single word out.

I get to my feet and watch as his van pulls out of the driveway; then I lean against the counter, wishing I could take back the last ten minutes. I grab the bottle of wine and top up my glass. No one else is going to drink it. I take a big swig, ignoring my dizzy head.

I continue to seethe about the whole evening and Henry interrupting my nicely planned meal, but I can't lay the blame all on him. I did bring up the whole university thing, without taking into consideration how it would make Max feel. Plus, I unintentionally made Henry feel as if this were some sort of date.

I take a large gulp of wine, holding it in my mouth for a few seconds before swallowing. I decide to try to forget about the weirdness with Henry and apologise to Max when he comes home, so I head into the lounge and settle on the old sofa with my wine.

MAX RETURNS home at almost midnight, by which time I've polished off the bottle of wine and am halfway through the second one when he walks in, shutting the front door behind him. I'm still on the sofa, but now I'm reading a book, but I haven't been able to absorb any of the words on the page for over an hour. I'm exhausted, but I can't go to bed knowing Max is mad at me.

'Thanks a lot, Mum,' he says as soon as he sees me, his eyes blazing. 'Megan and I had a massive argument. She kept asking why I dropped out of school. Now, she thinks I'm thick.'

'She doesn't think that, Max. You're not thick. You just … had complications during this past year at school.' I want to go further and say he should have focused more on his schoolwork like I asked him to, but I hold my tongue. It was my fault for not supporting him more. 'You can always study hard over the summer and catch up, ready for your final year in September. There's still time to look at universities.'

Max's jaw is clenched. 'Yeah, right. She's going to university to become an architect. How am I supposed to compete with that?'

'Why do you need to compete with her?'

Max looks down at the floor. 'You embarrassed me. I feel stupid now.'

I stand up and slowly walk towards him. 'I'm sorry. I didn't mean to. I merely asked her about universities. I didn't think.'

'Whatever.' Max turns to leave. 'Oh, and you inviting Henry to dinner like that was just plain weird.'

'Yeah, I'm sorry about that too, but he looked as if he wanted to join us, and I felt bad.'

'He clearly fancies you, Mum.'

The idea makes me cringe. 'I think he's just lonely,' I say by way of an explanation.

'Fine, but I don't want him creeping into this family. He seems nice enough, but he's a weirdo.'

'Right.' I can't say I don't disagree with him.

Max goes upstairs to bed, but I stay downstairs. I can barely keep my eyes open, but my brain won't switch off. It keeps replaying the events of yesterday in the garden and what Henry and I did. I need to confront Henry and make sure we're on the same page. Plus, I need to explain that there needs to be boundaries between us, and make my intentions and feelings perfectly clear. I've told him once already, but clearly the message hasn't sunk in, or he just refuses to accept it. The thing is, if I push him too hard, or upset him, then what's to stop him revealing my secret?

13

Henry is due any minute, and I'm still nursing a hangover at the kitchen table. I have work in less than an hour, which I'm dreading. I've never been a big drinker, yet I ended up finishing the second bottle too, mainly to try to knock myself out so I could sleep, but what little sleep I did eventually get wasn't decent. It was plagued by vivid dreams, blood and the smell of rotting bodies. I think the medication withdrawal is finally beginning to subside, but it's hard to tell whether it's the cause of my foggy head lately. We've been here six days now. It feels like a lifetime.

A knock sounds. I look up and see Henry waving at me through the kitchen window. I wave back, then begrudgingly stand up and let him in. He saunters through the door with a grin on his face, looking as fresh as a daisy. It rubs me up the wrong way, but it's not his fault I'm feeling so crap.

'Morning, Nat!'

'Er ... morning, Henry.'

'Mind if I put the kettle on? I skipped my morning coffee

so I could get here early.' He is carrying a bag of tools and plonks them down on the kitchen floor before heading straight for the kettle and flicking it on without waiting for my answer. I stare at him in utter amazement. He's treating my house like it's his own, which is ... weird.

'So, what's the plan for today, then?' he asks.

I sigh as I sit back down at the table and set my empty coffee mug in front of me. 'Henry, we need to talk.'

'Uh-oh, are you breaking up with me?'

'Listen, I need to know that we're on the same page about things.'

'What things?'

I gulp, fighting back nausea and dizziness. 'Well ... what happened in the garden, for a start, but also, I don't want you questioning my son on topics that clearly upset him, like his black eye. I've worked hard to put our past behind us. While I'm indebted to you for a lot of things, I'd like to keep our relationship on a professional level. I want to make it perfectly clear ... I'm not interested in you in that way.'

Henry folds his arms. He stares at me for an uncomfortably long time. So long, in fact, that I clear my throat and add, 'Do you understand?' Shit. I may have been too blunt. I've never been good at confrontation. I usually avoid it like the plague.

'Yeah, I understand, but I'm afraid *I'm* not comfortable with keeping *your* secret.' His voice has changed. It's sterner than before. Harder.

'What secret? You mean the ... what we found in the garden?'

'Not exactly.'

'Then what secret do you mean?'

'Well,' he says with a casual shrug of the shoulders,

nowhere as nervous and agitated as I am, 'something tells me that Max isn't quite the nice boy he appears to be. Maybe he had something to do with that stabbing in Birmingham the other night.'

'Wait ... *What*?'

'And perhaps I've been looking at all this the wrong way. What if you're the one who killed Prudence and buried her in the garden?'

A snort of laughter escapes before I can stop it. 'I'm sorry ... What did you say? You think *I* killed Prudence? I didn't even know she existed until six days ago. What the hell makes you think that?'

'Well, think about it. It makes sense. Maybe you knew about Harriet and Prudence all along. You wouldn't have got anything if Prudence was around, so you killed Prudence and faked her running away with some bloke who doesn't exist. Then all you had to do was ensure Harriet put you in the will and wait for her to die, and lo and behold, you inherit her house, everything in it and whatever money she had left.'

All words and rational thought leave my mind. I can't even form a coherent sentence or an aggressive retort against him because his suggestion is so ludicrous, so far-fetched and ridiculous that I'm flabbergasted.

Henry just stares at me, unblinking. Is he being completely serious about this accusation, or is he merely making it clear that he could ruin me by making these claims to the police if he wanted to? It's almost as if now he knows I'm not interested in him, he's turned on me. Did he think we were going to be some happy family? I've known him less than four days!

'Are you threatening me, Henry?' I finally spit out. My voice is shaking with both rage and fear.

'No, I wouldn't dream of doing such a thing. I'm just providing all the possibilities.' His body language is telling me the opposite.

We lock eyes, neither of us willing to back down, but I have to. I have more to lose than he does if this gets out. I owe this man more than money for the work he's doing on my house. He holds my life, my son's life, in his hands. If I piss him off or push him away, he could tell the police anything he likes. Hell, even the ridiculous story he's just concocted of me killing Prudence for the house would make sense in a roundabout, strange way.

There's no evidence, of course, but the fact we've now moved the body and re-buried it will be enough to prove to the police that I have something to hide. Fuck. I should have just reported the bloody body when I found it. Why did I let Henry convince me to hide it? Or did I convince him? Was this his plan all along? To hold this against me, to manipulate me into doing whatever he says.

'Henry, what is it you want from me?' I ask.

'I just want us to be closer, get to know each other and see what happens.'

'I ... I don't ...' I knew it.

Henry sighs, his angry demeanour shifting slightly. 'Look, Nat, I thought we had some sort of connection. You're lonely. I'm lonely. Max could do with a father figure around the house, don't you think? I'm happy to keep on working here and keep my mouth shut if you just play along for a bit.'

'What the fuck?' I spit. 'You're blackmailing me?'

'If that's what you want to call it, but I'm not calling it

that. Of course, all this nastiness could have been avoided had you just been nicer to me.'

'I have been nice to you, Henry. In fact, I've been more than nice. But you can't just expect me to pretend we're a happy family. I'm going to the police.'

'I wouldn't do that if I were you, Nat. I can make things very difficult for you.'

I'm about to open my mouth and argue when my phone rings on the table. Henry glances down at it. 'Who the fuck is Adrian?' he snarls.

I scoop up my phone. 'My solicitor.' I use this as the perfect excuse to back out of the confrontation with Henry. I turn my back on him and answer the phone. 'Hi, Adrian.'

'Hi, Natasha. Just wanted to tell you the good news. The money will be in your account by the end of the day.'

The relief is almost instantaneous. I close my eyes and take a deep breath. 'Thanks for letting me know. That's a massive weight off my chest.'

'Everything okay, Natasha?'

'Yes. Yes, everything's fine. Thanks, Adrian.' I hang up just as he starts talking again, and then I feel bad that I cut him off mid-sentence. I turn around and find Henry has taken several steps closer to me. I shriek, leaping back.

'Something you want to tell me, Nat?'

'What? No. Adrian's just my solicitor, and I … I don't have to explain myself to you.'

Henry glares at me. 'I'd best be getting on with the new bathroom, then. It's arriving later today.'

Shit. I forgot about that. If I don't agree to play along, then Henry will walk out and leave me with unfinished building work. And worse, he'll tell the police about the body and make things ten times worse for me.

I need a plan, but in order to make one, I need space and time to think things through.

'Listen, Henry, I really don't have the mental capacity to deal with this right now. I'm not saying I'll do it, but I'm happy to put our differences aside and give you another chance, but ... there's nothing physical between us, got it?'

Henry grins. 'Whatever you say, Nat.' He steps forward, inching his way closer to me, and I have to fight the urge to flinch away as he leans in and plants a kiss on my cheek.

FORTY-FIVE MINUTES LATER, I leave for work. Henry is already upstairs, ripping the bathroom apart, making short work of carrying everything downstairs and dumping it in a big pile in the driveway. I need to start removing the rubbish soon so the place doesn't turn into a tip. It looks like we'll be going without showers for a few days, depending on how quickly he can replace the bathroom suite. Luckily, we have a downstairs toilet just off the main hallway we can use in the meantime.

Darren waves at me as soon as I enter the pub. 'Hey, Natasha! How's the house? Was there much water damage in the end? Sorry I missed you yesterday to ask you about it, but I was taking a much-needed day off.'

It takes me three long seconds before I understand what he's asking me and remember the lie I spun him the other day. 'Oh, yeah, it's not great, but Henry's back at the house now, pulling the bathroom apart. Most of it needed replacing anyway.' Not too far from the truth.

'That's good. What caused the leak?'

'Just an old house, I guess. It was probably going to happen eventually.'

'Good job you had Henry there to lend a hand.'

'Hmm, yeah ... good job. Well, it's all under control now. Thanks again for your understanding.'

'No worries at all.'

I smile weakly, guilt niggling my insides, making me squirm. All I wanted when I moved here was a fresh start for Max and me, free from lies and stress, but all that's happened is more of the same. Now, instead of Max being in trouble and keeping secrets from me, I'm keeping secrets from him and doing illegal things.

During my break, I check my bank account and almost squeal with delight when I see just under ten grand in there. Now I have the money to pay off the dealer, I can get that whole thing sorted out. Luckily, I saved the dealer's number to my phone before throwing Max's phone away, so I sit in my car, take a deep, cleansing breath and call him. Time to get this particular weight off my back.

'Who the fuck's this?'

'This is Max's mother ...'

'You fucking bitch. It takes balls to run and hide from me.'

'I'm just calling to let you know that I have your money.'

'Do you now? Cash, I take it?'

'No, I can't take that much cash out. I'll have to transfer it.'

'No deal.'

'You never specified in what format you wanted the money, so it's either I transfer you the money now, or I disappear again, and you'll never get anything.' I'm shocked at my own bravery, but I still hold my breath while I await his response.

Then my phone pings. I look at it and see a text message has arrived with bank account details.

'Transferring now,' I say. 'I need your word that we're done. You leave Max and me alone.'

'You're not even worth the hassle,' he snarls at me before hanging up.

Once I've set up the transfer, he texts me to say he's got the money. I then block his number and delete it.

A calmness settles over me, but my shoulders are still tense, and the anxiety in my guts continues to swirl. It's not over. The threat from the dealer is over, but now I have a new threat.

A worse threat.

Henry.

14

I tell Max as soon as I get home about paying off the drug dealer. For the first time since we've arrived here, he smiles, and I see his hard, aggressive exterior melt away, revealing a normal teenage boy beneath. He says thank you. I want more than anything to wrap my arms around him, hold him close, but Max has never been that sort of kid, not since he was much younger.

Max has no idea about the issues I'm now facing with Henry and my fragile sanity that's clinging on by a thread. I don't want to burden him with it, especially now he's free from the dealer's threat. I decide to play along with Henry's plan for now. He may think he's using me, but I'm using him for cheap labour. If acting like a happy family keeps him happy and working and silent, then that's what I'll do until I can find some way out of it.

No more Miss Nice Natasha.

I throw myself into work at the bar and renovating the lounge over the next couple of days while Henry works on the rest of the house, including installing the swish new bathroom. I say it's swish. It's not. It's the cheapest one I could find, but it's a hell of a lot better than the bathroom suite that was there before, which was covered in black mould and mostly cracked. So I have a beautiful new black and white bathroom, which looks out of place against the rest of the house due to its shininess, but we're making slow progress.

Max and Megan appear to have made up. She drops him off from work and picks him up when she can before and after school. I'm still not sure of their relationship status, but it's not my business to ask. She even pops round some evenings to help with the painting and decorating, which forces Max to join in too.

Now I have some money coming in from my job at the pub and the few thousand pounds from Harriet's account, I can afford to pay Henry for his labour and the building materials he's ordered. He's a very professional builder. I don't have a lot of experience with building work, but even I can tell his standards are high. As far as his skills as a builder are concerned, I have no complaints.

Money is still tight, but at least I'm able to make a dent in paying off my overdrafts and bills. Having no mortgage payments or rent on this house is a lifesaver too. I'm even managing to quietly save money to buy Max a set of ten driving lessons for when he's ready.

When Henry is here, I'm as polite as possible to him. I'm not exactly sure how far he wants me to go with the whole happy-family charade, but he seems content with spending time with me and Max. He has dinner with us too, since he often works late into the evenings.

'Mum, why do you keep inviting Henry for dinner?' Max

asks me one evening as I'm dishing up. Henry's upstairs finishing off some sanding.

'He's doing a lot of work for us.'

'Yeah, that's his job, isn't it?'

I place the bowl of stew in the middle of the kitchen table. 'Yes, but ...' I stop, aware that I don't have a good enough answer to give my son, who's more clued up on what's been going on than I first thought. 'I think he's just lonely,' I say. 'I'm just trying to be nice.'

'You know he has a massive crush on you, right?'

I feel my cheeks heat up. 'Yes, I'm aware, but I've made it clear to him that I don't feel the same way.'

'Do you not think it's leading him on a bit?'

'I suppose so,' I respond with a sigh. 'Has he been okay with you?'

'What do you mean?'

'Do you like him? Has he been rude to you or anything?'

'No, I just find it weird that he comes to dinner every night. Megan doesn't want to come over when he's around.'

'She doesn't? Why?'

Max shrugs. 'I guess she finds him weird too.'

Max walks out of the kitchen.

I carry on with dinner, the sinking feeling of anxiety growing in my gut.

THE NEXT EVENING, Henry saying he's heading home early today means Max and I can have dinner in peace. At seven o'clock, Megan's car pulls up in the driveway, with Max at the wheel. I chuckle to myself as he slams on the brakes too hard, and the car jolts to a halt, sending both him and

Megan whiplashing forwards. They laugh together as they get out and walk into the house.

I'm just finishing the washing up, only a few minutes away from dishing up a meal of sausage and mashed potatoes with thick gravy.

'Hi, Natasha,' says Megan brightly.

'Hello, lovely. Thanks for dropping him off. How's the driving coming, Max?' I add.

Max rolls his eyes at me, but it's different to his usual eye roll. He's not mad at me or annoyed but enjoying my light teasing. 'Megan's brakes are really delicate,' he says, opening the fridge and pulling out a half-drunk bottle of Coke.

'My brakes are fine, thank you very much,' says Megan, gently punching him in the arm.

'Would you like to stay for dinner, Megan? Um ... Henry's going home early. He's just finishing off now.'

'Oh, no, thank you. I can't tonight. Have a late shift at work, so I have to head off now.' She turns to Max. 'I'll give you a text tomorrow,' she says, pulling him in for a quick kiss. My son blushes so red he almost matches the tomato ketchup bottle on the worktop.

I purse my lips together to stop from grinning. 'Bye, Megan.'

She gives me a little wave and leaves the house.

'Have I got time for a shower before dinner?'

'Um, yes, if you're quick.'

'Cool.' He chugs a few gulps of Coke and replaces the bottle in the fridge. Who is this person? The old Max would have left the bottle on the side with the cap off. He leaves the kitchen.

'Hi, mate,' I hear Henry say cheerfully.

'Er ... hi,' grunts Max.

I smirk at the fact Max is being awkward around Henry. Clearly, Max isn't as forthcoming with being a happy family as I am.

'Well,' says Henry, entering the kitchen, 'that's the upstairs mostly cleared apart from the beds, ready for me to rip up the rest of the carpets.'

'That's great. Thanks, Henry. Are you off now, then?'

'Ah, yeah, turns out I don't need to rush home after all. Dinner smells good.' We lock eyes, daring the other to back down first.

'It's sausage and mash,' I say with a fake smile.

He pulls out a chair and takes a seat. There are clearly only two places laid at the table, but I fetch a third and plonk it down in front of him a little harder than I plan. He frowns at me.

'Careful, Nat. Wouldn't want to break anything.'

I don't respond.

'I won't be working tomorrow, by the way.'

'Oh?' This surprises me because in the past eight days he hasn't had a day off at all. The man is a working machine. I've told him several times that he doesn't need to work every single day, but he won't hear of it. Perhaps he's got nothing else to do. He's an enigma, really, probably quite lonely. Doesn't he have any other building jobs on? He's not mentioned anything about doing any other work for people. I know he said at the start that he was taking time off, but there's been no hint of any other building work. I'm relieved that I'll get to spend the day by myself without him hovering around me like a bad smell.

'Yeah, taking the day off.'

'No problem at all. Thanks for letting me know. Got anything nice planned?'

'Maybe we could hang out.'

I freeze. 'Hang out?'

'Yeah, you know, like a couple.'

'But ... we're not a couple.'

'Maybe not, but would be nice to spend time together, right? Maybe go for a few drinks. I bet you're a right laugh with a few drinks in you.'

I turn and face the oven, squeezing the bridge of my nose and closing my eyes as I count to ten slowly. I busy myself by serving dinner. It's a good job I cooked extra sausages. I usually do anyway because Max always asks for a second helping, but he'll have to make do with one tonight.

Henry remains silent, but I can feel his eyes staring at the back of my head. Max breaks the tension a few minutes later.

'I thought you were going home.' Max's tone is harsh. I don't blame him.

'Yep, I was, but your lovely mum was kind enough to invite me again.'

I turn and plaster a fake smile across my face before plonking the ketchup bottle in the middle of the table with a little extra force than necessary.

Max pulls up a chair.

'You got a problem with me staying for dinner?' asks Henry. It's the first time there's been an air of aggression in his voice aimed towards Max. I hold my breath, hoping it doesn't turn into an argument.

Max glares at Henry, and Henry glares back.

Shit.

I need to step in here.

'Max, would you mind helping me strip the old wallpaper off the walls upstairs later, after dinner?'

Max drags his eyes away from Henry. 'Whatever.'

'Don't talk to your mother like that, young man,' says Henry.

'I'll talk to my *mother* however the fuck I want. You have no right to tell me anything. You're not a part of this family.'

Henry bristles and thumps his fist down on the table.

'Henry, it's fine,' I say quickly.

'No, Nat, it's not. You can't let him get away with the way he speaks to you.'

'And while I agree to a certain point, Max is my son, and I'll decide how to handle it.'

Henry clenches his jaw, staring at me. I brace for the fall-out, an explosion, something, but it doesn't come. 'Sure, no problem,' he says.

The kitchen falls into an awkward silence. I put a plate of food in front of Henry, trying not to scowl at him. He beams at me, the tension forgotten. 'Cheers, love.'

I see Max roll his eyes.

'I've had an idea,' says Henry while chewing with his mouth open. 'How about Max shadows me and learns a bit about the building trade? Nat, you mentioned it before, didn't you? Would be good for him to learn a trade, considering he's not doing anything else with his life.'

I open my mouth to reply, but Max gets there first. 'I'll pass.'

I let out a long breath. It's not that I don't want Max to go into the building trade, I just don't want him learning from Henry. I said at the start it might be a good idea, but a lot has happened since then. It's yet another thing Henry's trying to manipulate his way into, and I don't like it. I'd love for Max to be a builder, if that's something he wants to do, but I don't want Henry pressuring him into anything. I really need to speak up about this before it goes too far, but the fact that Henry has so much hold over me makes me hold my tongue. I still haven't decided what to do about this whole blackmail situation.

'Nat,' says Henry, 'what do you think?' He's ignored Max completely, and now I feel like I'm stuck between a rock and a hard place, but of course I'm going to side with my son.

'I think Max has enough to deal with at the moment with starting a new job and possibly starting school in a few weeks.'

Max grins at me, seemingly pleased I've taken his side. Henry grumbles something under his breath and busies himself with finishing his dinner.

Max slurps his glass of water, then stands up. 'Thanks for dinner.'

'You're welcome, Max.'

He leaves the kitchen. As soon as he's out of earshot, I round on Henry. 'Don't you dare talk to my son like that again.'

'Maybe you should be more concerned with how he speaks to you. He's disrespectful and rude. He could use some manners knocked into him. It's clear he's had no male role model in his life.'

'It's still not your right to speak to him like that.'

Henry gets to his feet and leans across the kitchen table towards me. 'You both could do with a strong male around here.'

'Get. Out.' I point stiff-armed to the door.

Henry grins at me. 'See you Sunday, Nat.'

I don't release my breath until I hear him slam the front door. He speeds down the driveway in his van, sending up a cloud of dust in its wake. This is getting way out of hand. He has so much control over me. My stomach is in knots as I stare at the empty driveway.

'You okay, Mum?'

I turn, having not heard Max come in. 'Yes. Fine.'

Max is quiet for a few seconds and then says, 'I know I gave you a hard time back in Birmingham, and I never said thank you for helping me out of that situation, but I'm glad we moved here. I like it here, and I'd really like to go back to school so I can attend university next year.'

'I think that's a wonderful idea. I shall contact the school next week and get you signed up.'

Max nods. 'Thanks. I hate to say this, but … you were right, Mum.'

I make a show of clutching my heart and stumbling against the worktop in shock.

Max laughs. 'Yeah, yeah, all right, don't rub it in. Oh, and I don't like Henry. He's a dick.'

I sigh. 'I know. I'm sorry, but … I need to find a way to tactfully tell him to move on.'

'Why don't you just pay him what you owe him for the work and tell him to fuck off?'

'Because … because … it's not that simple.'

'I guess some things never are.'

'You're right about that.'

It's midnight when loud bangs jolt me out of a deep sleep. At first, my anxiety spikes, and I struggle to catch my breath as I stumble out of bed and down the stairs, towards the noise. I know who it is before I even reach the front door.

Unlocking it, I find Henry standing on my doorstep,

gently swaying from side to side. He places his hand on the doorframe, slips and almost bashes his head on the door.

'Henry, what the hell?' I look past him at the driveway. His van isn't there, which means he walked from the village. He's blind drunk, barely able to stay upright.

'Y-you f-fucking women are all the s-same, aren't ya?'

'Excuse me?'

He wobbles and wipes a slither of drool from the corner of his mouth. 'Just taking advantage of u-us decent blokes. M-my fucking w-wife was exactly the same.'

'Look, I'm sorry your wife left you, but there's no need to have a go at me.'

He clenches his jaw and makes a sound that sounds like a growl. 'F-fucking bitch left me seven years ago. Cheated on me with some other b-bloke. H-haven't seen her s-since.'

'I'm sorry, but—'

'No, you ain't sorry! You're just lying to me again.'

'Henry ...'

He hacks up a load of phlegm and spits it out to the side of the door. He takes a step back, loses his balance and topples over. I can't let him walk home in the dark in this state. I know he managed to get himself here, but he can barely stand up now.

'Henry ... for fuck's sake. Come and sleep it off on my sofa.'

'I d-don't need your f-fucking pity, woman!'

'It's not pity. Believe it or not, despite the fact you've been unbelievably horrible to me, I'm not a bad person, and I can't let you stumble back home in the dark.' I walk over to him and crouch on the ground. The moment I do, he lunges to the side and heaves his guts up. I grimace and look away.

I instantly regret my decision to be a good Samaritan.

It's going to be a long night.

SOMEHOW, I manage to drag Henry through the front door and into the small toilet downstairs, where he continues to puke on and off for the next hour. He doesn't say much other than growling a few expletives at me and telling me he wants to die.

I clean him up, give him a drink of water and convince him to pass out on the sofa. I'm a little wary of leaving him in case he starts choking on his own vomit, but I'm pretty sure it's all out of his system now, so once he's snoring, I place a bucket on the floor next to his head and pull a blanket over him before heading back upstairs.

It's gone three in the morning by the time I crawl into bed. Max has slept through the whole thing, which is just typical of him. Not that he would have been much help. He probably would have told Henry to go away.

I don't hear Henry stir during the next hour, so after four I finally fall asleep. When I wake up, I creep downstairs to find Henry in the exact position I left him. I quickly check to make sure he's breathing and then decide to grab a quick shower to wake me up before starting breakfast.

As I lather shampoo into my hair, I take some deep breaths. The whole situation with Henry has gone beyond weird now. He's clearly lonely and in pain from his wife leaving him for another man, but what makes him think he can just barge his way into my life and force me to play happy families? I know he and I share a secret, but he seems to have taken a vicious turn ever since I turned him down.

I switch off the shower, pull back the curtain and shriek

when I see Henry standing in the open doorway. I locked the door. I know I did, so how the hell is it now open?

I grab the shower curtain and hide my body. 'Henry! What are you doing?'

'Just came to say thanks and bye and sorry about last night.'

My heart is pounding like a drum still, but I manage to nod, still soaking wet and very much naked behind a see-through curtain. 'Um ... yeah, you're welcome. It's fine. Well, it's not fine, but ... Now's not the right time to talk about it. I'll see you tomorrow.'

Henry looks terrible, pale and green at the same time. 'Yeah, see you tomorrow, Nat.'

And he's gone.

I still can't catch my breath even when I step out of the shower several minutes later. I check the lock on the door. The damn thing doesn't even work. Henry was the one who fitted it.

The pervert.

15

Once I know Henry is gone, I relax a little. I head off to work, looking forward to returning to an afternoon pottering about the house and gardens. Maybe I can return to the vegetable garden idea, but I'll move it elsewhere, away from the new patio with the body underneath.

It still doesn't seem real whenever I think about it. Sometimes I question whether it was all just a bad dream, and my medication-muddled mind made it all up. Then I remember how Henry is blackmailing me, and that anxiety-riddled knot in my stomach tightens again.

WHEN I GET BACK from work, it's to an empty house. The sun is out and beating down upon the garden. It's nice to have the doors open to allow fresh air in. It would be a pure nightmare to be renovating this place in the dead of winter, with snow and rain pelting against the windows. It also means Henry can leave the doors open and work clean too, not trampling in mud and leaves from the garden. He is a very tidy builder; I'll give him that. He makes sure to clean up after himself and says that once the new carpets are in, he'll wear plastic protectors over his boots to keep the carpet free from dirt.

I fetch the random gardening tools from the shed – a spade, fork and clippers – then wander around the garden, doing my best to avoid the patio area. I can't bring myself to go over there. It's a shame, really, because it really is a lovely little sun-trap and would be a perfect location to set up some chairs and a table, maybe an array of colourful potted plants.

I find a secluded area, just across from the house, that's flat and not too overgrown. Granted, it needs everything ripping out, including brambles and stinging nettles, but I don't see why I can't make a start on clearing the area. However, the last time I wanted to enjoy tending to my garden, I found a dead body, so as I begin ripping out roots and cutting back branches, I'm a little apprehensive.

I cut and dig for about thirty minutes, stopping every now and then to catch my breath. I pull at the weeds, find about a thousand slugs and spiders, and discover a few random buried items, old coins, nails and even an old metal watering can.

I reach down into the weeds to pull out a clump of roots and instantly yank my hand back.

'Ouch!' Something stabbed my finger. I watch as a bead of blood blooms on my skin. I avoid sucking it because my hands are covered in dirt.

Curious as to what's pricked me, I stamp on the long weeds to reveal the soil near the roots. A small, metal brooch lies half-buried, its sharp needle fastening sticking straight up, waiting for an unsuspecting, bare hand to attack.

I pick it up and scrape off as much embedded dirt as I can, revealing a glimpse of shiny gold and silver. There's an engraving on the back of it, but it's impossible to read. Who the hell wears a brooch anymore? It must be quite old.

My curiosity gets the better of me, and I carry the brooch towards the house, squeezing it tight in my left palm, which is moist with sweat. Despite needing a wee, I walk straight past the downstairs toilet and into the kitchen, where I run the water and start cleaning the brooch.

It's very delicate, and as the dirt comes away, I realise that it's riddled with rust, and the clasp at the back pops off and clatters into the sink.

'Damn it,' I mutter, picking it up and putting it on the side before returning to cleaning. Using my fingernail, I gently scrape away the embedded dirt in the engraving on the back of the brooch. The engraving itself is tiny, only a few millimetres in size, so my fingernail is too big to be of much use. In the end, I run the brooch under running warm water and allow the water pressure to melt away the dirt, finally revealing a glimpse of the engraving.

I hold it up to the light, turning it in different directions until I can read it clearly.

C.P.H.

That's what it looks like. The letter in the middle could be something else, as it's been worn away in places.

My mind automatically fills in the name for *H*: Harriet, but then why's it at the end and not the beginning? Maybe the *P* stands for Prudence (if it is a *P*).

Am I jumping ahead of myself? Perhaps it didn't belong to either one of them, but it's an old-fashioned brooch, something no one of this day and age would wear, not unless it's part of a fancy-dress costume. Harriet would have been more likely to wear it over Prudence, since she was around my age when she ... died.

'Hey, Mum.'

I'm so startled by Max's loud voice that I drop the brooch into the sink. 'Gosh, you scared me! I wasn't expecting you back so early.'

'Sorry, just back to grab a quick shower. What's that?' He points to the brooch.

'Oh, I found it while clearing the garden. It's got an engraving on the back of it, but I can't make it out. Here, take a look.' I hand the brooch to Max, who takes it and does the same thing as me and holds it up into the light, turning it from left to right.

'*C* ... not sure, possibly a *P*, or a weird symbol ... Is that an *H*?'

'That's what I thought, yeah.'

'Ah, well,' says Max with a shrug, handing the brooch back to me. I take it and look at it. I wish I were more like my son, who can just forget about something so quickly if it doesn't concern him. This brooch shouldn't matter to me, but it does. Because I know something that Max doesn't know.

There's a body buried only about thirty feet from where this brooch was found.

Did it belong to Prudence, and it fell off while she was being dragged into her grave, or did it belong to Harriet, and she was wearing it while she'd been doing the dragging, and it had been dislodged during the process?

So far, while I've been clearing the rooms over the past two weeks, I haven't seen any other brooches or old-fashioned jewellery. Maybe Harriet wasn't into wearing it. It may not belong to either one of them, but the fact is it was found very close to where Prudence's body was buried, so it seems likely it's connected somehow. It's been there a long time too, considering the damage and rust.

I place the brooch on the side of the worktop while I fill up the kettle to make a cup of tea. 'Do you want a cup?' I ask Max.

'No, thanks. Megan's picking me up in an hour, and we're going to hang out.'

'Okay. Have fun.'

Max frowns at me. 'Aren't you going to ask where I'm going and how long I'll be?'

I turn and face him. 'A lot has changed since we moved here, Max. Things are finally settling down, and I want you to have fun. Out of interest, what time should I expect you back?' I give him a grin to show I'm kidding.

'I'll give you a text when I know more. Oh, I bought a new phone. It's crappy, but it'll do until I save up for a new one. I'll text you my new number, but it shouldn't be later than ten tonight. She's taking me driving around and seeing some sights.'

'See you later, then. Oh, and you're free to create a social media account now.'

Max nods and then heads upstairs for a shower.

I go to make myself a cup of tea, but I can't find my favourite mug anywhere, which is odd because I used it earlier this morning before work. I open all the cupboards and double-check the lounge and my bedroom, but the mug is nowhere to be seen.

I sigh, annoyed that I can't find it, so make do with another mug. I stir the teabag a few times, allowing the water to turn black, then scoop the teabag on a spoon and carry it to the flip-up bin in the corner. The lid flips open.

There it is. My favourite mug. Smashed to pieces.

I pick up the biggest part, a sadness settling over me. Seventeen years I've had this mug. It saw me through pregnancy when I couldn't stomach anything other than green tea. It saw me through the late nights of breastfeeding when I needed as much water as I could take on board. It's seen several thousand litres of coffee in its time too when I was exhausted after Max was awake at all hours of the night, having his own private toddler dance party.

I put the broken piece back in the bin, along with the teabag, and close the lid.

If Max had broken it, he would have told me. I'm almost certain. Plus, he's never used it. He knows it's mine. But I've seen Henry use it several times now. Does he think I won't notice it's missing? Did he do it on purpose? Is he that petty?

Should I ask him about it and confront him?

My initial thought is yes because I'm fucking angry. He's broken it and tried to hide the evidence; not very well, I might add. Someone who didn't want me to find the broken mug would have tried to bury it deeper in the bin so it wasn't noticeable as soon as I opened the lid.

It must have been Henry. I trust Max. I don't trust Henry. Not even a little bit.

He has broken my mug and lied to me about it.

It isn't only a mug. Not to me.

I finally go to the toilet, then take my tea into the lounge, slipping my feet out of my shoes before tucking them underneath me on the sofa. I can't dwell on it too much; otherwise I'll just go round and round in circles. I tend to overthink and analyse everything, but this whole broken-mug business has at least distracted me from the brooch I found, which now leaps back into my mind, begging to be the centre of attention again. I'll have a quick tea break and then head outside to finish the weeding.

I sit on the sofa, pick up my tea and go to take a sip.

The doorbell rings.

Sighing heavily, I carry the tea to the front door and open it. I haven't had any visitors here apart from Henry on day two, so I'm intrigued as to who it can be.

A woman stands on my doorstep. She looks nervous, but she's very pretty and has gorgeous long black hair almost to her waist. She's wearing a white, flowing summer dress and minimal make-up.

'Can I help you?' I ask.

'Hi, is your name Natasha Moore?'

A solid lump forms in my throat. 'Um ... yes. I'm sorry, but do I know you?'

'No, I don't suppose you do. My name is Poppy Kalu.'

I narrow my eyes at her. 'Okay,' I say.

She laughs as she nervously tucks a strand of long hair behind her right ear. 'I ... I used to live here. Seven years ago, I was called Prudence Greene.'

I drop the mug of tea to the floor, where it smashes, and the hot liquid splashes across my feet.

PART III

16

Ignoring the hot tea soaking into my socks, my brain cells bounce back and forth like a ping-pong ball across a net. A million questions want to explode out of my mouth at once, but my bottom jaw just hangs open as I stare at the woman in front of me, who blushes and begins to fidget with her hands, tugging at her dress and looking down at her feet.

'I'm so sorry to just drop in like this out of the blue. I can imagine you're a little shocked to see me,' she says with a slight smile.

Hang on just one second.

Prudence Greene is buried under the patio in my garden. This random woman can't be her. Why is she pretending to be Prudence? Why is she here? I need to get to the bottom of this.

'I ... Y-yes, sorry ...' I manage to say. 'Um ... would you like to come in?' I step to the side and then bend down and pick up the shards of the broken mug. 'Excuse all the mess. I'm renovating.'

The woman who can't be Prudence nods as she steps over the threshold, looking around at the stripped walls, bare floors and piles of rubbish. 'Yes, I can see that. You're doing a wonderful job.'

I narrow my eyes at her as I attempt to recall the pictures I've seen of Harriet and Prudence around the house. Granted, she has long black hair like Prudence did, and she's slim like her too. I suddenly realise that I'm staring blankly at her.

She frowns at me. 'Are you okay?'

'Sorry ... still in a bit of shock. Um ... Would you like a cup of tea or coffee? I'll have to make myself a new one,' I say, holding up the broken mug.

'Tea would be lovely, thanks. It's been a long time since I've had a proper cup of English tea.'

I lead the way into the kitchen, flicking the kettle back on. How do I approach this? Either she's lying about who she is, or she's telling the truth, and that means ... who the fuck is buried underneath my patio?

I decide to test this woman. See what she says when I question her on certain things.

'I'm so sorry for my reaction when I saw you,' I say. 'As you say, it's a bit of shock. I was sent a letter by Harriet after her death, and she told me about the house and her leaving it all to me. She said she'd written you out of the will.'

Poppy smiles. 'Yes, of course. I completely understand your shock. Again, I'm sorry for the abruptness of my arrival.'

I make her tea and hand her the mug.

'Thank you,' she says. 'I guess I should explain myself and tell you why I'm here.'

I gulp hard, reach out a shaky hand, steadying myself

against the table as I lower myself down onto a chair. Poppy sits down opposite me, both her hands cupping the mug.

Oh God. She's here to try to take the house from me. That's all I can think about.

No. No. No.

She can't do this. I'm the legal owner. She was written out of the will years ago. She doesn't have any say anymore. And since she can't be Prudence, she has even less say.

Poppy clears her throat. 'Before I tell you what happened between Harriet and me, I just want you to know and put your mind at ease that I'm not here to take the house from you.' The relief must be immediately clear on my face as my shoulders visibly relax because she smiles. 'The house and everything in it belong to you, Natasha. Harriet changed her will, and I accept that. My being here doesn't change anything.'

I nod, but my gut tells me she's lying. She hasn't convinced me about her identity yet.

'So why are you here?' I ask. 'Where have you been for the past seven years? Why have you changed your name to Poppy Kalu?'

Poppy shifts in her seat before taking a small sip of tea and replacing the mug back on the table. 'I'm here to pay my respects to Harriet and the house. She wasn't an easy woman to live with. It took me a long time to realise that. However, upon her death, I also received a letter, which explained who you are and that you'd be taking the house. Abioye and I – sorry, he's my husband – we've been living in Nigeria with his family for the past five years. Before that, we travelled around Europe for a while, every so often going back to Nigeria. I've never regretted leaving Harriet. She was very manipulative, and I couldn't spend any longer living under her roof.' She looks uneasy for a moment and shifts in her seat. 'Have you ever wished you could run away and start a new life, have a new identity and just forget the person you used to be?'

I almost laugh at the question because she's hit the nail on the head for me, but I can't admit that, so I merely nod. Her explanation certainly seems sincere. I'm not an expert at telling if people are lying, but the more I stare at this woman, the more familiar she becomes.

'I suppose I can understand that,' I say. 'Before a few weeks ago, I didn't even know you or Harriet existed. My mother never told me about Harriet. She and I lost contact when I was seventeen.'

Poppy gasps. 'Gosh! Why? ... Sorry, forget I asked. It's none of my business.'

'No, it's okay. I was pregnant, and my parents didn't agree with my decision to keep the baby.'

Poppy's eyes light up. 'Wow, you have a child?'

'Yes. Max.'

'I've always wanted a child, but ... unfortunately Abioye and I haven't been able to conceive yet.'

'I'm so sorry.' And I really am. I know Max was an accident, but even before I found out about him, I knew I wanted children one day. The idea of not being able to conceive is a horror I wouldn't wish upon my worst enemy.

My body has visibly relaxed around this woman now. I think I believe her, but there's a rising panic blooming in my chest, travelling slowly up my throat.

Who is the woman buried in my garden?

Poppy/Prudence is still talking, so I do my best to ignore the anxiety.

'... Harriet took me in when I was young, after I lost my parents in a car accident.'

'I'm so sorry to hear that. So ... your mum was ... Joan?'

'Yes, Joan. She was older than Harriet, I believe. Harriet was firm but kind in her own way. However, as I grew up, I realised how manipulative she really was, but when I met Abioye, she refused to let me marry him. Turns out she was a complete racist. He's from Nigeria, and I fell head over heels in love with him.'

'How did you two meet?' I ask, realising that I'm enjoying having an adult conversation for the first time in a very long time.

Prudence takes another sip of tea as she looks at the ceiling, as if recalling the happy memory. 'I was on holiday, backpacking in Scotland, and he was the tour guide for one of the mountain walks. We hit it off straight away. He told me about his life in Nigeria, and I fell in love with him there and then, but when he told me he was moving back to Nigeria to be closer to his parents, I realised I had a decision to make. Harriet flew off the handle about it. I realised she was a manipulative old lady, so I chose to disappear and start a new life. I didn't want anything to do with her. Not her money, her house or anything. I had nothing here to stay for, so I chose Abioye, and I don't regret my decision, not even for a second.'

Frowning, I watch her fiddling with the mug, thinking over my next set of questions carefully. 'If you and Harriet had an argument and you left on such bad terms, then why are you here? I'm still not sure I understand.' I hope I don't come across as rude, but Prudence, luckily, doesn't take it the wrong way.

'As I said, she wrote a letter to be delivered to me after

her death. I'm not too sure how she managed to track me down. Maybe she hired an investigator, I don't know. But I wanted to meet you. I never knew about you either. You're the only family I have left.'

I smile. 'So ... we're ... cousins?'

Prudence nods.

'When did Harriet find out about me? My mum didn't tell me anything about her family. Did Harriet ever want to meet me before?'

'Apparently, she and your mother had a huge falling-out when they were young. I have no idea what it was about. Probably some pointless argument. Our family is weird and holds grudges for a stupidly long time. Anyway ...' Prudence flips her long black hair over her shoulder and then continues, 'your mum told Harriet to never contact her again. When your mum died, Harriet was in her will, but she didn't want anything from her so refused what your mum had left her.'

'What was it my mum left her? She didn't leave a thing to me, and I was her daughter.'

'No idea, I'm afraid. Harriet never said, but anyway, during this whole reading-of-the-will thing, Harriet found out about you. When I left her, she must have changed her will and left everything to you.'

'Did you keep in contact with her? You left a note, but what happened after that?'

'No, I never contacted her again, and she never looked for me as far as I knew, although she must have known where I was because she had that letter delivered to me.' Prudence finishes her tea and takes a deep breath as she looks around the kitchen. 'Lots of memories in this house.'

'I ... I should tell you that my son and I have been going

through your belongings that you left behind, and we've donated or thrown away most of it. I'm sorry. If I'd known you were coming, I would have kept it.'

Prudence shakes her head. 'No need to apologise. As I said, I don't want a thing from this house. It's yours to do with as you like. Did you find the box of cash under the floorboards in the back bedroom, by any chance?'

'Yes, my son found it.'

Prudence grins. 'Good. Any other surprises you've found?' She fixes me with a stare, and I feel my heart leap in my chest.

Is she asking me what I think she's asking me? Does she know about the body in the garden? Does she know who it is? Do I dare ask her about it?

'I ... like what?' I manage to ask quietly.

'Harriet hid and stored all sorts of things in this house. It wouldn't surprise me if you'd come across some odd objects.'

A thought suddenly springs into my mind. 'Did Harriet ever own a brooch with the initials C.P.H. engraved on it?'

Prudence tilts her head slightly to one side. 'Hmm, not that I can remember. She wasn't big into jewellery, to be honest. C.P.H. you say?'

'Do you recognise those initials?'

'No, I'm sorry, I don't. Why do you ask?'

'I found an old brooch upstairs while I was sorting through the rooms and thought it might have belonged to either you or Harriet at one time.'

'I'm afraid not.'

My heart sinks a little. Of course it would never be that simple. 'No problem,' I say with a small shrug. 'Another tea?'

'No, thank you. It's been so lovely to meet you, but I think I'll be off.'

'Did you come all the way from Nigeria to visit me?'

Prudence laughs. 'No, not exactly. Abioye and I like to travel. His family is quite wealthy in Nigeria, you see, and we often visit other countries for long periods of time. Australia is fabulous.'

My eyebrows rise. Is he Nigerian royalty perhaps? No wonder she isn't fussed about the house and the small amount of money Harriet left behind.

'We're touring a little of the UK, and I thought I'd pop in and see what was going on with the house and meet you. However, I'd really appreciate it if you didn't tell anyone I was here. Only you and one other person knows.'

I nod quickly. 'Yes, of course.' I'm quietly relieved because it would be much simpler to keep pretending that she doesn't exist.

Prudence stands, and I quickly follow, walking her to the front door. As she passes the dining room, she stops in her tracks. I follow her gaze. She's spotted Henry's bag of tools. It has his name and logo on it.

'Is Henry Clayton the builder who's working on the house?' she asks.

'Um, yes,' I say, scratching behind my left ear. 'He knocked on the door and offered his services at a very reasonable rate a few weeks ago. Do you know him?'

Prudence turns slowly around. Her facial expression is completely different to what it's been like since she's been here. While we chatted, she was smiley and upbeat, open, but now there's a frown across her face, and her eyes are narrow.

'I ... Yes, I do know him. At least, I knew his wife mostly. Catherine. We were friends.'

At the mention of her name, a flicker of recognition

ignites in my mind. It begins buzzing and tickling me, sending me off guard. I didn't expect her to say that at all, but then Henry did let it slip once that his wife and Prudence knew each other well, but he never told me his wife's name.

'Did you say he offered his help with the house of his own accord?' continues Prudence. She's stopped directly in the middle of the hallway, no longer heading towards the front door.

'Yes, he did,' I say brightly, but inside, a shadow of doubt is growing.

'Can I offer you some friendly advice?'

'Okay ...'

'Fire Henry and get yourself another builder as soon as possible.'

I feel as if I've been punched in the chest. 'W-why's that? I asked around, and his references checked out. He's an excellent builder.'

'Yes, I know he is,' she says. 'He did some work on this house a long time ago, but ... I don't trust him.'

'Can you elaborate on that?'

'Catherine told me he drank a lot and would get violent with her sometimes. I never saw any bruises or anything on her, but I get the impression that it wasn't mainly physical violence he hurt her with.'

'You mean he was emotionally abusing her?'

'I believe so. That's why she left him.'

'She ran off with another man, right?'

Prudence shakes her head. 'Yes, but it wasn't the main reason she left. She just couldn't take his crap any longer. I feel bad because I ran away myself not long after she left. She told me she was going somewhere down south, but because I changed my name and moved away, I never found out if she ended up happy with someone else. I think I might try to look her up while I'm in the UK. She was always very lovely to me, and I always felt bad for never standing up for her when I had the chance. Has anything happened ... with Henry, I mean?'

'No,' I reply a bit too quickly.

Prudence smiles as she leans forwards and gives me a gentle hug. The gesture is so out of the blue that my body tenses, and I just stand there like a rigid pole. She steps away. 'Please be careful,' she says. 'He has a mean streak.'

I gulp back the lump in my throat.

Prudence walks to the front door. I follow at a distance, searching my mind for any further questions I can ask. She turns and gives me another light hug. This time, I hug her back.

'It's lovely to meet you, Natasha. I'll write to you, okay? And I'll give you my address so you can write back once I'm back in Nigeria. I don't do phones or email.'

'I'd like that. Thank you for coming. It's nice to know you're alive and well.'

Prudence gives me an odd look, as if she wants to question me further on my choice of words, but she doesn't. She turns and begins to walk down the driveway. It doesn't look like she drove here. Maybe someone is picking her up at the end of the lane.

I watch her until she disappears.

My pulse quickens as I think about what she said about Henry.

What is going on here? Am I missing something?

I rush back into the kitchen and retrieve the brooch from the counter, having just had a thought click into place. I slip in my haste on the tiled floor but manage to stop myself from colliding into the worktop. I grab the brooch, lifting it up to the light. The symbol or letter in the middle still looks unreadable, but the C and the H are perfectly clear.

This brooch *could* have belonged to Catherine, Henry's ex-wife. Quite why she'd be on the property, I don't know, unless she was here visiting Prudence.

But the fact is that Prudence is alive.

There's a female body with no name underneath my patio.

Henry's wife is called Catherine, who left him seven years ago.

Prudence and Catherine knew each other and were friends.

C.P.H.

What if that *P* in the middle isn't a *P* at all?

What if it's a symbol?

What if it's C & H?

What if it's Catherine who's buried under my patio ... and what if Henry put her there?

17

Holy shit.

Then the reality of that being true hits me like a punch to the gut. The brooch drops to the floor as my brain connects the dots. All this time I thought Henry was keeping *my* secret, but what if I've been keeping *his*?

Did I stumble upon Henry's wife's resting place and then unknowingly help him re-bury her somewhere else, protecting his secret without realising it? Or did he not know it was her? He was the one who suggested it was Prudence right from the start. Maybe he doesn't know that Prudence is even alive. Does he know his wife is dead? But then, if he knew it was Catherine, of course he wouldn't have admitted it to me, so that was why he suggested it was Prudence to throw me off the scent, but now I know it's not Prudence because she's alive and well. And Henry has no idea that I know this. Either Henry is a brilliant actor, or he's just as clueless as me.

Prudence's warning about Henry pops into my thoughts.

Is he dangerous? Granted, he's creepy and annoying and seems to pop up at the most inappropriate times, but he has never been aggressive towards me, not physically anyway. He's blackmailing me, but a killer?

I SPEND the rest of the day going over and over this new information, trying to connect the dots and fill in the blank spaces. It all fits. There was a reason why Henry turned up at my door. Perhaps it wasn't to play happy families after all, but to keep an eye on me, an eye on the property.

By Sunday morning, my anxiety about Henry arriving is sky-high. I can't catch my breath or stop trembling and sweating. I'm a nervous wreck. He'll take one look at me and suspect something is up.

Henry's van pulls into the driveway, the tyres crunching loudly over the gravel. I'm sitting at the kitchen table and clasping the brooch in my hand so hard that the sharp edge digs into my palm. I scramble to my feet and press my back against the nearest wall, as if I'm afraid of him seeing me, which I immediately realise is ridiculous because this is my house. I have nothing to hide. He's the one who's hiding something. This man can't be trusted. I'm just feeling a little jumpy. I need to pull myself together because I can't let him see my uneasiness. He's like a firecracker ready to explode at any moment, and I must not give him the ignition to do so.

Henry has a hell of a lot more to lose if his wife's body is found than I do now. This is what I've been waiting for. Two can play this blackmail game.

I have a plan. I just need to calm the fuck down.

I will ask him about his wife, to see if he gives anything away. Maybe he'll contradict what Prudence told me. I want him out of my house, but I can't just throw him out for no valid reason, or can I? I don't want to get the police involved. But if I piss him off, then he could easily tell the police about the body in my garden. But if it is his wife, then surely he wouldn't do that? It's clear I may have the upper hand now. All this is too much to comprehend, and the panic rises in my chest as the van door slams. I can't stop it. Can't control it. Even deep-breathing exercises won't be enough to calm the storm raging inside. But I'm close to getting rid of him now. I just need to tread carefully. Very carefully.

Henry knocks at the door a minute later. I open it. He's carrying a bag of something or other as he walks straight past me to the stairs as he says, 'Morning, Nat.'

'Henry,' I say as calmly as I can, 'can we talk?'

He stops halfway up the stairs, turns and looks down at me. I walk to the bottom of the stairs and look up. I don't like it that he's higher than me. It feels like he has the upper hand.

'I found something in the garden earlier. It has an engraving on it, but I can't work out what it says. Would you mind looking at it? Maybe you can figure it out.'

Henry slowly walks down and joins me on my level. 'Sure.'

I hold my breath and hold out my shaking palm, the brooch resting on it. There are little red marks from where I squeezed too hard, and the metal has left tiny indentations. I watch him carefully, studying his body language, looking for any sort of reaction.

He blinks once.

'Oh my God,' he says, gasping. A smile lights up his face. 'Where did you find this?' He picks it up and turns it over, reading the engraving.

'Like I said, in the garden, sort of buried under a load of weeds. Do you recognise it?'

'It belonged to ... m-my wife.'

'What does it say on the back?'

'C & H. Catherine and Henry. Our initials. I bought it for her for our first anniversary.'

'How do you think it ended up in the garden?' I ask casually.

'A few days before she left me, she visited me here at the house while I was working for Harriet. I was in the garden, digging the pond. We had an argument, and she threw it at me in a fit of anger before storming away. I picked it up and put it in my pocket, but it must have fallen out at some point while I was working in the garden. I did look for it, but I couldn't find it anywhere. I was gutted because it's the only thing she left me of hers. She took everything else.'

I take in his words, but the alarm bells are ringing so loudly in my head that it's hard to stay focused. He's staring at me too, like he's daring me to say or do something to discredit him. It's him against me.

Henry is the most convincing person I've ever encountered, but the thing is, I don't know if he's lying or not.

'You're shaking,' he says. Then he does something that makes my insides turn to ice. He reaches out and brushes his hand against my bare arm, bringing goosebumps to the surface of my skin. 'Are you cold?'

'I ... No, I'm just ...'

'Thank you for finding the brooch. I may hate my wife for what she did to me, but I still love her. This brooch means a lot to me.'

I nod, quickly looking down at the ground away from his prying gaze. 'Where did Catherine move to?' I ask.

'She didn't say. Somewhere down south.'

'Have you heard from her since?'

'Only to finalise the divorce proceedings.'

'So, you are divorced, then? She didn't just disappear. You had further contact with her after she left you?'

'Yes, that's right.'

'What was the name of the man she ran away with?'

Henry shifts his body slightly, and that's the moment I realise I've said too much, asked too many probing questions. I step back, determined to make some space between our bodies. Having him so close is making me queasy, and I can smell his musty body odour.

'Sorry, I don't mean to pry,' I say.

'Nat ...' he says sternly, 'if you have something to say to me, then now's the time.'

'No, nothing. Sorry.'

I turn and scurry away as quickly as I can without seeming like I'm sprinting for my life. I can feel Henry's eyes on the back of my head until I turn the corner into the kitchen and lean against the wall, puffing and panting. I clutch my chest, taking a deep breath.

Something isn't right here.

I'm in danger.

Max is in danger.

There's no concrete evidence that Henry killed his wife and buried her in the garden, but one thing is for sure: He knows I suspect him of something.

I wouldn't put it past him to do something drastic to keep his secret safe.

18

Max messages me to say he will be back at eleven that night and not to wait up, so I make dinner for one, eat in silence and then spend the evening stripping more wallpaper and sanding down walls, which turns out to be a very therapeutic process. It's repetitive and requires little concentration other than a bit of brute force. My arms ache, and sweat beads on my forehead after only a few minutes. I play some music on my phone just so I don't have to listen to the deafening silence of the house. I'm not sure I like it. Henry decided to only work for half the day, considering it's a Sunday, and I was more than happy about that. I don't miss Henry being here, but not having Max around as much is making me realise that me being alone is something I'm going to have to get used to. I don't know what the future holds for him, but he's pulling away in the right direction now, and I must let him go when he's ready. Being alone is something I've not had to worry about for seventeen years, but now it's constantly in the back of my mind, like a silent alarm.

The music helps combat the inevitable quiet.

I head upstairs at ten, thoroughly tired but pleased with my progress, take a shower to wash off the dust and sweat, and then crawl into bed, but I can't sleep. Eleven o'clock passes, and then I hear Max come in at ten minutes past. Relief washes over me that he's back safe, so I'm hoping it's enough to send me off to sleep after working hard all day, but my brain refuses to switch off.

I try counting sheep, but only make it to around one hundred before I lose count. I start again; however, I then get bored and give up.

I try the sleep app my therapist suggested, but even the meditation and soothing water sounds don't help switch off my racing mind. I've never been one to find meditation in any form helpful. The quiet just seems to make the voices and anxiety in my head louder, more pronounced, so that I end up focusing on them even more.

I think about the routine I used to have, and a realisation hits me: I don't really have a proper routine here. I have tried, but between renovating the house, worrying about money, stressing about Henry, discovering the body in my garden, Prudence turning up and starting a new job, I haven't been able to get myself into a solid routine.

My therapist would have said it was good for me to step outside my comfort zone. She probably wouldn't have recommended stopping my medication so abruptly though. Perhaps I should see a doctor about starting up again.

My main problem now is Henry and the possibility that he killed his wife seven years ago and buried her under my patio. I know I should just leave it alone. Max and I are happy and safe, but for how long? What if Henry finds out I suspect he murdered his wife? He could turn on us. Would he kill us to keep his secret safe?

I sit up and punch my pillow into a different shape, turning it over so my head rests on the cold side, but it's no use. I can't sleep. I may as well get up. I've always read that if you can't sleep, getting out of bed is the best thing. It helps your mind and body reset. Then when you feel tired again, you go back to bed and try again.

Sighing heavily, I fling back the covers and get out of bed, pulling my dressing gown over my pyjamas. It's a little chilly tonight. I creep down the hallway so as not to disturb Max and head down to the kitchen, deciding to make myself a hot chocolate. The light from the moon isn't enough to give me a clear view of the room, so I turn on a nearby lamp, choosing that over the large light in the ceiling, which would no doubt blind me. Even the dim lamp hurts my eyes.

I stagger into the kitchen and let out a shrill scream as my eyes land on a message scrawled on a piece of paper in red pen on the fridge door.

Hi, Nat. xx

My hands fly to my mouth, snuffling out the remainder of my sob. I step forwards and pull off the note, which is being held in place by a fridge magnet of a frog Max bought with his pocket money when he was seven.

Thundering footsteps down the stairs make me spin on the spot. I scrunch up the paper, hiding it behind my back as Max rushes into the room, his hair sticking up at odd angles, and only wearing a pair of trouser bottoms. Bless him, he's carrying a broom, I assume to fight off an intruder or to protect me.

'Mum! What the hell? Are you okay? I heard a scream.'

'I'm fine. I'm sorry. I saw a mouse.'

He lowers the broom. 'A mouse?'

'Yes, I couldn't sleep and came down to make a hot chocolate, and a mouse ran in front of the fridge just as I was about to open it. I'm sorry if I woke you.'

Max yawns as he props the broom up against the wall and then rubs the back of his neck. 'It's fine. I only got back about half an hour ago.'

'I heard you. Did you have a fun day with Megan?'

'Yeah, she took me to a local castle, and then I took her on a date to a local pub.'

'That's nice.'

'Are you sure you're okay?'

'Yes, perfectly fine,' I reply in a sing-song voice. 'Just not a fan of rodents.' I'm not sure if my son buys my performance, but maybe he's too tired to worry about it.

'Okay, well, maybe we should get some mouse traps.'

'Yes, good idea. Well, goodnight.'

'Night.' Max yawns again as he turns and walks back upstairs like a zombie.

I stand frozen to the spot, the note still clutched in my hand behind my back. It's not a menacing or threatening note, but the fact it's there on my fridge tells me that someone has been in my house and left it. My only thought is that it was Henry who left it.

I rush to the bin, flip the lid and stuff it inside. Out of sight, out of mind.

But it's not, is it?

It's ingrained into my mind's eye just like that engraving on the back of the brooch.

I fetch the milk from the fridge and pour some into a

small saucepan on the hob. My body won't stop trembling. It may be cold tonight, but that's not the reason.

How did Henry get into my house to leave this note, and when did he leave it? He left here at two in the afternoon, almost ten hours ago. I've been either in the kitchen, lounge or my bedroom all day. I didn't hear or see a thing, and the note wasn't there when I turned off the lights and went upstairs to bed earlier. I heard Max let himself in half an hour ago, so why didn't I hear Henry sneak in? He's not exactly small and nimble like Max is. Plus, I would have heard his van pull up in the driveway. Unless ...

Henry's still here.

He must be.

He must have parked the van further down the road so I couldn't see it, then snuck back and hidden himself some-where, waiting for the right time to leave the note, but why leave it in the first place? To mess with me? To prove to me that he can come and go whenever he likes?

I leave the milk simmering on the side and pull my dressing gown tighter around my body. All my senses are on high alert. I can barely catch my breath as I turn and scan the kitchen area, my eyes seeking out any potential hiding place for a six-foot-two man. There can't be many.

My brain keeps telling me I'm being ridiculous and jumping at shadows, but my heart is screaming at me with every beat that he's here and he's dangerous. He's threat-ening me not to keep sticking my nose in where it doesn't belong. Prudence's warning pops into my mind.

I know the safest thing to do is to ignore it and get on with my life, but how can I with this threat looming over my head, over Max's head?

The long curtains I hung the other day in the lounge are

twitching slightly. I flick on the low light to get a better look. Surely, he wasn't hiding in the lounge the whole time I was there stripping and sanding the walls? I was at it for hours.

Heart pounding like a drum, I reach out my shaking hand and yank back the curtains.

He's not there.

The window is cracked open ever so slightly, enough to cause a draft and make the curtains twitch.

I take a large inhale, allowing the curtain to fall back into place. This is stupid. No one is in the house. I make a conscious effort to always keep the door locked, even when I'm inside.

I shake my head, turn and walk back into the kitchen to finish making myself a hot chocolate. As I stir, my ears pick up a slight rustle. I stop, place the spoon down and pick up the hot saucepan of milk, ready to launch it at Henry's face should he be standing behind me with a knife.

I turn and find myself looking at nothing.

The rustle was my own damn feet on the tiled floor.

For fuck's sake. I need to get a grip. I'm scaring myself with my own vivid imagination.

I pour the hot milk into a mug, take it upstairs and get into bed after checking the wardrobe, behind the curtains and then placing a chair underneath the door handle.

I still don't sleep.

THE NEXT MORNING, I barely have the energy to keep my eyes open. All the hot chocolate did was make me need a wee an hour later, so I had to traipse out into the hall and then freaked myself out in the bathroom when the shower curtain pulled across the bath gave me visions of the film *Psycho*.

Max saunters in at eight. 'You got work today?' he asks.

'Not till later.'

'Is Henry in today?'

'Um ... I think so. I don't know.'

The toast pops up from the toaster, but I ignore it. 'Max, I'm thinking of asking another builder to finish the renovations.'

'Good.'

'I think you were right. He gives a weird vibe. I don't feel safe around him.'

Max stops what he's doing, which is pouring himself a glass of orange juice from the fridge. 'What do you mean? Has he done something to hurt you?'

'No, no, nothing like that. It's just a feeling I have sometimes. I think he might be lying about the whereabouts of his wife, and I'm not sure I trust him.'

Max takes a long slurp of juice. 'What happened to his wife?'

'She ran off with another man.'

Max scoffs. 'No wonder he's trying to weasel his way into our family. He's probably been trying to replace her with you.'

The fact my son can see something that's been right in front of my face the whole time astounds me. Why have I been so blind? Has the withdrawal from my meds affected me this much? Not only has my brain fog been debilitating, but I've been making all the wrong decisions, sleepwalking through the past couple of weeks, allowing a man to blackmail me, and not having any clear direction on what I'm doing.

While I'm mulling this over, Max keeps a frown on his

face as he walks across to the bin with the empty carton of juice. I hear him step on the pedal and the lid flip up.

I begin to butter my toast.

'Mum ... what's this?'

'What's what?'

'This note. Who wrote this?'

I gasp and spin on the spot, clutching the kitchen counter behind me.

Max holds the note up, still holding the empty juice carton too. 'What is this?'

'I ... Nothing. It's nothing. I guess maybe Henry was about to write me a note but then decided not to in the end.'

'Then why are you freaking out right now? Did you find this last night? Is that why you screamed in the middle of the night?'

'No! I ... Yes.' I hang my head. It's time I came clean to Max. I can't keep this up any longer. The stress and anxiety it's causing me is going to push us apart all over again, and over the past few days I feel as if we've turned a corner in our relationship. He no longer answers me with one-word answers. He asks me how I am and seems genuinely concerned for me. If I continue to lie to him, I'm just going to go backwards to where we were in Birmingham, and I don't want that to happen ever again.

'Look, I didn't tell you the whole truth about Henry. The truth is that he has something on me, something bad, and he's blackmailing me. But now I think I have something on him. I think he killed his wife.'

'What the hell? Why would you think that?'

I take a deep breath. 'Because I found a dead body underneath a patio in the garden, and Henry helped me re-bury it, and I think it's his wife, and that's why he convinced me not to tell the police. I made the wrong decision. I know I did, but now I'm stuck, and I don't know what to do.'

Max slowly lowers the glass of orange juice and places it on the counter. 'Did you just say you found a dead body in our garden?'

I look at him and nod, tears filling my eyes. 'Yes.'

'Holy fuck,' he whispers.

'Kind of makes the idea of you dealing drugs seem like nothing,' I say, hoping to inject a little light-heartedness into the situation. I have no idea how Max is going to react to this, but it's time I trusted my son.

'Hmm,' he says.

'Was I right to tell you?'

Max takes a deep breath. 'Yes.'

'I just need to find proof or get him to admit that he did it somehow. Then he'll leave us alone.'

19

I spend the morning finishing off the sanding, which has taken me longer than expected, and then do some painting in the hallways upstairs. Painting is just as soothing as sanding. The repetitive motion of the paintbrush ensures my mind is focused on that rather than the million and one things fighting for front position in my head. Even though my arms ache, it's an ache I've come to relish because it means I've worked hard, and knowing I'm adding my own flourish and hard work ethic to this house is making the process all the more special.

The sun is shining delightfully this morning, so once I'm done with the sanding and painting, I take a cup of coffee and walk around the garden to get some fresh air. The fumes from the paint were causing my head to feel a bit foggy.

Now I'm not painting, I don't have the distraction, so my mind replays the conversation with Max earlier. I stop when I reach the new patio.

Shit. I didn't realise I walked over this far.

Tears fill my eyes as I stare down at the slabs, imagining

the horror that lies underneath in the dark, cold soil. Before I know it, I'm on my knees, the coffee mug on the ground, crying my eyes out.

The truth is, I'm in too deep now. How can I possibly get out of this situation without putting myself or Max in danger? The worst thing would be for me to get locked up in prison and for Max to be by himself. Since he's still under eighteen and has no other relatives, he'd probably go into foster care, and then what? It doesn't even bear thinking about.

The one thing that needs to happen is for Henry to leave us alone. I need him out of my life. He knows too much, but I know more. I'm almost certain his wife is buried underneath my feet, and he was the one who put her there. If only the dead could talk.

I need to be brave, put a plan into action and let him know that he doesn't scare me. He's not the only one who could lose everything if this goes wrong. And he needs to know that I hold the power too, even though it doesn't feel like I do.

THE NEXT DAY, Max heads off early to work, and Henry arrives a little later than usual. He looks like utter shit. His face is pale, and the shadows under his eyes make him look like he hasn't slept in a week, and look menacing. In fact, it wouldn't surprise me if he keeled over or vomited at some point today. The man looks positively sickly.

'Yeesh,' I say when I see the state of him.

'I'm fine,' he says with a grunt, seeing my expression. 'Just a hangover.' Henry coughs violently and wipes his mouth with the back of his hand. 'Yeah, well ... seeing that brooch brought back a lot of old memories, and I sort of fell down a dark hole. Sorry about the other night. I always get a bit crazy around the time of year my wife left me.'

I fold my arms across my chest, signalling that I'm putting up my defences. I'm not sure I even accept his apology. 'Were you here last night, Henry?'

He scoffs. 'Why would I be here? I left yesterday afternoon at two, went home and started drinking. In fact, by last night I was so far gone again, I had my head down the toilet most of the night; then I passed out in a puddle of my own piss and vomit.'

'And yet, no one can confirm all that and that you were actually drinking all night at home?' I continue.

'Why else would I look like this?'

I shrug nonchalantly. 'I don't know. You tell me.'

'Why do you keep doing this, Nat? Why can't you just leave me alone? I've done nothing wrong here. All I've done is help you the whole time, and how do you repay me? By accusing me of fucking stupid things and thinking I have some weird vendetta against you.'

'What was the note about, then?'

'What note?'

'The note you left on my fridge door!' I shout. His insistence at being innocent in all this is grating on my last nerve and making me snap. I hardly ever shout or lose my temper. I'd rather bottle all my feelings inside than make a scene or have a confrontation with someone. But Henry is slowly turning me into someone I'm not.

'You've lost it,' he says with a laugh, turning to walk away. 'I never left anything on your fridge door.'

'I'm warning you, Henry. Leave me and Max the hell alone, or you'll regret it,' I say to his back.

I squeak as he turns and lunges towards me quicker than I expect a man of his size to move, especially since he's feeling so delicate today. His large body ploughs against mine; one large hand grasps me around the throat, the other pointing a stiff finger right in my face. He is so close that spittle flies from his mouth and splashes against my face.

He squeezes his hand tighter around my throat, hissing through his teeth as he says, 'Don't you fucking threaten me, you heartless bitch. I'm warning you, Nat. The last woman who crossed me ...' He stops, his mouth opening and closing, like he's trying to take his words back.

'Y-yes?' I manage to stutter. I'm struggling to breathe, but I will not beg him to let me go. I have more self-respect than that.

Henry releases his grip around my throat ever so slightly. The tips of his fingers are still digging in so hard that I can feel a sharp sting from his fingernails piercing my skin.

'Just remember, Nat. I can ruin this perfect little life of yours in an instant. I can deny everything. I never helped you re-bury Prudence. You were the one who put her body in the ground. Not me.'

'You're forgetting about something, Henry.'

Henry's grip tightens again, and I cough, desperately trying to pry his fingers away from my throat, but he's so strong, his muscles tight and built from years of hard labour. He loosens up enough for me to speak.

'There's a very professional patio covering that body now. A patio I'd never be skilful or knowledgeable enough to lay by myself. How would you explain that to the police?'

Henry's lips curl into a snarl, and he presses his lips so close to my ear, I feel them brushing my lobe. 'Don't even think about it, bitch.'

'I don't blame your wife for cheating on you,' I say, sounding more confident than I feel.

Another snarl, this time a growl emanates from his lips. 'It's a shame I never found out who was shagging her.'

'Or what? You would have done something to hurt him, like you did your wife?'

'What? I never hurt my wife. Do you just like making shit up about me?'

Damn, this guy is good.

'So you didn't kill your wife and bury her in the garden?'

Fuck. Why did I say that?

I expect him to explode at me, hit me, shout expletives at me, deny it, something. But he does none of those things.

In fact, he grins, and it sends all the hairs on the back of my neck and arms to standing.

Henry takes a step back, finally letting go of my throat. I cough and lean forwards, gulping in air, which stings my delicate throat.

'Nice try, Nat,' he says with a chuckle.

I don't point out to him that he hasn't denied it.

'I don't want you here anymore, Henry. I want you to leave us alone. If you don't, then I'll tell anyone who'll listen that you murdered your wife and buried her in my garden.'

'Are you saying there's two bodies in your garden?'

'No, Prudence is alive.'

'What? How would you know that?'

'Because she came to visit me.' I suck in more air, but my throat is screaming at me. It burns like a match has been lit and held against my throat.

'Whoever that woman was, it wasn't Prudence. Prudence is dead and buried in the garden, and my wife ran off with some bloke. Get your facts straight, Nat, and stop accusing me.'

He walks away, and my legs crumple underneath me. I slump to the ground, burying my face in my hands, and sob. All the while my throat is on fire, and I can barely swallow back the bile that rises from my stomach.

MY THROAT BURNS SO MUCH the only thing I can swallow for the next few hours is sips of cool water. I manage to choke down some painkillers, but they get stuck halfway down my throat, and I retch until I bring them back up again, coughing and spluttering. I study my throat in the bathroom mirror, running my fingers delicately over the obvious bruising and finger marks on either side. It looks like I have several giant hickeys decorating my neck. Perfect.

How the hell am I supposed to hide these contusions from Max and Darren and other people? I dab a bit of foundation over the bruises, but my make-up is the cheap stuff, barely covering it at all, just making them slightly lighter.

I wear a top with a higher neckline than normal, but it doesn't reach all the way up my neck. It's too warm anyway. I'm just going to have to make up something on the spot if anyone asks me.

Darren clearly sees the damage straight away. 'Jesus, Natasha, what the hell happened to your neck?'

'Um ... some sort of reaction to something I dug up in the garden. I kept scratching it last night, and now it's spreading. I may have scratched a bit too hard in my sleep.'

'Ouch. Looks sore.'

'Yeah.' I quickly get on with my usual jobs and duck out

of sight before he can question me further. It's going to be a long day.

Max and Megan come in halfway through my shift and order some soft drinks. Megan's eyes spend a fraction longer on my neck than is deemed normal, and we lock eyes as I hand her the two Cokes. She smiles, but it doesn't reach her eyes. I have a feeling she knows exactly what the marks on my neck are. I hope she keeps it quiet from Max, who hasn't seemed to have noticed yet.

I watch them take their seats in the corner of the pub, smiling and laughing and touching each other lightly on the arms, holding hands and every so often sharing a light kiss. They are so cute together, and when Max is with her, he practically glows.

Twenty minutes later, Megan walks up to where I'm standing behind the bar, washing up glasses. She keeps her voice low as she says, 'It was Henry, wasn't it?'

'W-what?'

'The marks on your neck.'

'How did you—'

'He did it to me once.'

'What!' I shriek, then wince as I realise just how loud it was. It also hurts my throat. I grasp her arm and pull her into a quiet corner while the customers around us go back to their food and drinks. 'What do you mean he did it to you? When?'

'About a year ago.'

'Why didn't you report him to the police?'

'Because he threatened me.'

'Fuck,' I mutter. 'Why didn't you tell me this before?'

'I'm sorry, I guess I just thought it was a one-off. I mean, I did antagonise him and say some stuff about him that I shouldn't have. I was having a hard time at school, and he said something a bit inappropriate, and I just snapped. I called him a loser, and worse, I made fun of the fact his wife left him. It was wrong of me, but he cornered me outside and squeezed my throat, threatened to do more than that if I ever mentioned his wife again. He really has an issue with people talking about her, especially when it comes to her cheating on him.'

I gulp and wince as my throat burns at the action. 'Listen, thank you for telling me, but please don't tell Max about this. I don't want him to worry.'

Megan flicks her eyes over to him. 'He should know, Natasha. Henry is clearly dangerous. You should fire him.'

I shake my head slowly. 'I'm trying. Believe me. I wish it were that simple. I really do.' I reach out and gently place my hand on her arm, giving it a quick squeeze. 'Please, please, just don't tell him. I'll find a way to tell him on my own. It should come from me.'

Megan sighs. 'Okay, I won't, but be careful, okay? Tell the police. Don't let him get away with it. Not like I did.'

'I won't. I promise. I just need some more time.'

Megan gives me a hug and then rejoins Max at the table. He glances over at me, probably wondering what the two of us were talking about so secretively in the corner. I give him a reassuring smile, and he turns to Megan. I can't hear what they're saying, but it seems she's putting his mind at ease that it's nothing to worry about.

I reluctantly go back to my shift, counting the minutes until it's time to go home and take a long, hot bath. I'm still struggling to swallow solid food, so I keep myself going with water and juice.

. . .

THE REST of my shift drags, and by the end of it, I can barely speak because it hurts too much. My stomach is also growling with hunger. I need to try to eat something, but every time I do, it feels like I'm swallowing razor blades. I escape out the door the second my shift is over and race to my car, slamming the door hard enough that it vibrates the whole frame. I drive on autopilot home, forgetting that I needed to pick up more milk and only remember as I pull up into the driveway. It's too late now. The milk can wait.

Max is in the lounge, finishing the sanding of the far wall when I walk in. I must have missed a bit. My heart skips a beat when I see him. I'm hoping it's dark enough that he won't notice the bruises, which seem to have gotten darker over the last few hours.

'Hey, Mum.'

'Hey,' I manage to croak.

He looks up. 'What's wrong?'

I clear my throat, immediately wincing as the pain engulfs me. 'I ... um ... Henry attacked me.'

'Shit. Are you okay?' Max walks up to me and looks at my neck. 'What the fuck? They look like finger marks.'

'He was pretty angry, but he denied everything. He's still convinced that it's Prudence who's buried, but I know for a fact it isn't.'

'How do you know?' Max's face is full of confusion. He's searching for the answer before I answer him.

'She turned up at the door the other day and introduced herself. At first, I didn't believe she was Prudence, but the more she talked about her life here, I believed her. Plus, she looks like the younger woman in the photos we've found around the house.'

'Why did she come here?'

'To meet me and to sort of say goodbye to the house. Anyway, we got talking, and we got onto the subject of Henry working on the house, and she told me to be careful of him. She said his wife's name was Catherine. It was at that point I realised the brooch read C & H on the back. Catherine and Henry. The brooch belonged to Henry's wife. I asked him about it, and he didn't deny that it was hers.'

Max nods along, taking it all in.

'Anyway, I ... think he killed her. At the time, when I found the body, I hadn't paid the dealer back, and I was scared about the police turning up and being on the news and putting you at risk, so between Henry and I, we somehow made the decision to keep the body a secret. Now, thinking back, Henry was merely playing along, convinced me it was Prudence, and re-buried the body deeper in the ground.'

We spend a couple of moments in silence, neither one of us knowing what to say to move the conversation forwards.

'Maybe we should move again,' I say eventually with a long sigh. I've been toying with the idea, but it really does seem like the only safe option. Would Henry try to find us? The last thing I want is another dangerous man chasing us across the country. If we ran again, would we be running forever?

'No, Mum. We ran away once before because of me and the situation I got myself into, but this time we're not going to run. Besides, you said it yourself, we're happy here. I'm happy here. I have Megan, and you ... well, you're happy here, right?'

'Yes, of course I am. If it weren't for Henry, I'd be perfectly content to stay here forever.'

'Then we need to make Henry go away.'

'I wish it were that simple. If I report him to the police, then he could easily just tell them about the body and spin it so that I'm the one who made him bury her.'

'But if you're right and he killed his wife, then he's the one who's guilty. Not you.' Max stares at me for a few moments. I'm expecting him to blow up at me, like he used to do, accuse me of being a hypocrite, tell me that it's all my fault, but he doesn't. His eyes just blink rapidly as he looks at the bruises around my neck. 'Has Henry done anything like this before?' he asks.

'What do you mean?'

'You say you think he killed his wife ... He's clearly dangerous. Has he ever hurt anyone else?'

I know exactly what he's trying to get at. I gave Megan my word that I wouldn't tell him, but he's figured it out for himself. I can't deny it; otherwise he'll know I'm lying to him, which will make him lose his trust in me.

'Yes,' I say. 'I believe so.'

Max clenches his fists at his sides. 'He hurt Megan, didn't he? That's why she never wants to stay at the house when he's around.'

I nod once. 'I believe so,' I repeat.

'Now I'm really going to kill him,' says Max. His body is practically vibrating with anger.

'Max, let's not go rushing into things, okay? We need to tread carefully. Just follow my lead. I think I may have an idea. If we pretend that we're going to sell the house and stop the renovations, then maybe Henry will realise we don't need him anymore. He'll move on.'

'But he lives around here, doesn't he?'

'Yes, but at least he won't be visiting the house every day. If he continues to watch us, then that's reason enough to go to the police and report him for trespassing or stalking or something.'

Max unclenches his fists, but his shoulders are still tense. I know he's angry and wants to protect Megan and me, but he's just a boy. If he confronts Henry, there's no telling what could happen. I can't risk it. Max could get seriously hurt.

'Promise me you won't talk to Henry or mention anything about it to Megan either.'

'Fine, but if he's not gone by the end of the week, then I'm going to have a word with him.'

I let out a long breath. I have three days to get rid of Henry before my son puts himself in danger.

The trouble is, Henry is smart.

Anything could set him off.

I must be careful how I play this moving forwards.

What's my next move?

20

The next morning, I'm a bag of nerves, shaking and sweating, waiting for Henry to arrive. I hate that he makes me feel this way, and I can't even blame it on the medication withdrawal anymore because it's been almost two weeks since I took a dose, so it's out of my system now.

Max has gone to work, leaving me to bite my nails while I look out the window, waiting for Henry's van to trundle up the driveway. Max wanted to stay with me, but I told him no and had to practically shove him out the door and into Megan's car. She gave me a sweet wave, and I waved and smiled back, pretending like I wasn't about to confront a possibly dangerous killer.

Henry waltzes through the front door a few minutes later.

'Morning,' he says. I find it fascinating and unsettling that he can act so normal around me considering the run-in we had yesterday. He's a psychopath, possibly a narcissist. It's as if it never happened. At least he looks brighter this morning. Clearly, all the alcohol is out of his system now.

My hands instinctively go to my neck, feeling the tender areas. 'Henry, I'm afraid I have some bad news.'

He stops and drops his tool bag. 'What now?'

'You remember I said that Prudence turned up on my doorstep the other day? Well, she has contacted my solicitor, demanding I move out of the house straight away.'

Henry's eyes narrow, the cogs whirring in his brain. 'You're lying.'

'I promise you, Prudence is demanding I move out.'

'Even if that were true, it's too late. You signed the deed, right? The house is legally yours. You were left it in the will, not her. She has no say in its ownership. I'm not stupid, Nat.'

I gulp and continue my speech. 'Yes, but she's very insistent and feels she's owed some compensation. Therefore, I've decided rather than fight her on this, to sell the house and give her half the money. I'm not happy here, and to be honest, the renovations are too expensive, and I'm struggling to pay all the bills. It will be easier to move somewhere smaller and cheaper.'

Henry turns and faces me, his hands on his hips. 'And she's agreed to that, has she?'

'Yes. I'm putting the house on the market as it is, so I'm afraid I'll no longer be needing your building services. I'll happily pay you the money I owe for the work you've done. You can threaten me all you like regarding the body in the garden, but I have proof that you're responsible for killing your wife. I spoke to Prudence about you, and she said she saw you that day in the garden when you and Catherine argued. She saw you strangle her, Henry. That seems to be your MO for hurting women. There's no point in denying it.

There's a witness. Maybe you didn't mean to do it. Maybe you only meant to scare her, like what you did to me and Megan, but whatever happened, your wife died, and you buried her in the garden. Prudence saw you, and she has agreed to testify if you continue to harass me or Max. She doesn't want the intrusion on the property either. I think it's best for all of us involved that you leave Max and me alone. We'll keep your secret if you keep ours.'

My breathing is ragged, and I must fight my lungs to not draw in too much oxygen; otherwise I'm at risk of hyperventilating and giving away the fact that I've just lied through my teeth.

'Wow,' he says. 'That's quite a story, Nat. Well done.'

'It is. You're right. You thought you'd got away with murder all these years. Now, it's time for you to decide. Leave this house and don't come back, leave Max and me alone, or risk going to prison for the rest of your life.'

'What about you, huh? If I go down, then I'm taking you down with me.'

'With Prudence's testimony, the police won't have anything on me. I can easily say that you threatened me to keep the body a secret and move it elsewhere. I have no motive for killing your wife. I didn't even know her. I was living elsewhere, miles away from here at the time. I have a solid alibi.'

Henry steps towards me, and I take a step back, but I bump into a wall. He leans in close. I hold my breath so I don't smell his odour. 'I didn't kill my wife. Prudence is lying about what she saw.'

'Can you really afford to risk it though?' I reply, my words shaking at the end.

Henry smiles at my nervousness. 'Whatever. You win this

round, Nat.' He winks at me, picks up his tool bag and heads upstairs.

'Where are you going? I said you needed to get out now.'

'A good builder never leaves his work unfinished. Don't worry, I'll be out of here by the time you get back from work this evening. You have my word.'

I grind my teeth. He's baiting me. He won't leave straight away. He's trying to prove that he still has power over me. There's nothing I can do, so I accept his decision and get ready to leave for work.

A sense of relief has washed over me at the thought of this being over soon. But another part of me knows Henry is still playing a game with me.

And it frustrates me beyond belief that he's still winning.

I KEEP REPLAYING the conversation with Henry in my head all day. Did I say enough? Did he even believe me, or was he faking his acceptance of the matter, lulling me into a false sense of security? Did he let me win that round, or has he got something else planned for me? I'm glad Max is going to be with Megan most of the day. The last thing I want is Max and Henry alone in the house without me. Max is hotheaded, and I can't guarantee he won't explode at Henry should he be given half the chance.

Adrian left a message on my phone during my shift, asking me to call him back when I can, but I haven't had the chance to return his call yet, so I make a note to call him tomorrow morning before my shift. It's too late now, almost ten o'clock at night by the time I pull up in the driveway.

Henry's van is still here, parked just off to the side.

My blood boils as I get out and slam the car door. Why the hell is he still here?

Didn't I make myself perfectly clear I wanted him gone? He even said himself he'd be out of here by the time I was back from work tonight. He gave me his word. Not that his word means fuck all to me.

As soon as the car slams shut, a loud shout pierces the darkness.

I recognise Max's slightly high-pitched voice straight away. A mother always knows the sound of her son's cries for help.

My head perks up. It came from inside the house.

My legs are running towards the front door before my head realises what I'm doing. I barge into the house, ready to defend my child.

'Max!' My head snaps from side to side as I desperately search for the origin of the shout. 'Max!' The lights are all on in the house, blinding me.

He's not in the lounge, so I spin and race to the kitchen.

A shrill scream erupts from my lungs as I see Henry and Max grappling against the worktop. Henry has his large hands wrapped around Max's throat, and Max's eyes are bulging out of his sockets, the whites streaked with red veins. There's blood trickling from his nose.

'Leave him alone!'

Henry doesn't even acknowledge my presence. He keeps squeezing, his jaw clenched and his arms shaking with the force it's taking to hold Max in place. Max is gasping, coughing for breath, doing his best to pull on Henry's arms to loosen his grip, but Henry is rock solid. I know I don't have the strength to pull Henry off him myself, so I do the only option available to me.

I yank the nearest drawer open, grab a sharp knife and throw myself towards Henry.

I don't think. I just act.

The knife slides into his side easier and quicker than I imagined, like a hot knife through butter. Warm blood squirts out and splashes onto my hand clenching the handle of the knife.

Time stands still while Henry's brain connects the pain receptors to what's happening in his body. The grip on Max's neck eases, and Max coughs, gulping in air and shoving Henry to the side. Henry grabs the worktop to stop himself from falling over. I yank Max away from Henry as Henry grunts and clutches his side, finally collapsing onto one knee.

'I told you to stay away from us!'

Henry opens his mouth, but only blood spurts out as he gives an almighty cough. Blood splatters the worktops and the pale walls, like an abstract painting. He is still pressing his right hand against the knife wound in his left side, which is pulsing and oozing rivers of blood. His foot slips in the viscous liquid spreading out across the tiled floor, and his body goes down hard with a loud thump.

Max and I stand shaking, our arms gripping tightly around one another as we watch the life slowly drain from Henry's body. I'm not sure what organ I've punctured, but it's enough to inflict serious injury.

He starts to mutter obscenities at me. 'Fucking b-bitch ... Call an a-ambulance!'

Max clutches my arm so hard that it hurts, but I don't pull away from him. I pull him closer instead, my arms around him, using my body as a shield.

'M-Mum? Should we call an ambulance?'

'No,' is my immediate response. I don't even need to think about it. 'No, we can't, Max.'

'Why not? I know he's a shitty guy, but you've just stabbed him. He's going to die if we don't help him.' Max is close to tears. I can see his eyes swimming with them.

I squeeze his hand. 'Listen to me, okay? If we call an ambulance, whether he lives or dies, the news is going to get out. You and I are going to be questioned. If he dies from his injuries, then I could be arrested and sentenced for murder. If Henry survives his injuries, then he could make a lot of trouble for us. We spoke about getting rid of Henry. He's threatened and attacked me. He's done the same to you. I can't let him manipulate me any longer.' I take a deep breath. 'Either way, whether he lives or dies, if we call an ambulance, we're done for. Do you understand? This will never stop.'

Max stares at me, his eyes finally drowning in tears. They stream down his face. 'W-what are you saying?'

I turn and look at Henry, who has grown very still. He's still alive, but barely. The blood is still oozing from his wound, the knife now lying on the floor next to him, having been dislodged as he fell to the floor.

'We let him die, and we bury his body in the garden. I know the perfect spot.' I lock eyes with my enemy. His face is contorted with rage and pain. He doesn't have long left. He knows exactly what I'm talking about. It's rather poetic, really. He killed his wife and buried her in the garden, and now he's going to join her there for eternity.

Henry lets out a low growl in response.

Max shakes his head. 'I don't know ...'

'Max, I told you that you need to trust me on this. We cannot allow this man to ruin our lives, do you hear me?

We've been through too much to give up now. It's better for all of us if he just ... goes away ... quietly.'

'Goes away! You're talking about a man *dying*, Mum.'

Henry coughs violently. Max and I turn to look at him.

'D-didn't ... k-k-kill ...' He coughs one last time, and then every last ounce of life leaves his body. He lies in the puddle of blood as his hand falls away from his wound, splashing down into the liquid.

Max stumbles to the nearest chair and grabs the back of it, his knuckles turning white with the effort of holding on, fighting to stay standing. He looks like he might vomit at any second.

I need to keep control of this situation. I wish it hadn't come to this, I really do, but I didn't have any other choice. Henry could have killed Max. If I had arrived at the house only a few minutes later, it could have been too late. My son could have been dead.

We needed Henry to disappear from our lives, and now he will, just not in the way either of us were expecting. Max and I must work quickly and come up with a convincing story to explain his disappearance. Maybe he went off on one of his drinking binges and never came back, ending his life on his own terms. Perhaps he took on another job elsewhere and left suddenly because it paid more. As far as I know, Henry doesn't have family in the area. He never mentioned his parents.

It could work.

No, it *will* work.

'Max, listen to me. We need to get him out of the house and into the garden. There's shovels and things in the shed. Go and get them and the wheelbarrow out the back. Now.'

Max can't drag his eyes away from Henry's body. He's turned catatonic.

'Max!' I clap my hands once in front of his face, jolting him out of his trance.

He looks at me, his face pale.

'Help me. We can do this. We'll be okay.'

Max's eyes still swim with tears as he nods and shuffles out the door, leaving me in the kitchen with Henry. His cold, dead eyes stare up at me, wide and glassy, but full of hate. I bend down and gently close them, blocking out that evil glare forever.

The weight I've been carrying around for the past few weeks since Henry started causing trouble has disappeared from my shoulders again. I told myself I'd do anything to keep Max and me safe, to keep hold of the life we're building here. I didn't realise it meant having to kill someone to do it.

Max returns with the wheelbarrow and a roll of carpet. It's the old carpet Henry ripped up from the upstairs room. I haven't had the chance to take it to the dump yet. We lay out the carpet next to the body and then roll Henry onto it, sealing him up in it like a large burrito.

Between us, we manage to lift him into the wheelbarrow and push him out into the garden. Max grabs a torch, as the darkness has settled in now. The chilly air makes goose-bumps appear on my skin, but I know it won't take long before I'm dripping with sweat. Another hole needs to be dug.

I can't believe this is the second grave I'll have dug in less than three weeks of living here.

I direct Max through the garden until we reach the patio where Henry's wife is buried. There's no way I'm digging up the patio again, so I'll have to settle for burying Henry next to it and then perhaps lay another patio myself on top. I watched Henry do it; it didn't look too complicated. It doesn't even need to be a professional job. I just need to extend the current patio over the area. There aren't any slabs left, but there are still some bags of cement and rubble left over that I can use.

'Here,' I say, pointing at the spot next to the patio.

'Why here?' asks Max, out of breath after having pushed the wheelbarrow through the overgrowth and long grass.

'This is where his wife is buried.'

Max pales and looks down at the ground.

'Plus, it's out of the way. We'll put him in, mix up some concrete, then pile the earth on top. Tomorrow, I'll buy some more slabs, and we'll lay an extra bit of patio over the top of the grave so no animal or anything can dig in the earth. Henry explained exactly how to do it properly.'

Max merely nods.

He picks up the shovel that's laid across the wheelbarrow. 'I guess there's no turning back after this, is there?'

'No, I'm afraid not.' I pick up the other spade as I watch my son begin to dig a hole. I always imagined him and me working together on a project, enjoying each other's company, but this wasn't what I had in mind. Not by a long shot.

IT TAKES us almost two hours to dig Henry's grave. Henry's a large guy, but at least this time I have help with the digging. We tip Henry into the deep hole, mix up the cement, pour that in, then pile the dirt back on top. We mostly work in silence, neither of us wasting energy on talking. We know what needs to be done.

Once we've thrown the last of the dirt on top of the grave, we walk back to the house and begin to clean the kitchen. By the time we're finished, the whole house reeks of bleach, and Max and I are covered in sweat, dirt and bloodstains.

It's almost two in the morning by the time we're done. Max takes a shower, and then I do the same once he's done, sealing our stained clothes in a black bag, ready to burn in the open fire pit in the garden.

We eventually sit at the kitchen table with a hot chocolate each, staring at each other. My son and I now share a deadly secret that could rip our small family apart if it were to get out. I know I made the right decision to protect us, but it doesn't make me feel any better. I'd do the same again if it meant protecting Max. There's nothing I won't do to protect my son.

Henry was a bad man. He was trying to control and manipulate me. He threatened Max and tried to kill him. He tried to kill me. It's better that he's gone.

Now, I just need to make sure that no one misses him.

21

It's gone eleven in the morning, and Max is still asleep. I call his manager at the Co-op and tell him that Max is sick and has a high fever and won't be in work today. I also text Megan, letting her know she needn't pick him up later. Megan texts me back, asking how he is, and I explain that he's still asleep and isn't well. She says she'll call in on him after her shift.

I drive into town and buy more slabs and cement. I used up the last of the cement bags in covering Henry, but I still need more to lay the slabs. I silently thank Henry for showing me how to mix cement. Never did I think I'd end up needing those skills again only a few weeks later. In a round-about way, he unknowingly sealed his own fate.

I begin to sow the seeds of Henry's disappearance when I tell the building merchants that Henry didn't turn up for work this morning and has left me in the lurch with regards to the house renovations. They are apologetic and sympathetic, but don't ask too many awkward questions. Thankfully.

Adrian waves at me as I cross the road. Damn, I forgot he'd tried to call me, and I never returned his message. I don't even know when that was. Time seems to have all rolled into one lately, the hours and days blurring around the edges.

'Hi, Nat!' He jogs up to me with a smile on his face. Since when has he started calling me Nat?

'Hi, Adrian. I'm so sorry I haven't called you back. I've been so busy at the house, and it completely slipped my mind.'

'That's no problem. Is everything okay at the house?'

'Not really. You remember that builder I hired? Henry Clayton? Well, he's buggered off to a new job somewhere and left me with unfinished work at the house.'

A frown quickly replaces Adrian's smile. 'I'm so sorry to hear that. I really am. I didn't like him as a bloke, but he's a decent builder. It's the first time I've heard of him leaving a job half-finished. He usually takes great pride in seeing things through. I can't believe he's done that to you. Any idea where he's gone?'

I shake my head. 'No, not a clue. He just left me a note last night to say he wasn't coming back because he's been offered a better job elsewhere.'

'How odd,' says Adrian, scratching his chin.

'Anyway,' I say, desperate to change the subject, 'what was it you called me about?'

'Oh, um, I mean, well ...' Adrian blushes pink and looks away, avoiding eye contact.

Oh God ... I know that look.

'I was wondering if you wanted to grab a drink some-time, after you finish work one day this week?' He scratches the back of his neck, finally swivelling his gaze around to meet my eyes.

Now, it's my turn to blush red.

Even though I guessed correctly, I still didn't expect to be asked out on a date by Adrian, or by anyone, to be honest. It's been a long time since a man has asked me, and I have to fight my automatic urge to say no.

It's always been my go-to answer over the years.

I gulp, realising he's still waiting for my answer. 'Oh, um … sure, yeah, why not? I finish work at eight tomorrow night. Would that work?'

The smile is back across Adrian's face. 'Brilliant! Yes! I'll pop into the pub, shall I?'

'Sure.'

'Great. And listen, Nat, I'm really sorry about Henry walking out on you like that. Have you still got that list of builders I recommended?'

I nod my response.

'Good. Any one of those guys will help you out. I promise.'

'Thanks for your help. See you tomorrow.'

'Bye, Nat. Have a good day.'

I can feel his eyes on me as I walk to my car. Normally, after being asked out on a date, I'd feel elated and buzzing with excitement, but all I feel is fear gripping my insides because going on a date is the last thing I need right now.

I've got a patio to lay today.

The building merchants are dropping off the slabs in an hour, so I need to get home and prep the area a bit more. I'll have to start without Max. If he's still asleep, I'll leave him be. He's already deeper involved than I'd like him to be.

· · ·

WHEN I PULL up in my driveway, yanking the hand brake on harder than necessary, another problem stares me directly in the face, one that I completely forgot about and walked straight past earlier without giving it a second thought.

Henry's work van is still here.

I can't be telling people that he's done a runner on me but leave his van here for all the world to see. What builder wouldn't take their van and all his tools with them? Where the hell am I supposed to hide the blasted thing? I have less than an hour before the building merchants arrive with the slabs.

I squeeze the bridge of my nose with my fingers and then tap my fingers together, hoping it calms my anxiety. Things are slipping again. I keep forgetting what I'm supposed to do and in which order. I can't let things get on top of me. I used to think I was good at prioritising, especially as a single mother who had no choice but to juggle a million and one jobs. No one else was going to do it. Now, I have another job to do.

And that's to get rid of a dead man's van.

The patio will have to wait a while.

I had the sense to check Henry's pockets before rolling him up in the carpet, but all I found was a stick of gum. There had been no van keys. When I open the door, they are still in the ignition, so I could just drive it somewhere and dump it, but then what? How would I get back here? What if someone sees me driving it? What if the van is found without Henry in it? It will look like he's been abducted or something.

I need a quick, short-term solution while I can come up with a more solid, long-term one. There's a garage on this property, around the side of the house, but the last time I looked, it was full of junk, boxes and tools. There's no way I have enough time to clear it out and hide the van inside.

A reckless thought pops into my head: the pond.

But then, how would I get it out again to dispose of it properly? What if the pond isn't deep enough to submerge the van?

I stand and stare at the van with my hands on my hips and don't hear Max creep up behind me.

'Mum?'

I jump and turn around. 'Max, you scared me.'

'What are you doing?'

'I have the building merchants arriving in less than an hour with the new patio slabs and bags of cement to cover … you know what, and I have Henry's van parked in my driveway after I've already told people he's done a runner on me.'

'I'll drive it round the back of the house and hide it under a tarp.'

I let out a breath and nod. Sometimes the best solution is often the simplest. It's not perfect, but it will do for the time being. The building merchants won't have any need to go around the back of the property, and there's no way of seeing anything from the driveway.

I let Max drive the van, making sure he wears gloves and wipes down the surfaces; then we park it next to the garage and use a tarp to cover it. It could very well be just an old car left to rust here. It will be moved eventually, but that's a job and problem for another day. Just one thing at a time.

A horn signals the arrival of the building merchants, who begin unloading the slabs and piling them in the driveway, along with the bags of cement. Max and I watch in silence.

We swap glances when the building merchants drive away with a toot of a horn.

'Time for you to learn how to lay a patio,' I say.

FOUR HOURS LATER, a crude patio is laid. It's not perfectly even and doesn't match up to the finish of the patio that Henry laid, but after a bit of wear and tear, no one will be able to tell the difference. Besides, it's not like I'm going to be holding BBQs and garden parties here and telling people how proud I am that I laid this patio all by myself and to check out my DIY skills.

THE NEXT DAY, even though yesterday I buried Henry in my garden, I still feel a growing sense of anxiety. At first, I put it down to the date with Adrian tonight, but then I realise that going on a date is child's play compared to what I did yesterday to protect my son. I killed someone. I buried their body in my garden. I can't just brush past that fact as if it didn't matter. Henry was a threat, and now he's gone, but at what cost to my soul? Does this make me a bad person? Does protecting my son justify the action of taking some-one's life?

I should just cancel the date, say I have a headache or I'm exhausted after a long day, but I don't want to draw any unnecessary attention to myself. I don't want to cause trou-ble. Plus, perhaps it will be a good distraction for me, take my mind off the fact it still feels as if I have blood embedded into the creases in my palms, no matter how many times I scrub my hands.

I've had a few people chat to me throughout the day,

asking about the renovations on the house. I tell them about Henry leaving abruptly. It gets easier every time I use the lie. He just left for another job. That's it. Done and dusted. I know nothing more about it.

The best thing is that no one is surprised because he has been unreliable in the past. They say maybe he's gone on a massive bender and will drink himself to death. I accept their sympathy and nod. I haven't organised a new builder to come yet. I don't want to invite anyone onto my property until I've disposed of Henry's van and tools.

I'm thinking the bag of tools will sink to the bottom of the pond, but the van is a different matter altogether. Max had the idea of stripping it apart, piece by piece, and taking it to the local tip, which isn't a bad idea, other than the fact that neither of us know how to take a van to pieces. It's not like we can take a crowbar to it and expect it to come apart. The engine would need to be dismantled properly, not to mention all the panels, wheels, seats and more. It's a big job, one I don't relish doing on my own, and I'd rather not google how to strip a van apart, just in case anyone ever looks at my browser history.

Adrian walks through the door of the pub bang on eight. He looks like he's come straight from work himself, in a suit and jacket, minus a tie. He's sporting a five o'clock shadow, and his salt-and-pepper hair is slightly dishevelled. He's an attractive, older man, not the type I'd usually go out with, but pleasant and friendly.

My heart speeds up as he waves at me, but not because I'm happy to see him, but because I'm overthinking everything, including what the hell we're going to talk about for however long this date lasts. I'd sooner just go home and have a bubble bath.

I don't know anything about the man, so I guess I could start by asking him about his hobbies and interests. The idea of making small talk is already exhausting me.

'Hey, Nat,' says Adrian. He awkwardly steps forwards and gives me a weird hug and kiss on the cheek. 'Good day?'

'Not bad, thanks. Um, I've bagged us a table over there,' I say, pointing to the far corner. I didn't want to have to sit in the middle of the pub, surrounded by prying eyes and ears. Darren has already ripped me to shreds over having a date in my place of work, all joking of course, but now I feel very awkward and self-conscious as I weave through the array of tables to the corner booth.

'What can I get you?' he asks.

'A house white would be great, thanks.'

'Coming right up.'

I'm glad he didn't make the obvious joke about me pouring our own drinks or getting them on the house. I probably would have walked out there and then if he did.

I take a few deep breaths, attempting to calm my nerves and stomach flutters while I wait for Adrian to return with our drinks. He does, a few minutes later, and slides into the booth opposite me, pushing my wine glass across the table.

'Thank you,' I say, picking it up.

'Cheers.' We clink glasses and each take a sip. I resist the desire to chug the whole thing.

'So, I have to say, I was a little nervous about asking you out. I know you've had a lot on, and I wasn't sure if it was appropriate, and … I guess I'm a little older than you.'

I let out a little laugh. 'You make me sound like I'm a teenager. Me too … I mean, I was nervous too. I hadn't really considered going out with anyone just yet. It's all very new to me.'

'I'm sorry. Please feel free to tell me to mind my own business, but ... are you divorced or separated or anything like that?'

I take a small sip. 'Oh, no, it's fine. No, not divorced or anything. Single mum. I've raised Max by myself since day one.'

Adrian raises his eyebrows. 'Wow, that's ... impressive and very commendable.'

'Thank you.'

'You must be a very strong woman in more ways than one.'

'I certainly don't feel like it sometimes, especially lately. This whole house renovation has been a huge undertaking and ...' I stop, realising I'm entering dangerous territory. When I'm nervous, I tend to blab too much, especially with a drink in my hand.

'You've been here less than a month, and you've done amazing things with the house. I know Henry's left you in the lurch, but I'm sure you'll find someone to take on the remainder of the work. You're not one to back down from a challenge.'

'You've got that right,' I reply with a smirk.

We clink glasses again and fall into an easy rhythm as we chat back and forth, swapping stories and learning about our backgrounds. It surprises me how easily we converse and how at ease I feel despite my nerves beforehand. Adrian makes me feel relaxed, and within a few minutes, I'm enjoying his company.

Adrian moved here five years ago. He has a twin brother called Alex, but they aren't identical. Alex works in France as a private chef, which seems a world away from Adrian being a family solicitor near Newcastle. He's never been married but does have a son called Harris from a long-term relationship, but he hasn't seen him in over a year. I don't ask him too many questions because I can tell it's a sore subject. Plus, it's none of my business. If I ask him too many questions, then he may ask me lots too.

However, I tell him about my parents disowning me when I got pregnant with Max and some of the struggles I've faced being a single mum: the odd looks from other mums at the school gates, the disapproving frowns from strangers when I celebrated my nineteenth birthday and had a two-year-old on my hip, the judgemental looks when Max started acting out at school because he was being bullied about not having a dad. I heard it all over the years. Even the whole 'Oh wow, you don't look old enough to have a seventeen-year-old child!' It's not always the compliment it's probably meant to be.

'How is Max settling in?' asks Adrian.

'Really well, thank you. He has met a girl. He pretty much met her the day after we moved in, and he's now going to be attending the local school, continue studying for his A levels, then hopefully apply to universities for next year.'

'That's brilliant. I'm so glad he's thriving here.'

I smile as I twiddle my empty glass round and round on the table, causing a sweat ring.

'Refill?' he asks me.

'No, thank you. I shouldn't. I'm driving. Actually, I'm sorry, but do you mind if I call it a night? I'm really tired. Thank you for a lovely evening. It's the first time I've sat down and had an adult conversation for a long time.'

'The pleasure's all mine, Nat. Maybe ... Maybe we can do it again soon?'

'I'd like that.' And it surprises me that I mean it.

We say goodnight, and he walks me to my car, leaning in to kiss me on the cheek. Even in the dark, I can see a faint blush on his cheeks. I spend the drive home smiling like a moron, wondering how one day something catastrophic and awful can happen, and the next day something wonderful comes along. It doesn't make any sense. I feel as if I'm constantly on a rollercoaster.

Up and down. Up and down.

Yesterday, I killed and buried a man in my garden. Down.

Today, I went out on a first date with an attractive man and enjoyed it. Up.

THE NEXT MORNING, I'm washing my hair in the shower when Max knocks on the bathroom door. I spit water out of my mouth and shout, 'Yeah?'

'Um, Mum ... the police are at the door.'

Fuck.

Back down the rollercoaster I go.

22

E yes still stinging from the shampoo, I stumble out of the shower, grab a towel and get dressed as quickly as possible, although my damp skin impedes my every attempt to pull a vest top over my head, and it ends up getting bunched up under my armpits. But I finally make it downstairs, where two stern-looking police officers sit at my kitchen table, merely inches from where Henry bled out on the floor only days ago.

'I'm sorry to keep you waiting. I was just taking a shower. Would you like a drink or anything?' As soon as I ask the question, I realise it's the wrong one. I should have asked, 'What's this about?' because that's what a normal person would ask when two police officers show up at their house.

'No, thank you,' says the taller officer, whom I recognise from him having a drink in the pub a week or so ago. I can't remember his name. 'This shouldn't take long, Mrs Moore.'

'Oh, um, it's Miss Moore.'

'My apologies, Miss Moore. I'm DS Wilson, and this is

Sergeant Blake. Has a man called Henry Clayton been working here and doing renovations on your house?'

Max is standing behind the two officers with his arms folded. I try to keep my focus on the officers rather than the startled rabbit-in-headlights look my son is giving me.

'Yes, that's right. He's been working here as a builder for the past two and a half weeks.'

'And you've been telling people he walked out on the job two days ago?'

'Y-yes, he left a note and said he wouldn't be back because he got a bigger job down south somewhere.'

'May we see the note?'

'I'm sorry, but I threw it away. I didn't think to keep it.'

Plus, it never existed.

DS Wilson nods while the other writes in a notebook, his lips pressed together.

I do my best to disguise my racing heart by taking a deep breath and holding it.

'Did he say anything to you before he left about going somewhere?'

'No, nothing. He was never very talkative. I'm sorry, but ... why are the police involved in Henry's disappearance?'

'So you do think he's disappeared?' comes the quick reply.

'What? No. I just meant that he left so suddenly. Why are the police involved?'

DS Wilson shakes his head. 'No need to worry. We're just following up on a few queries regarding him leaving town. Apparently, some people think it's a little out of character for him.'

'Oh ... Okay. Is there anything else I can help you with?'

'Just one last question for now. Did you like Henry Clayton?'

I baulk at the question. 'I'm not sure what you mean. As a builder, I couldn't fault him. He did a brilliant job on this house, but he did make me a little uneasy at times while he was working here.'

'In what way?'

'He ... um ...' I flick my eyes towards Max and then back to DS Wilson. 'He was inappropriate towards me a few times. He was standing and watching me shower even though I could have sworn I locked the door.'

'I see ... Anything else?'

'He often stayed longer than necessary and invited himself to dinner.'

'Anything else?'

'No.'

DS Wilson stands up, followed closely by Sergeant Blake. 'Thank you for answering my questions. If there's anything else that comes up, I'll be sure to call ahead next time.'

'Thank you.'

I walk them both to the door, and we exchange goodbyes. DS Wilson gives me his card and then pauses before getting into his car, scanning the area. Thank goodness we hid the van around the back of the house yesterday. It needs to go. Today. If the police come back with a search warrant or for any other reason, then they'll find it easily.

The second their car is out of sight, I call Max to come outside.

'Mum, are you okay?'

'Yes, fine. Just a little shaken.'

'Why do you think they're suspicious of Henry leaving so suddenly?'

'I'm not sure. I think they're just checking up on all avenues. Just precaution. But we need to get rid of his van and tools.'

'But how?'

'We don't have a choice. We're going to have to drive it out of here and hide it.'

'No, Mum, I've got another idea. Megan's dad is a mechanic, remember. She knows a lot about cars because he's taught her lots of stuff. I can ask her how to dismantle it; then we can hide the parts individually by taking them to local dumps, like I mentioned before.'

I shake my head. 'Max, we can't bring Megan into this. The fewer people who know, the better.'

Max sighs. 'Fine, it was just a suggestion.'

'Let's use some paint to cover up his name on the side so if anyone does see us, they won't immediately recognise his van. Then, tonight, we'll drive it out of here under the cover of darkness.'

THE NEXT FOUR months pass without any further incident. The police drop Henry's case. The house is almost finished. Well, finished in the sense that all the jobs I started are now complete. I'm not sure you can ever truly finish renovating and updating a house. People say renovating a house is stressful and expensive, and while that's true, it's also been the most rewarding experience of my life. In the end, I did hire one of the builders from the list Adrian gave me, who managed to finish the jobs Henry left behind. The new builder did a brilliant job too, and he didn't once invite himself to dinner and make me feel self-conscious or threaten to kill my son. I wish I'd hired him in the first place.

There's only one room left to finish, which is the kitchen. I can't afford a new kitchen, so I'm saving up, but I've redecorated it and added finishing touches that make the whole area feel spacious and fresh. I'm proud of how far Max and I have come.

My anxiety, although still there, doesn't control my life anymore. I have managed to set up a routine of sorts, but I'm not as strict at keeping to it. It took several more weeks before my medication withdrawal went away completely, and I touched base with the local doctor, who scolded me for going cold turkey, but she didn't see any need for me to go back on it again.

It's mid-October now, and the garden is just beginning to fade after being in full bloom all summer. A lot of it needs cutting back now, but I am going to leave certain areas to grow wild to help the local wildlife. The other day, I saw a heron fishing in the pond and a hedgehog scurrying in the undergrowth. I love nothing more than tending to the garden in the warm, dry evenings too. Adrian often pops round to help as well. He's not afraid of getting his hands dirty and doing a spot of cleaning or gardening.

We've been dating casually for four months. While I wouldn't say it's super serious, I do really enjoy his company, and we have a proper laugh. Plus, it's been a long time since I've felt a connection with another person. I'm happy with Adrian, and he brings me flowers, cooks for me and always asks about my day, listening intently, never flicking through his phone at the same time; his focus is always on me.

Max likes him too, although he's a little apprehensive

about becoming too friendly with him. I don't blame him, to be honest.

Max and Megan are a proper couple now. She's spent the night here several times and has settled in as part of the family. She's been so good for Max. I managed to get him accepted into the local school. The headteacher was honest with us and explained that it would be difficult to catch Max up, him having missed so much learning. However, she gave him a chance, and he's worked his butt off over the last couple of months of the year and over the summer, eventually coming away with some half-decent predicted grades for his A levels. He's now started the new term, his final year in school, and has set his sights on applying to universities next year.

The thought of him leaving is enough to give me heart palpitations. I try not to think about it, but I couldn't be prouder of him and his accomplishments in such a short time. I know now that this house renovation was the best thing for us as a family. It's brought us closer than I ever thought possible.

Henry's disappearance has fizzled out in the local community. We managed to completely get rid of the van by taking it to a scrapyard, where they crushed it into a cube.

I often feel guilt over the fact that Henry's wife, Catherine, is buried under my patio, but her disappearance is never brought up by anyone. Henry's lie of her leaving him for another man has never been questioned. Only Max and I know where she is, so I visit her often. I like to think she's pleased that her husband is dead. Maybe not so pleased that he's buried a few feet away from her.

The autumn sun is slowly disappearing behind the horizon. Max is staying at Megan's tonight, and Adrian is at his place. I never stay at his house. He stays here maybe once a week, but tonight I'm spending an evening by myself with a glass of wine.

I take it and walk out onto the driveway, smiling at the delightful sounds and smells of the garden. I've even managed to start a vegetable patch, but so far, my bounty has been a couple of measly carrots and a few stringy runner beans, but next year I'm determined to make a proper go of it, to grow vegetables and fruits to eat. Max still reckons I'm nuts, but when he goes off to university in a year's time, what else am I supposed to do to keep myself entertained in this big house by myself? I don't know what the future holds for Adrian and me, so I have to think about myself for once.

'RED OR WHITE?' calls Adrian as soon as I open the front door.

I quickly close it, closing out the cold, place my handbag on the table in the hallway and walk into the kitchen to find him cooking a meal, wearing a yellow apron and humming along to the tune on the radio. I've just come home from a long shift at work, and my feet have their own pulse.

'White, thanks,' I reply with a happy sigh. I could get used to having a home-cooked meal waiting for me after work. 'How did you get in here?' I ask with a giggle, taking the glass of wine he offers me. I sit down at the kitchen table and watch while he expertly moves around the kitchen, finishing chopping a few vegetables. We haven't got to the point of swapping keys yet.

'Max let me in,' he says with a wink.

'Ah. Is he upstairs?'

'No, Megan picked him up a few minutes ago, actually. We have the evening to ourselves. How was work?'

'Long. Something went wrong with the beer pump, so we couldn't pull any all day.'

'Ouch. And on a Saturday night. I bet some of the locals weren't happy.'

'You could say that.' I take a sip. 'Hmm, this is good wine.' I reach across the table and pick up the bottle, reading the label.

'Thanks. I thought you might like it. The red's good too.' He picks up his own glass of red.

'When did you become such an expert at picking out wine?'

Adrian gives me a sly look over his shoulder. 'A gentleman never reveals his secrets.'

'Oh, a challenge. I like it.' I smile coyly at him and take another sip. I can feel the tension draining out of my body already. I'm happy at work, but it exhausts me. 'What are we having?'

'I got us a couple of filet steaks from the local butcher, and I'm doing some chunky chips with them and roasted veg.'

'Sounds amazing. Do I have time for a shower before you serve?'

'Yep.'

'Okay, won't be long.' I take a quick sip, place the glass down, and to say thank you, I wrap my arms around his waist from behind and plant a kiss on his neck. 'Thank you for this.'

'No problem.' We kiss.

Adrian's phone is lying on the kitchen counter next to

him. It buzzes and lights up. My eyes are drawn to it, but he snaps it up before I can see who's calling.

'Hi, Poppy,' he says. 'Can't talk now. Can I give you a call back tomorrow? ... Okay, cool. Bye.'

I slowly release my arms from his waist and take a step away from him. Something feels wrong. Why are my internal alarm bells ringing? It's not the fact a woman is calling him. I'm not a jealous person, but it's the name ... the name sends a jolt of adrenaline through me, and I can't quite figure out why.

Poppy.

'Are you okay? You look pale.'

'I'm fine. Sorry ... wine's gone to my head.'

Adrian laughs. 'You're such a lightweight, Nat.' He moves towards me, but I flinch away. 'What's wrong?'

'N-Nothing.' I shake my head.

Poppy ...

It hits me like a lightning bolt.

'Was that Poppy Kalu?' I ask.

Adrian's face drains of colour. 'How do you know about Poppy Kalu?'

'How do *you* know about Poppy Kalu?' I echo.

We lock stares. My heart is beating so fast I can barely breathe.

'Adrain,' I say slowly, 'why are you in contact with Prudence Greene?'

'I ... I didn't realise you knew about her. When did you find out?'

'She came to visit me a few months ago. We've been in contact a few times, writing letters back and forth, but she's never said anything about knowing you. Why was she calling you?'

Adrian takes a long drink of red wine. 'She visited me a few months ago, probably when she was in town to see you. I was shocked to see her after so many years. I knew her well when she lived here. She'd received the letter from Harriet that I'd sent out to her upon Harriet's death, and she needed to confirm a few details about the house. That's all. I'm not sure why she's calling me again.'

Something doesn't add up. My mind flickers back to our first date and him telling me he moved here only five years ago, yet Prudence disappeared seven years ago. How did he know her well if he didn't live here at the time?

'But I thought you moved to town after Prudence left? You became Harriet's solicitor in 2017, right?'

Adrian leaves the peppercorn sauce bubbling on the hob and takes a step towards me. This man is lying to me, and I don't trust him unless he tells me the truth.

'No, I was here before she left. I'm sorry I didn't tell you.'

'And you knew her well?'

'Yes. Prudence and I ... we dated once about twelve years ago, but then we broke up. I met someone else and moved on, and then she met Abioye and ran away with him.'

'Did you know she was planning on running away with Abioye?'

'No, I swear, I even asked Catherine about it, but she didn't—' He stops and gulps.

Catherine.

Henry's wife.

Was that whom he was dating and moved on with?

Adrian opens his mouth, but no words come out.

Oh, fuck. How did I not see this before?

'Do you mean Henry's wife, Catherine?'

Adrian runs his hands through his hair and takes a deep

breath. 'Shit,' he says. 'This is all coming out now, isn't it? Yes, Catherine and I were having an affair. Henry never found out it was me. If he did, he probably would have torn my head from my body a long time ago.'

'But ... Henry said she ran off with the man she was seeing. If the man she was seeing was you, and you never left town, then ... where is Catherine now?'

Adrian gives me a look out of the side of his eyes, like he's scared to even turn his head to face me. Because I've just put two and two together and finally realised the truth.

I take a step back. I need to get out, to get air. It's suffocating in here. My blood turns to ice in my veins, and a lump almost chokes me. I inhale, but the air feels as if it's evaporated. All this time I was focused on Henry, accusing him of stalking me, killing his wife and threatening me ...

'It was you.' My voice wobbles.

'What was me? Yes, I was having an affair with Catherine. We've already covered this.'

'No ... No ... I mean ...'

Adrian doesn't blink, doesn't move, doesn't say a word.

He doesn't need to.

Henry was innocent all along. He may have been a horrible human being. He may have strangled Megan and me and tried to kill Max, but he didn't kill his wife.

Adrian killed her.

He's known all along that she was buried in my garden.

'You killed her, didn't you?'

'Why would you think that?'

He hasn't even denied it.

I open my mouth to scream, but Adrian lunges forward and shoves a hand over my mouth before any sound escapes. He pushes me back against the wall and leans in close to my left ear, his lips brushing against it as he whispers, 'If you say a word to anyone about what you know, I'll gut you like I did that traitorous bitch. She thought she could break it off and go back to her husband. No one leaves me. No one. Got it?'

He's pressing me up against the worktop, the edge digging into the small of my back. He removes his hand from my mouth. 'Adrian ... stop. Please.'

'Say it. Say you won't leave me.'

'I ...' My eyes flick to the side. I see the knife Adrian was using to chop vegetables on the side. 'I won't leave you. I'm sorry I accused you of killing Catherine. It was wrong of me.'

Adrian releases the pressure from my body and backs off, like a switch has been flicked, and he's back to being nice Adrian. He turns his back on me and picks up his wine glass.

I'm not putting up with the shit again.

I grab the knife from the side and hide it behind my back as I walk up behind him. 'Let me make it up to you,' I say, just before I stab him straight through the side of his torso, pull it out and then slice his throat from ear to ear.

No more Miss Nice Natasha.

EPILOGUE

Nine months later – August

Reaching the patio, I position the folding chair facing the sunset. The patio Max and I laid is uneven, which makes the chair wobble as I sit down. I cross my legs over at the ankle and breathe in deep, my eyes closed. The summer evening warmth is delightful on my face.

'Hey, Mum, mind if we join you?'

I crack an eye open and see my son and Megan walking towards me. There are two other chairs laid out on the patio.

'The more the merrier,' I say with a smile. 'I'm going to miss you two when you head to university.' Megan has been accepted at Bath University, and Max is going to Brighton in October.

'Don't worry, Natasha,' says Megan with a smile as she takes a seat. 'You know we'll always come back to visit.'

'I hope so.'

'It's a shame that things didn't work out with Adrian,' says Megan.

'Hmmm.' I reach forwards to the patio table and pick up my wine glass, taking a small sip. 'Just wasn't meant to be,' I add. 'Besides, I spent seventeen years without a man around. I'm happy here by myself.'

Max and Megan glance at each other and smile. It's so wonderful to see them so happy. I know young love doesn't always work out, but I truly hope that they will thrive, and their relationship works out while they're both studying away from each other.

'Wow, Mum, good work on the veg garden,' says Max, nodding over in that direction.

I'm super proud of my vegetable garden. I bought large wooden sleepers and laid them out in squares to create raised beds, then taught myself how to plant, tend and grow various vegetables, including runner beans, potatoes, carrots and green beans. Plus, nearest the house I also have strawberry plants and have tended to the overgrown orchard out the back.

'Thanks,' I say. 'It must be all the extra nutrients in the soil I've added.'

Max and I lock eyes for a moment.

He looks away and starts chatting with Megan.

I smirk slightly as I pull my cardigan tighter around my body with one hand, watching as the yellows and oranges bleed across the sky. I sip my wine and enjoy the last warmth of the day on my face, listening to Max and Megan talk about their summer plans.

I guess I was wrong.

And Henry was right.

I can sit on this patio with three dead bodies beneath it and enjoy a glass of wine of an evening.

Cheers.

THANK YOU FOR READING

Did you enjoy reading *Under Her Skin*? Please consider leaving a review on Amazon. Your review will help other readers to discover the novel.

ACKNOWLEDGMENTS

I'm pretty sure that with every book I write, the acknowledgements section gets bigger and bigger. I have so many people to thank now and as I write this; I'm still blown away by the amount of people who continue to support me through my author career. I can't mention every single person, but those who know me personally, know how thankful I am to every one of you.

First, as this book is dedicated to my husband, Scott, I need to thank him first. He had nothing to do with the book itself, but during the writing process he was renovating our own house, making it ready for us to move in. Our own house renovation progress gave me the general idea for this book and as this book was written and finished, so too our house was renovated alongside.

Thanks also go to Connal Orton at Inkubator Books who helped to iron out some of the plot points during the planning process. His guidance and help are truly second-to-none. To all the people at Inkubator Books behind the scenes; the editors, marketing professionals, proofreaders, formatters, cover designers and all the other jobs that go into creating and publishing a book – thank you! Your expertise and attention to detail are hugely appreciated and valued.

Lastly, a big thank you to my readers, who continue to support me, read and review my books. Without you, I wouldn't have a job, so ... the biggest thanks go to you!

ABOUT THE AUTHOR

Jessica Huntley is an author of dark and twisty psychological thrillers, which often focus on mental health topics and delve deep into the minds of her characters. She has a varied career background, having joined the Army as an Intelligence Analyst, then left to become a Personal Trainer. She is now living her life-long dream of writing from the comfort of her home, while looking after her young son and her disabled black Labrador. She enjoys keeping fit and drinking wine (not at the same time).

www.jessicahuntleyauthor.com

Sign up for her newsletter on her website and receive a free short story.

ALSO BY JESSICA HUNTLEY

Printed in Great Britain
by Amazon